THE
AFTERLIFE
OF
KENZABURO
TSURUDA

THE
AFTERLIFE
OF
KENZABURO
TSURUDA

A NOVEL

ELISABETH WILKINS LOMBARDO

SHE WRITES PRESS

Published 2018
Printed in the United States of America
ISBN: 978-1-63152-481-3 pbk
ISBN: 978-1-63152-482-0 ebk
Library of Congress Control Number: 2018941495

For information, address:
She Writes Press
1569 Solano Ave #546
Berkeley, CA 94707

She Writes Press is a division of SparkPoint Studio, LLC.

For Rosemary, Joe, and Alessandro

A NOTE FROM JOE,
BETH'S HUSBAND

When Beth first told me about her book idea, we were walking together at the Tōdai-ji temple in Nara, Japan. It was April, and people all around us were celebrating *hanami*, the custom of viewing the cherry blossoms. Beth and I, two ex-patriates living in Kobe, noticed plates of special foods left at Tōdai-ji. She said the offerings reminded her of Obon.

Obon is a weeklong Japanese summer holiday when families anticipate the return of their ancestors' spirits—sort of Memorial Day and Thanksgiving mixed with Mexico's Day of the Dead. Beth said she wanted to write a novel about Obon but told from the perspective of someone who had recently died.

I remember that spring day at Tōdai-ji because the idea of Obon written from a dead person's perspective interested me. It felt unique and exactly like something my wife would imagine.

At the time, she hosted a Japanese radio show. She was also featured as a television and print advertising spokesmodel—a Midwestern native from Illinois dressed in full kimono and selling Japanese products like tea, candy, and pudding. You can probably still hear her voice on the train to Kansai Airport, welcoming passengers to the terminal.

She lived such a creative life, I was not surprised that one of her goals was to write a novel. When we eventually returned to the United States, she completed a graduate degree in fiction writing, and the idea she once shared with me beside the Tōdai-ji cherry trees became a manuscript that quickly won a PEN/New England Award for new writers.

And then she died.

Beth wrote a novel about the delicate veil between life and death—and now she is, herself, dead. Beth would see humor in that. She loved to laugh.

During the last awful week of Beth's cancer, her friends and I promised to find her novel an audience. Thanks to you, reader, we are keeping that promise.

Beth believed in an afterlife, and through her story of a complex Japanese family—both living and dead—I can see, smell, hear, and taste exactly how that afterlife existed in her mind. Those descriptions comfort me, as well as the other people who knew her best.

Just like the Tsuruda family she created in these pages, I believe Beth's spirit will find her way home.

OBON

The Buddhist holiday known as "The Days of the Dead" which takes place in mid-August. During the week of Obon, the Japanese believe the spirits of our ancestors are permitted to come back from the afterlife and visit the living world. When the festival is over, the spirits return to the afterlife to await the opportunity to come home again the following year.

Inari

The Japanese Shinto goddess of fertility, prosperity, healing and agriculture. Appearing alternately as a beautiful maiden or an old man surrounded by bags of rice, Inari is often accompanied by two white foxes, one male and one female. Together they may carry any number of magical objects: a jewel that illuminates the dark, a sheaf of rice that brings good harvest, a sword, or a key. Inari is the goddess of luck, change, and transformation and is known for her ability to alter her form and cross any boundary, earthly or otherwise.

Empty-handed I entered the world
Barefoot I leave it.
My coming, my going –
Two simple happenings
that got entangled.

—Kozan Ichikyo

1

OBON
THE DAYS OF THE DEAD
1990

The Obon holiday, and at last I am home. I am a reluctant ghost, studying my wife and child—an old woman and her middle-aged daughter—as they play out their remaining days. I worry that I may be too late.

While my wife Satsuki sleeps, I send her visions of underwater bubbles clinging like pearls to hairy kelp, the taste of fresh oysters, and the memory of her own strong legs pumping in flight over the sand.

Obon—the journey back. In the heat of mid-August during the Days of the Dead, we spirits are allowed to visit our old lives. We loiter in the living world to watch our family lines dwindle from a torrent to the intermittent drip, drip, drip of water off a cedar bough. We are here watching, but we cannot eat or drink, we cannot embrace our children or even feel rain on our shoulders. We cannot eat a sour red *umeboshi* pickle, feel a skein of silk slide through our fingers, or make love in winter under layers of heavy futon. And yet, being here is the closest we are able come to that lushness, to the feeling of flesh. I would even welcome the pain of polio again if it meant I would also be able to feel Satsuki's palm against mine.

"Do not complain," cautioned my great-great uncle Benkei on the day of my first Obon as a spirit. "Just thank the gods we are not hungry ghosts. Those unfortunate spirits spend eternity starved for food and drink that turns to hot coals in their hands." He shakes his head and shudders. "Water becomes molten metal and burns their throats, but the poor creatures continue trying to drink. Their thirst in death is even greater than their greed was in life."

I sniff and look away when he speaks, pretending something interests me in the garden. I do not remind my uncle that every spirit in our family line still in Yamato is in danger of becoming a hungry ghost if I am unable to complete the task assigned to me in the afterlife. I do not remind him that I have one year, until the next Obon, to complete it.

So I stand and watch my bedridden wife and our only child, our daughter Haruna, as they spend their days, studying them with the same intensity I reserved for my beloved insects when I was a living man and respected professor at Kobe University.

I am dismayed to see how ill Satsuki has become in the year since my death. On the first day of my visit, I knelt next to her bed and touched her forehead, her arm, her twisted leg. Now while I wait by her bedside each night, I try to ease her discomfort by whispering to her, telling and re-telling the story of our life together. I recite memories that flare and dim before I lose them in the haze of imperfect recollection: Walking through the tunnel of red *torii* gates and bowing to the statues of white foxes on Mt. Inari the first time Satsuki took me home to her village. A picnic on Mt. Rokko when Haruna was two years old, her chubby fingers wrapped around my thumb as she bent to examine a large horned beetle I'd found. I bring out these moments from our past each night during Obon and am rewarded when Satsuki smiles and murmurs in her sleep. Through her, I see how the phases of death repeat those of birth, the body reversing itself into the infancy of old age.

During the day, I wait in the garden or follow Haruna as she tends to Satsuki. My daughter's life has become a worn path on the tatami mats of our house as she cleans and cares for her mother. Most days Haruna falls onto her futon as soon as it's laid out and sleeps within seconds. At night, she dreams of faded scars, a man's laughter, and a silver fish that slips from her hands and swims away. On those nights, she moans in her sleep and shouts out words that sound like names, but I cannot tell who she's calling.

A year has passed since my death. There are times when I wonder if I'm not already a hungry ghost of sorts, though food and water aren't what I crave. I stand at my wife's bedside at dusk watching her body rise and fall with each breath and realize that I am starved for other things: the scent of Mt. Rokko in the evening, the chance to make my daughter laugh again, and the touch of Satsuki's hand on my sleeve, pulling me toward her.

On the third night of Obon, I hear a noise in the garden and look to see who is watching, but it's only the nightingale on the branch outside Satsuki's window. The small brown bird fluffs her wings and tips her head in my direction before flying off.

I see that the other spirits from my family have begun to gather around the garden wall; they enter the house at twilight. My childhood home is also the Tsuruda ancestral home, and so our family comes: my grandparents and their parents, stretching back to the very beginning of our name. We are here for two women who represent the last of the Tsuruda family line—my wife and my daughter Haruna, the final stroke of our family's pen in the living world.

I have yet to see my mother, father, or brother here, though they all passed into the afterlife years before me. "In due time," says Benkei. "Be patient, Kenzaburo." Patience, I have found, is difficult in death.

There is one spirit who I cannot place, and it troubles me. He doesn't seem to be a family member, nor does he respond to my greetings or gestures to come closer. Instead, he stands shimmering at the periphery of the garden, where the wall is crumbling and bamboo has taken over. When my daughter Haruna ventures outside, he watches her. He is an unblinking statue who shifts toward Haruna when she passes by a window or walks around the garden in her wooden *geta* sandals. I cannot tell if her presence starves or sustains him. He does not have the swollen belly or ravaged face of a hungry ghost, who Benkei warned will try to trick other spirits into giving them their souls. The way he stands watch over my family annoys me. I wonder why he has come here and what he wants. His glasses reflect back at me in answer, two unseeing discs. Shoulders bowed, he holds his hat in his hands, and his legs fade into the mist. His lips move, but no sound emerges.

He reminds me of the gray moths on which I performed experiments for Kobe University. To study their nocturnal habits, I set up lamps on one side of an empty aquarium, and food on the other. As soon as I turned on the light, the desperate creatures beat against the bulbs until all the silver fell from their wings, their bodies drying into lifeless husks and dropping to the bottom of the cage. Other scientists might explain this instinct with biology, and at the time I'm certain I did as well. Now I know better—they did it out of hunger for the light and a desire to get inside of it. In the same way, we spirits are attracted to what we loved in the living world.

In life, and even in death, I did not at first comprehend the delicate balance the living and the dead share, the two worlds connected like wings to a butterfly, pulsing open and closed, brushing against each other in flight, cleaving together at rest.

But it is not desire alone that brings us back; our family's remembrance also pulls us home. It is their need that attracts us, like a related group of errant fireflies in the night, conjured up out of the mist for ten days in late summer. I understood this on the first day of Obon, when I saw the grief my absence caused. A hole existed where I had been; it made my wife and daughter stumble when they passed over it, to forget their words in mid-sentence.

Now their anguish, fresh and sharp as vinegar, has become my compass.

At night, while the young boys of the neighborhood beat the drums at the temple for the Obon festival, I wait by my wife's bedside for her eyes to flicker, for her to see me and give up her slight hold on the living world. There can be no proceeding, no continuation of our story, without Satsuki. I wonder if I will have the courage to do what I must to make certain that we meet in the afterlife. I worry that I will fail her again.

Saaaaaaa. As twilight begins to fall, I exhale along with the wind. Nearly time to go inside the house and take up my station next to Satsuki's bedside. The leaves of the cherry blossom tree, petals long since faded and fallen to the ground, expose their silvery underbellies to the breeze. When I was alive, and our daughter was still a young girl, she fell asleep each night lulled by the sound of the wind and my wife's animated voice explaining the workings of this world and the next. "Satsuki, why do you fill our daughter's head with such tales?" I would scold. "Spirits are no more real than *kappa* or *Oni*."

"Ah, and how do you know that the *kappa* doesn't wait at the bottom of murky ponds to pull children down by their feet with his frog hands, or that the giant demon *Oni* never existed?" Satsuki would answer. "Professor Tsuruda, you are a clever man, but how are you certain that spirits aren't around us, always?" In her pocket, she grasped the small statue of Inari the fox goddess, which she reached for whenever I expressed doubt.

Now I am thankful that Satsuki was not swayed by my scientist's logic or my belief that spirits, demons, and gods were created by men to soothe their fearful dreams. In life, I was blind to the ease with which spirits move back and forth, like the patrons of a neighborhood ramen restaurant ducking under a short blue curtain, shifting from dark to light. My foolish arrogance about the world in which I once lived, and the one I now inhabit.

And so it is that I find my garden crowded with spirits during the Obon holiday, just as Satsuki always said it was.

Somewhere in the house, I hear the sound of water running. Haruna, drawing her evening bath in the blue-tiled *ofuro*. One by one, by the tens and twenties, the ghosts of my family members pause then enter our house to take their places around each room.

I turn just before going inside. The stranger stands alone, the only indication he remains being the flicker of his glasses in the fading light.

Water

2

HARUNA

"*Omizu.*"

The croaking request for water came from Satsuki's bedroom. Haruna's mother was forever thirsty—a side effect, the doctor said, of all the medications she was taking. Haruna sighed. The bottles of pills Satsuki took filled two trays, and still her mother's condition seemed to worsen each month.

Haruna stopped short of invoking the Japanese mantra, "*Shikataganai.*" She remembered what her father used to say when he was alive: "The way to keep moving forward is not to admit defeat by saying, 'It cannot be helped.' No, Haru-chan. Don't look to the left or right—just keep going."

"I will keep going, Father. As you did," Haruna said to her empty bedroom. This month marked the first anniversary of his death. The head of the university's biology department had called asking her to consider donating his "invaluable collection" of insects to their program. But giving away the cataloged specimens felt like losing her father again. The familiar weight of grief and regret filled her when she remembered her *otohsan*, and what had been left unsaid between them. Again, she saw the look of disappointment on his face during their last conversation. If only she had been able to tell him the truth. Some days, the heaviness of the shame she felt was almost too much to bear.

"*Omizu.*"

Her mother's call for water came again. Haruna took a deep breath and banished thoughts of her last argument with her father from her mind. No time to dwell on that now—she needed to begin her *okaasan*'s routine for the day. Gathering up her long black hair, she twisted it into a tidy bun at the nape of her neck and secured it with a black band from her pocket. She stopped in the dark kitchen to fill a glass pitcher and cup with water and set them on a red lacquer tray her mother liked best. Before going to her *okaasan*'s room, she took a deep breath, preparing herself for what she might find.

On any given day, her mother might believe Haruna to be a relative, a childhood neighbor working the terraced rice fields of Inari, or a bullet train attendant offering local delicacies to passengers. Haruna found herself unable to do anything but surrender to her mother's perspective, where time, events, and memories slipped and merged in a revolving pattern of shapes and colors.

When she explained what it was like to Chiaki at the coffeehouse one day, her old high school friend said, "*Arara.* It is like that little toy you bought Tae-chan at the museum when she was small—that kaleidoscope. Each time you look through the end and twist the tube, a new picture emerges. Oh Haru-chan, *taihen desu ne.* This must be so difficult for you." Chiaki's understanding gaze forced Haruna to look away. Either that or embarrass herself by crying in the *kissaten*.

But Chiaki had been right—a new picture emerged from Satsuki's memory each time Haruna walked into her mother's room. And yet,

when the light hit Satsuki's face at certain angles, Haruna remembered the woman who had been strong and quick-witted, able to tell
her the names of every wildflower, plant, and mushroom in the forest
behind their house. Her mother knew how to use leaves to dress a
wound, brew tea or form into a compress for moxibustion. The last
time her mother had placed the burning *yomogi* on Haruna's skin,
she'd whispered, "This will stimulate the blood flow, it will clean your
body," holding Haruna as she wept. But this was before her father
died and before her mother's stroke had weakened Satsuki's health,
allowing innumerable afflictions to begin claiming her body piece
by piece.

Haruna shook her head to clear her thoughts and called out
"*Ohayo*," as she entered her mother's bedroom, breathing in the familiar smell of urine and medicine in the air. A warm smile greeted her,
and her mother replied, "Good morning," and tipped her chin in an
attempt to bow.

"Tetsuko-san, *ne . . . oyogouka?* Shall we swim?" *Ahsoka*, thought
Haruna. Today her mother imagined she was speaking with Aunt
Tetsuko, who had promised to visit them this Obon. Her mother was
no doubt remembering a family vacation they'd taken to the Japan Sea
when Haruna and her cousins were small. Haruna's father and Uncle
Zaemon had both been off traveling—her father to Indonesia to search
for Luna moths, and her uncle to America to negotiate a business
deal for his medical equipment company. It was August and all the
children were on vacation from school for the month, so Satsuki and
Tetsuko had decided to meet on the Japan Sea. They bought roasted
corn and whole squid on skewers from street vendors and the children
swam in the ocean all day until their skin turned the color of polished
chestnuts. Haruna remembered the sound of her mother's laughter
when a watermelon came floating in on the tide on the last day of their

stay, and how she and her cousins all broke it open with a baseball bat and gorged themselves on the sweet red fruit.

Haruna said, "Aunt Tetsuko is coming to visit tomorrow, *Okaasan*. It will be good to see her, *deshou?*"

"Have you found it yet, the thing that is hidden?" asked Satsuki with her soft slur, a leftover, the doctor explained, from the stroke she'd had. "You must keep looking, Tetsuko. It's in the house in Hajiyama. Kabocha will show you."

Haruna's shoulders slumped. This conversation again. What was it her mother wanted Aunt Tetsuko to find? While it could be nothing—just part of Satsuki's dementia, another in the long line of things she looked for that weren't really there—for some reason, Haruna believed this was different. Her mother hadn't wavered from her insistence that "this thing that was hidden" was at the country house in Hajiyama, where Satsuki stayed with Aunt Tetsuko for safekeeping during the war.

"What do you mean?" whispered Haruna. "What should Aunt Tetsuko look for? Let me help you, *Okaasan*—both of you."

But Satsuki continued as if she hadn't heard her daughter's question, instead remarking on the beautiful red sand caves and the bright water of the Japan Sea in August. She was back at their vacation of more than thirty years ago now, reliving the days when Haruna was young and death hadn't touched them with its methodical hands.

Haruna sighed and looked around her mother's room to assess what needed to be done. This had once been their Japanese-style living room, but they'd needed the twelve-tatami-mat space for the adjustable hospital bed and oxygen tank. When her mother became too ill to walk, they had moved her downstairs to the first floor. The beautiful cherry wood *tokonoma* alcove, where Satsuki had once displayed hanging scrolls and flowers, was now the corner where the medicine cart and a television stand stood.

Haruna shook her head at the mute TV. One year ago, her father had died. And just six months after that, Haruna had come home from grocery shopping to find her mother on the kitchen floor beneath an overflowing sink, half of Satsuki's body slack and hanging, the other struggling to move. The nurses at the hospital said that it was fortunate Haruna arrived when she did.

"The effects of the stroke would have been much worse had your mother been left for many more hours," said Dr. Ishikawa in his office. "You are lucky." Haruna did not feel lucky, but she did not contradict the doctor, who might be able to tell her how to aid her mother's recovery, as was her inclination.

"It happens like this with many older couples," Dr. Ishikawa continued. "One goes, and the other . . . " He did not need to complete the thought. Haruna nodded, the weight of his words pushing her down further into her seat. Since her father's death, her mother had lost her *ki*; her spirit was elsewhere. The stroke was one more physical sign of something Haruna already suspected.

After a week in the hospital, Satsuki wrote Haruna a message in the hand of a second grader. Two simple pictographs: Crane and Fox. The animals, Haruna knew, represented her father and mother— Kenzaburo, the careful crane, and Satsuki, the white fox from Inari, where the Fox Goddess had been worshipped for thousands of years. Haruna smiled and held Satsuki's good hand. Those first few days, she could not bring herself to touch the other one as it lay curled like the fingers of a dead child on the white sheets of the hospital bed.

Although her mother regained some of her speech, the stroke started a chain reaction in Satsuki's body, a series of gentle earthquakes moving down a precarious fault line. Despite the fact that Haruna tried her best to manipulate her mother's limbs and perform the exercises the doctor prescribed, atrophy was beginning to set in. Now her *okaasan's* legs and arms were starting to petrify at odd angles.

Haruna began Satsuki's morning massage, willing her to regain some flexibility. She sprinkled her mother's legs with baby powder and then took the sheets off the bed, replacing them with clean ones. When she was finished, she turned Satsuki on her side—the first of many rotations she would make throughout the day.

Perspiration gathered on Haruna's forehead and between her shoulder blades while she worked. The heat in the room was rising, as if someone was standing outside the house turning the heat up one degree at a time. She looked at the clock: 7:30 a.m. She was glad the acupuncturist was coming today for his weekly visit. Oh-san's ministrations seemed to help to alleviate the pain in her mother's joints. Haruna admired the acupuncturist's gentleness as he attended to her mother. She thought of his broad, good-natured face and the crisp cut of his salt-and-pepper hair above his white collar and smiled.

Now she said, "If I do the wash now and hang it out, everything should be dry by noon." She gathered the bedclothes into her arms and turned to leave the room. Haruna often talked aloud around her mother, even though Satsuki didn't often respond; the doctors said this might help her recover some language ability. And if nothing else, thought Haruna, it broke through the silence of falling dust motes.

Her mother's voice, with its trace of a soft slur, startled her.

"Haru-chan? Today . . . it's the beginning of the Obon Festival, *ne*. To go see the firelight Noh Theatre tonight in Kyoto . . ." Satsuki was lucid. Haruna turned back toward her mother and nodded, afraid to speak.

"Your father loved Noh, Haruna, do you remember?"

"*Hai,*" Haruna said, locked in place in the doorway. She licked her lips before she spoke, and her words came out in a rush. "Father always said that a great actor could make any mask show emotion. He said the man behind the *O-men* gave Noh its mystery." Her mother's eyes continued to focus on her, so she continued. "B-but you always said it was the other way around," she stammered. "That the mask took on its own life by inhabiting the spirit of its owner. You said it was the *O-men* that possessed the actor and made him great."

At that moment, the memory of their ancient debate was more real than the soiled sheets in Haruna's hands. She looked up at the ceiling, her cheeks scalded with salt and heat. One year since her father's death, and the pain of missing him—and what she hadn't been able to explain—was a heaviness that never left her.

Haruna wiped her face with her upper arm and tried to smile at her mother. She set down her bundle and approached the bed. She wanted to prolong this conversation, this sudden gift, and talk with her *okaasan* for as long as possible. She was afraid to look at her, afraid she might undo the delicate ties, fragile as spider's silk, that bound her mother's thoughts to this moment.

"I saw him last night," said Satsuki.

"Who?" asked Haruna, her voice coming out as a puff of air. She cleared her throat and said again, "Who did you see, *Okaasan?*"

"Your father, of course. He is here for Obon," she said. "I can still smell his scent in the room. Books and cedar and ink—and *Kao* soap." She paused and looked at Haruna. "He is worried about us. He said there is another spirit watching us, a man with round glasses. Who is it, Haru-chan? Do you know?"

A slight breeze rolled through the room, moving the curtains, stirring the papery leaves of a houseplant, brushing the back of Haruna's neck. Grief rose to the surface again, shimmering and hot. She took a step toward her mother and forced herself to breathe. "What do you mean, *Okaasan*? What else did *Otohsan* say?"

But while Haruna stood and watched, the spark in Satsuki's eyes went out like an aperture closing in a camera lens. Her mother's clarity vanished at the exact moment the cicadas started their rasping late-summer chorus.

3.

SATSUKI

Satsuki lay on her left side, the paper shoji doors of her bedroom open so she could look out the windows of the veranda into the garden. She watched as figures slid in and out of the room. They swung back and forth, resembling curtains; sometimes they gathered around her in a circle, whispering, "*Mo soro soro iku yo. We're going soon. Sssooon . . .*"

At other times Satsuki believed she was on a boat—a shallow-bottomed canoe that held only her body and a cargo of burning reeds. The flames licked the bottom of her nightgown until her whole body was alight, moving across the water toward the sun.

"*Hooo-hokekyo.*" The nightingale sang outside her window. Satsuki saw the shadow of his body thrown onto the window screen. The bough on which he perched bobbed wildly when he launched himself into the air.

Satsuki closed her eyes. When she opened them again, she was puzzled to find it was nighttime. The room wrapped around her like a black velvet box. Kenzaburo was standing next to her. Hands folded, hat in hand, he waited.

Satsuki smiled and exhaled. The sound joined with the breeze and became the night air.

"Is it time?" she asked. "*Dekita?* Have you done what you need to do?"

"Soon," he whispered. "Soon."

4

TETSUKO
THE VISIT

On the third day of Obon, Tetsuko stepped onto the bullet train, bound for Satsuki and Haruna's home in Kobe. Had it really been a year since Kenzaburo had died—and a full year since she had last seen Satsuki?

Her niece's recent letter, written on floral stationery in Haruna's flowing hand, had prompted Tetsuko to buy the ticket. "We keep going, Aunt Tetsuko. Some days, my mother remembers names of people from years ago. She mentions your name often and also Uncle Zaemon's. But lately *Okaasan* has been quite agitated; she talks to me as if I am you and asks me to 'find what is hidden' in your old country house in Hajiyama. She gets upset, but I have no idea what she means and wonder if you do. Perhaps on your next visit, you could ask her what she wants you to find? Seeing you would do her so much good, Auntie."

Tetsuko had no idea what Satsuki's words meant, but the fact that her sister-in-law mentioned her husband Zaemon's name piqued her curiosity. If this was real and not a product of Satsuki's dementia brought on by the stroke, could this "thing that was hidden" be the reason her husband had been so irrational when it came to Satsuki? Tetsuko had never been able to understand her husband's aversion to her sister-in-law, especially after what Satsuki's had done for their family during the war. Perhaps Zaemon had argued with her and never told Tetsuko? Maybe her sister-in-law had written a letter of apology that she wanted Tetsuko to find in the old house in Hajiyama. The mystery of it all bothered Tetsuko, who prided herself on having her life in order.

The train rocked and Tetsuko shifted in her gray velour seat. Besides going to see Satsuki, she also wanted to check on her niece. Beautiful Haruna, who devoted all her time to taking care of her mother, never to have a husband or children of her own. Tetsuko felt as guilty, as if her niece's spinsterhood was her fault.

Not that Tetsuko hadn't tried her best. When Haruna was twenty-four, Tetsuko placed a call to her sister-in-law. She had rehearsed her speech and was determined that Satsuki agree to her proposal. It was rare for Tetsuko to be refused by anybody, but Satsuki was someone who could not be convinced if her mind was made up—and she had proved she was not afraid to stand up to Tetsuko.

"Satsuki, it is time for us to find a husband for Haruna. Next year, when she's twenty-five, they will start calling her 'Christmas Cake.' No man wants a woman past her expiration date."

Tetsuko heard the hesitation in Satsuki's voice when answered. "Tetsuko-san, it is so kind of you to offer help. But Haruna . . . she does not want an arranged marriage. She says she wants a love match, or nothing at all." Tetsuko drew in her breath. Although Satsuki and Kenzaburo had met and married on their own at a time when it was considered highly irregular, most love matches were known to be unstable and ill-fated. At this point in Haruna's life, giving up on a proper *omiai* arranged by a matchmaker was unthinkable. Haruna was Tetsuko's niece after all, and Tetsuko felt it her personal obligation to find her a husband. She owed Satsuki this much, at least. And truth be told, it bothered Tetsuko that she could never repay her sister-in-law for what she had sacrificed for her during the war. As a result, instead of giving up on the idea of Haruna finding a husband, Tetsuko changed tactics.

"Well, who is to say she can't have both? Perhaps one of these young men will spark a *ren-ai* feeling in Haruna, and they'll 'fall in love,' as they say . . ." she paused, glad Satsuki could not see the look of distaste on her face. "And then everyone will be satisfied. After all, some day we won't be here to take care of Haruna. You don't want your only child to be alone, *deshou*. Isn't it best for everyone if she has a family and her own household?"

In the end, out of fear for her daughter, who seemed to spend more and more time in the company of female friends or alone reading her books, Satsuki yielded. The next week, she filled out a resume for Haruna and sent it with her daughter's photo to Tetsuko, who in turn sent it to a well-regarded matchmaker in Kobe. The *nakodosan* had asked for a "good picture that would show off Haruna's traditional Japanese beauty," but the best Satsuki could send was a blurry snap-shot taken when Haruna was caught unawares. In spite of the poor quality of the photo, the matchmaker sent dozens of offers from likely young men wanting to meet Haruna.

Tetsuko sighed. It could have all gone very well, too, if Haruna hadn't been so stubborn. Her niece went along with the dates out of obligation to her parents and her aunt but showed such lack of interest when being introduced to candidates as to be taken for rudeness. When Haruna was twenty-nine, the third matchmaker quit on the spot.

"How do you expect me to find a husband for a girl like that?" the woman hissed to Tetsuko in the lobby of the Miyako Hotel. Baba-san had sour breath and greasy gray hair tied up in a tight bun. Her black kimono smelled of mothballs, but she was one of the best in her field. Tetsuko had it from reliable sources that Baba-san could wrangle a proposal in even the most difficult cases and had found suitable matches for young suitors with lazy eyes, club legs, and port wine stains on their faces, no less—but even she had failed to find Haruna a mate.

"He was the son of a razor blade manufacturer. *Razor blades*, Uribo-sama," she said. The matchmaker used the politest language and form of Tetsuko's family name with which to rebuke her. Tetsuko was mortified.

"I do not have to tell you that this family produced swords for the emperor's army during the war, nor should I have to remind you what a valuable commodity razor blades are. Your niece gravely offended the father of the family. He is an elected member of the ruling LDP party, Uribo-sama. Why would your niece criticize their policies the very first time they met? In all my years as a matchmaker, I have never heard of such a thing. You would think she doesn't even want to find a husband," Baba-san sniffed. "Now I'll have to go in person to apologize to the family tomorrow." The matchmaker wrung her hands until Tetsuko apologized and pressed an envelope filled with 10,000-yen notes into the woman's palm—enough for her to pay her rent for a month and then some. A weak smile crossed the matchmaker's face before she bowed. "I am truly sorry Uribo-sama. But your niece . . . maybe she should join a sewing club, learn how to behave in a more feminine way."

When Haruna turned thirty, Tetsuko admitted defeat. She could not understand why her niece wished to remain alone, yet she had to acknowledge that no man would marry a woman past her prime child-bearing age. *Shikata ga nai* . . . it could not be helped. Tetsuko caught the dim reflection of her frowning face in the train window. Even now the thought that she had not succeeded annoyed her. She was not used to defeat, and the suggestion that she had fallen short of her goal—that she had indeed failed Haruna, Satsuki and Kenzaburo—was like a pebble she could not shake from her designer shoe.

If only Zaemon were here—he would understand. Her husband had also been someone unused to failure, which was why the two had been such a good match. When they married, Zaemon had been adopted into Tetsuko's family, as there had been no sons born to carry on the Uribo name or run her father's trading company. Following the *youshi* tradition, Zaemon had taken Tetsuko's surname and had his name erased from the Tsuruda family register when they wed. It was all part of the arrangement, and their union—and her father's company—had prospered beyond all expectations.

After the war, Zaemon made a calculated move and decided to produce medical equipment, and it had been a good bet on his part: Tetsuko was proud of the fact that the Uribo name was now known in hospitals all over the world. But all the years walking the factory floors and chain smoking had taken a toll on Zaemon's lungs. He died strapped to one of the ventilators his company produced.

It was hard to believe that Zaemon had been gone for these past ten years. There were times when Tetsuko allowed herself to miss her husband, but for the most part, she put her head down and moved forward. She nodded and took out her compact. When a man attempted to sit next to her on the train, she frowned until he backed away. She glanced into the mirror, powdered her nose, and reapplied her bright pink lipstick, all the while wondering what situation she might find at Satsuki's home when she arrived.

Would Satsuki even recognize her? From Haruna's letters, it sounded as if her sister-in-law was no longer aware of the world around her. It had been a year since she'd made the journey to Kobe for Kenzaburo's funeral, and even then, Satsuki had appeared fragile, a faded version of the woman Tetsuko had known and admired for most of her adult life.

She remembered Haruna's words after the funeral ceremony. "Don't wait too long before coming back," she'd said. Yet, to Tetsuko's shame, she'd put off her visit, coming up with excuse after excuse. The marriage of her sister's son, the birth of another grandchild. These occasions, while important, did not prevent her from taking a two-hour train ride to see her widowed sister-in-law and niece, even after Satsuki had her stroke.

She could not bring herself to explain to Haruna that her letters and phone calls scared her, that the idea of seeing Satsuki this way frightened her. In truth, her petite, countrified sister-in-law's strength and good sense had been a constant she'd relied on since the end of the war, when their friendship, which started in such an inauspicious way, began to blossom in earnest.

A line from Haruna's letter came to mind again: "Mother said your name again last night, Aunt Tetsuko, and I thought I heard her say the word 'kabocha.' Did you grow pumpkins when she lived in your house outside of Hiroshima? I thought you might know what she was speaking about. Perhaps it's just another silly thought."

Kabocha. Tetsuko hadn't thought about that dog in forty years. His name brought back memories that Tetsuko had kept packed away for decades.

Listen,
all creeping things—
the bell of transience.
—Issa

5
THE LAST DAY OF OBON
KENZABURO

On the third day Obon, I stood in the garden outside my home, a dusty guest, reliving the moments that led up to my death. I would write it all down, in time, but first I needed to remember.

The morning of the last day of my life, the mountains behind our house glowed indigo in the haze, their stiff shoulders hunched to block the sun. Waiting for some precise, mysterious mixture of heat and light to arrive before they began their chorus, the cicadas had not yet started calling to each other in their harried attempts to mate.

How odd to have found myself here—a ghost on the far edge of my former waking life. I saw myself as I was on my final day as a living being on earth, retracing my last steps over and over again, hoping that in the reliving of those moments I would find some new peace.

Satsuki slept beside me that morning, her long gray hair curling on the pillow around her. Her scent, that of sandalwood and growing things, clung to her. I bent to kiss her ear and got up from the futon limb by limb. The dull ache in my leg was there, as ever. In spite of the pain, I held my breath and backed out of the room, my bare feet sliding backward over the tatami mat like a pair of slow-moving carp. I could not stand the thought of waking my wife, so serene was the expression on her face.

The pair of weasels who had taken up residence in the small space under the peak of our roof had kept us awake for the better part of the night.

"We cannot ask them to leave," Satsuki had whispered in the dark. "It is good luck to have weasels in our home. Besides, they keep the snakes away." Armed with that logic, Satsuki prevailed.

I watched myself in my mind's eye as if I were watching a movie. I was impatient with my stiffness, with a lifetime as the owner of legs that would not cooperate. I walked down the stairs, leaning on the railing and trying not to put weight on my left foot.

Our kitchen smelled of ginger, soy, and the night garden just beyond the back window. I foraged for breakfast in the cabinets and put the kettle on to boil. When I was living, I could not start my day without green tea. I switched on the small television in our dining room that day—more news about the ailing emperor and fears for his imminent demise, which had been on the news every day these past months, commentators skirting around the *Tennō Heika's* war record. The news anchor reported on the emperor's health that morning and avoided the question of whether or not the head of Japan's royal family was the mastermind of the war or a simple gardener controlled by hawkish men. Men who, if they had been lucky to escape hanging after the war, went on to become businessmen and political leaders growing fat and prosperous in the decades of Japan's post-war industrialization.

Annoyed, I turned off the television. I wanted nothing to mar the perfection of the day I had planned. I turned back to my breakfast and plotted my course on Mt. Rokko. I was pleased to note that my dormant appetite had returned. In the year leading up to my death, my desire for food had become more difficult to capture than the rare insects I hunted in the mountains behind our house. That morning my need to eat rivaled the hunger I'd felt during the war, when all we had were rice rations and the scraps of food Satsuki and my mother managed to horde. I paused, remembering that for one month, we ate only salted fish, and the next, *daikon* pickle. So much salted food my urine burned for months. Still, we were more fortunate than many. We heard that some families who evacuated to the countryside were forced to eat boiled weeds when they ran out of war grade rice.

Now, in the final year of the emperor's reign, the young people in Japan had only known prosperity. Our daughter had always been different, more inclined to like a two-hundred-year-old *tansu* rather than a brand new factory-made cabinet, and for that Satsuki and I had been grateful. Most young Japanese people favored shiny, modern things. They didn't care for traditional Japanese homes or furniture and tossed out their grandparents' antiques on *sodaigomi* day for the trash picker—and jubilant foreigners—to collect and sell in the temple sales of Kyoto and Osaka. Now these *gaijin* from America, Australia, and Europe, with their raucous laughter and crude behavior, seemed to be overrunning Japan, making good salaries teaching English to bored housewives and schoolchildren. I almost preferred the soldiers of the occupation, who had been much less inclined to stay.

In truth, my own countrymen had disappointed me most. Some of Japan's greatest losses occurred in the decades after the war, when everyone pushed to erase the darkness associated with that time. The generation born after the war simply turned away from the traditional Japanese way of life. Instead, they bought bright shiny fluorescent lights and all the latest appliances—and joined the western world in promoting all that was new and progressive.

I shook my head again to clear these unpleasant thoughts away and peered into our refrigerator. Some left-over noodles and cold salmon from the previous evening's dinner awaited me, along with the pink *umeboshi* plums Satsuki pickled every autumn. While my morning miso soup was warming, I rummaged in the drawer and found my favorite pair of *ohashi* in their bamboo case. I polished each ebony chopstick with my handkerchief, noting how like an insect's pincers they were. I clicked them together, and my thoughts turned to the beetles I would hunt that day. Anticipation made my heart beat fast as a schoolboy's the moment before classes are dismissed for the month of August.

While I ate, I contemplated my morning outing. The salty miso mingled with the flavors of fish, rice, umeboshi plum pickle, and sea-weed. Many times, I have wished to return to that moment and tell myself to truly enjoy the food, to take time to savor every bite. Instead, I rushed, eager to be out the door. I slurped up the remaining noodles and held my hand up, palm facing the pale light that seeped through the sliding shoji doors, my habit to test the intensity of the coming day's heat.

Although the first floor was still cool, the warmth from the porch on the other side of the doors pulsated through the heavy white paper that covered them. A perfect day for the hunting of the Japanese horned beetles, the *kabuto mushi* that were prized by collectors and scientists alike. In my waking life, nothing was more enjoyable than searching for them in the quiet of a summer morning. My ritual after a successful hunt, was to come home and bathe in our blue *ofuro*, cool water up to my chin, and sleep through the hottest part of the afternoon.

Later, Satsuki would wake me with a call of, "Dinner time, Professor Tsuruda!" and we would enjoy our meal together. If our daughter Haruna was home, the three of us would eat on the *engawa* porch in the cool evening after the sun had slipped into the ocean far below us. If we stayed and talked on the veranda, enjoying cold sake and the sound of crickets in the garden, we would see the lights of the passenger trains moving in their endless procession from Kobe to Osaka and back again, like long strands of brightly lit DNA coupling and uncoupling in the darkness.

The night preceding my death had been just such a night. Satsuki and I spent the evening talking about my research, her garden plans, my sister-in-law Tetsuko's upcoming visit. Haruna did not come home, and when I thought of this, my mood darkened. I did not tell my wife the secret I knew about our only child. Better to keep it from her, spare her worry and shame.

Thinking of this, my head began to hurt again, and I stopped in the bathroom to take some aspirin. "An old man can't drink like he used to," I said to the gray reflection in the mirror. Before splashing my face with water, I removed my round spectacles and placed them on the basin. When I opened my eyes, I saw my face again, as it had looked when I met Satsuki—round and younger than my years. I had cultivated a thoughtful expression to convince people to take me seriously, but my future wife saw through it in an instant, mimicking my furrowed brows and nicknaming me "Professor" long before I became one. I smiled, remembering how fearless she was, how more than one man at the munitions factory had gotten in trouble for watching her when they should have been working.

In better spirits, I shook my head, dried my hands, and smoothed my thinning hair back from my forehead. I found my bag where I'd left it on top of the shoe cabinet and checked its contents. Within its folds were contained small nets and mesh cages for the beetles, a set of binoculars, a compass, and an old pocket watch of my father's. Three rice balls and a bottle of *mugi-cha,* my favorite summer drink of cold buckwheat tea, completed my lunch.

I will admit there was another compelling reason why I wanted to go out that morning—I had received a call from Mori-sensei, the new head of the Zoology at Kobe University.

"I hope you are not too busy to write an article for the spring edition of our scientific journal. There has been renewed interest in horned beetles of late, as their numbers are in rapid decline." Mori-sensei's voice became greasy with flattery. "After all, you are one of Japan's foremost experts on *kabuto mushi.* The university would be indebted if you would contribute some of your latest findings."

"*Saaa,* I will have to think it over, Mori-sensei. But perhaps I *might* be persuaded to consider sharing some recent discoveries with the academic community."

If I had told Mori-sensei the truth, I would have said I was elated to be asked to present my theories to my former colleagues. My passion for insects and their behavior had not dimmed with the passing of years. The fact that I would once again enjoy the respect of the academic community was more important to me than I cared to admit.

I reserved my greatest fascination for horned beetles. In their black armor with their great curling horns, they looked like nothing so much as samurai warriors wearing the *kabuto* helmets for which they were named. It comforted me to observe the bugs as they moved through the vegetation, intent on finding food or mating. There were no puzzling emotions under the surface of their shiny wings to discern, no complex political motives to untangle.

And the truth was that I hated the thought of my former colleagues knowing just how dull my days were. In the three years since I'd retired, I'd begun to feel as if I was pinned to a piece of cardboard like a specimen, frozen under glass, a piece of yellowed paper beneath my feet with my name printed on it: Tsuruda Kenzaburo, Homo Sapien.

As on countless other days, I dressed in loose-fitting khaki pants and a white cotton shirt unbuttoned at the collar. I decided against wearing the pocketed vest that Haruna had gotten me for my birthday. "A pocket for each insect," she'd teased when she'd given it to me the year before. The thought of my daughter again made my mouth tighten in disapproval. Shame took the shape of a tight, hard fist clenching and unclenching in my chest.

"*Otohsan?*"

My posture stiffened when I heard Haruna address me. She spoke in an earlier voice, soft and childlike, contradicting her forty-one years, and for a moment I melted. A nightingale sang *"Hooo Hokekyo,"* filling the silence that followed. I found myself resenting the clumsy weight that had tilted balance of our family. I had no map for this, no way to comfort or advise our only child.

When I spoke, my own voice was harsher than intended. I am ashamed to admit I felt glad, because my daughter jumped when I barked, "Haruna? Go back to sleep. It is only six in the morning."

"But Father, the letter you found. I wanted to explain," Haruna stared at the floor. One hand held the fabric of her nightgown together at her stomach.

"We will talk later, Haruna. Now go back to sleep," I repeated, my voice flat and cold even to my own ears. I did not let my daughter see that my hands were shaking with the effort it took me to talk to her this way.

My daughter lifted her chin and looked at me with—could it have been anger? With no words, she returned to her room. I heard her door slide on wooden grooves, its mute jaws snapping shut. Another chance for me to correct something that was wrong, wasted because of my own pride and stubbornness. Instead of making things right that day, I justified my actions by saying, "Haruna does not understand what she has done," as I opened the shoe cabinet. I was certain that she would soon come to see things as I did. I turned and arranged my boots in our sunken tiled hall, planning to step down into them.

I was not prepared for what happened next. A hot spasm of pain knifed its way toward my pelvis, and my breath was sucked from my throat. Grimacing, I leaned against the wall. I must have called out, because the mourning dove that lived under our azalea outside the front door took flight, its call making the sound of a squeaky door as it fled.

Over the months leading up to the day of my death, the old sickness and pain of my childhood insinuated its way into my life again, curling up inside my body like a cat sleeping on its favorite cushion. I had begun to remember the taste of polio, the ache of solitude and constant pain I'd had as a child.

I did not tell my wife, but she noticed, as she always did. She had commented on my condition during our evening stroll two weeks earlier.

"You are limping again, Tsuruda-sensei." My wife still called me by my surname and title, "Professor Tsuruda," when she wanted my attention.

"I must have twisted my ankle on Mt. Rokko," I replied.

"So-oh?" She answered, with more doubt than question in her voice. "Perhaps you should make an appointment with Doctor Ishikawa. I will call tomorrow."

That week, I was subjected to interminable poking and prodding and an endless series of tests at Kaisei Hospital. Dr. Ishikawa had been one of my students at Kobe University, but now his thick black hair was receding at an alarming rate and a paunch had grown around his middle. Like most in his field, he would not divulge an unappealing prognosis to his patient, even a patient he had known for twenty years. But what Dr. Ishikawa wouldn't tell me concerned me more than I cared to admit.

"You are fine, Tsuruda-sensei," he said now with forced cheerfulness, his yellow teeth and dry lips spreading into his best professional smile. He looked out the window as he said, "You are as healthy as one could expect for a man your age." He shifted from one leg to another and fingered his keys in the pocket of his white smock. I followed his gaze to where a woman pushed her adolescent son in a wheel chair in the gardens outside the hospital. The boy's misshapen body was twisted like a dried root. His arms and hands curled toward his face in a frozen pose, as if he were trying to defend himself from an unseen attacker.

"Tell me. Ishikawa, Please. One scientist to another." I said, addressing him as I had when he was still a student. The only difference was the pleading tone of my voice.

Ishikawa smiled again, trying to be reassuring; I could not disarm him. "You are fine, Tsuruda-sensei. Please. Go home now. I have no further information."

He would not show me the x-rays the hospital had taken. He was afraid I might decipher their meaning, see the deterioration of my limbs, the breakdown of bone and cartilage. It was not difficult for me to catalogue the symptoms of a system giving way, of my body's gradual and unstoppable disintegration.

I wanted to say: "You are a coward."

Instead, I bowed and left.

"Slow down," he said as I walked down the pale green corridor. "You're not a young man any longer, Professor Tsuruda."

I ignored him and hurried out of the hospital, away from the smell of sickness and antiseptic. On the way through the reception area I bumped into an old janitor, his back bent by years of labor and poor nutrition, sending his bucket of floor cleaner skittering across the entryway until it stopped with a clank at the front desk. People in the waiting room glanced at me in alarm, then looked away.

"I will not give up my research or my walks," I said aloud, as if Dr. Ishikawa was standing there in his white lab coat, stethoscope around his neck, blocking my exit. When no one replied, I sputtered, *"Baka!* Stupid old man! Get out of my way." The janitor stayed bowed at the waist until I limped out the door.

The memory of the doctor's evasive expression filled my thoughts as I waited for the aching in my legs and torso to subside in my front hall that morning. When my breathing returned to normal and I coaxed on my boots with renewed determination. But when I bent to tie the laces, new waves of pain, small and sticky like the grasping hands of children, pulled me downward. I recited facts about *kabuto mushi* aloud until the throbbing in my head and leg subsided.

"The horned beetle, indigenous to Japan, Asia, and Africa, subsists primarily on vegetation, though it will eat other insects," I panted as spoke. "Their mating season ranges from June to September. Their horns can reach lengths of five centimeters or more."

My canvas hat hung on the hook by the door, just out of reach. I stood with difficulty, bracing myself against the wall, and swung my arm upward until I knocked it from its perch and trapped it with my shoulder. My walking stick waited for me in the corner, and I grabbed it, still panting. My father had fashioned it for me from the sakura tree that once graced our garden. "The cherry tree will help make you strong," was all he said when he handed it to me.

I stepped outside onto the stone path of our walkway. In the first lick of August heat, the air was thick, green, and liquid and enveloped me like a warm bath. Blotting my forehead with a white cotton hand-kerchief, I headed up the road toward the mountain, commanding my legs to move, my lungs to inhale, my hands to stop shaking.

From our bedroom, Mt. Rokko appeared to be unyielding and solid, but here on the ground familiar paths led into the hills. In the soft mud of the mountain trail, I noted that some of the footprints were made by men and some by animals. As always, it was the animals I understood best, their prints traveling along the path like an unfurl-ing scroll.

I decided to look for the trail of the wild boars that foraged in the brush behind our house and in the neighborhood trash bins at night. During the summer months, we heard their tender grunts of pleasure under our open windows when a tasty root was found, their indignant squeals when a dispute of ownership arose over apple cores or water-melon rinds.

In the dark soil, I found their hoof prints, tiny indentations that were surprisingly delicate for such cumbersome beasts. A bed of bent grasses to the side of the trail was the size of the sow whose comings and goings I had been observing. She must have lain there to sleep and nurse her latest brood of piglets, dreaming her piggish dreams. The boar had chosen a good place to shelter, near the stream that ran down the mountain into a shallow ravine.

Peering into the darkness of the thicket, a flash of dark blue caught my eye and I turned to see its source. The bushes rustled, and I heard a boy laugh and call to me:

"*Omae!*"

You. The way Satsuki said it in Kansai-dialect before I harvested the eyelashes from her cheeks, her pillow, even hanging from her eye-lids, about to fall, and pasted them into a small book, always careful to record the date, time, and place. I kept every one that I'd found since the day we took our first walk together along the Shukugawa River. She found it amusing and would laugh and say "*Omae,*" shaking her head.

Again, the flash of blue, and I saw my younger brother Zaemon run by in his school uniform, looking as he had at the age of ten. He was three years my junior, but always the faster runner, the better athlete. I hurried to follow, dragging my left leg, forgetting the pain and my doctor's warnings in my excitement.

"*Oi, Oniichan!* Catch me if you can, Big Brother!" He laughed at me over his shoulder, and shouted, "Come and find me!"

"Zaemon, *matte!* Wait! I need to talk to you," I yelled, forgetting everything and struggling to keep up with him. But at the clearing, I came upon an old piece of knotted black fabric hanging from a tree, nothing more. I stood. As silly as I felt, I could not shake the odd feeling of disappointment and regret.

Later I learned that these were the signs that this was my last earthly day, that the closer you are to the exact day of your death, the more time shifts and changes. My brother, Zaemon, dead for some ten years, was the first sign I failed to decipher.

I removed my pocket watch from my satchel with difficulty and cupped it in my palm. The second hand spun around the dial in fits and starts, as if a spring had broken. "*Ara?*" The metal grew hot and I dropped it with a cry. Panicked at the thought of losing my father's gold watch, I leaned against a nearby birch tree and used it and my walking stick to help me slide down to my hands and knees. I kneeled there for some time until at last I spied a glint of metal between the roots of the tree. The timepiece, now cool to the touch, had stopped dead.

Fishing in my bag for the *mugi-cha* I'd brought, I leaned against the tree and took a long draught. Tiny rivulets of cold brown tea escaped from the corners of my mouth, running down my face and neck. When I had caught my breath, I used the tree and my walking stick to stand again. From between the trees, I could still make out the roof of our house and our front gate. Standing there waving to me was my long-dead mother in her favorite purple kimono, the one that was the bruised color of an eggplant's skin.

"Ken-chan," she called, her voice high and panicked. "Where are you? Come home now. I'm waiting for you!" Pushing branches out of my way, I shouted out "*Okaasan?*" but she evaporated in the heat waves that were already starting to rise from the street.

The hangover from the sake we drank the night before was making me see things, I decided, and the salt from the sweat in my eyes had blurred my vision. Rebuking myself, I grumbled, "*Bakayaro.* Simple old fool." As I turned back to the trail, tree boughs swooped and closed their arms behind me until I was encircled in the damp green world of Mt. Rokko.

I walked to where the half-dead oak marked the first bend in the trail. Pausing there to drink more tea, I was able to make out the burbling of the creek to my left and follow it. I climbed another twenty minutes, stopping to rest every few minutes, before reaching a narrow rocky ledge overlooking the foothills of the mountain and the town beneath. I had guided Satsuki here when we were first married, I remembered, and kissed the back of her neck as she exclaimed over the view.

The memory, fresh as cut green melon, was interrupted by the sound of a woman crying. This time, I did not look toward it source, but hurried away. "I need to douse my head in the river and clear my mind," I thought. Yet in spite of my determination to focus the insects I was hunting, more memories came rushing back, swallows to their home, darting inside the cracks of my resolve.

The sound of the woman crying reminded me of the arguments I'd had with Satsuki during the height of the war. The air raids in Kobe had grown more frequent until they were raining down on the city almost every day. Citizens carried crank-handle air raid sirens to warn neighbors whenever they saw the allied planes flying overhead. After my father was killed in a fire bombing that engulfed China Town, I took Satsuki to my brother and sister-in-law's house outside of Hiroshima. "Until it is safe, again, Sa-chan," I coaxed my wife, trying to make her see the logic of my plan. I would remain in Kobe with my mother. My *okaasan's* health was failing and I feared she would not make the trip to Hiroshima.

Satsuki begged me to let her stay in Kobe. "My place is here, with you and your mother, not in Hiroshima with your brother and his wife. They haven't even replied to your letter," she said. "How do you know they are willing to take me in?"

"War time mail is unreliable," I replied, shifting in my seat. "Besides, Zaemon's wife comes from a wealthy family. He told me once that their country home is twice the size of our house here. Surely they will have room to spare." As I talked, I convinced myself that I was right. In truth, my fear for my wife's safety—and panic at the thought of losing her—dictated my every decision. "This is what I have decided," I said, my voice firm and unwavering.

Satsuki was silent for a long moment and I knew I had convinced her. "I must say good-bye to Mt. Rokko," she whispered, head bowed. She did not know that I followed her up the mountain and observed from behind a tree as she knelt, tracing characters in the dust. After she left, I saw that she had written the *Jizo Bosatsu* sutra, meant to protect those journeying into hell. Somehow Satsuki knew, although she obeyed my wishes. How had she never reprimanded me after all these years? Even in death, I have not been able to answer that question.

Again, I thought of Zaemon, his blue-black hair combed back with pomade, his broad shoulders, his quick temper always lying just under the surface of his smile. At Osaka University, Zaemon was friendly with men who drank too much whiskey and women who smoked and didn't cover their mouths when they laughed. His girlfriends wore their hair in short bobs and favored Western dress over kimono. I envied my brother's confidence and quick wit, his ability to charm. I covered my shame and laughed along with him when he teased me for the amusement of his friends. He moved through life unimpeded by illness or a hesitant nature. In the silence of my room, I pretended I rode on his shoulders, my legs encircling his neck like bent branches.

"Your younger brother has no respect for what is proper," my mother would complain, tight-lipped, after Zaemon had left for the evening in a cloud of cologne and smoke. "It will hurt him eventually." She smiled at me. "*Okagesamade*, I thank the gods that they gave me one son with sense." My stomach, slippery and weak. I felt embarrassed both by her favoritism and my need for it.

The sound of my brother's laughter echoed through the trees again.

"Zaemon?" I whispered. A tiny fissure let in suspicions I'd kept behind glass, neat and frozen, for decades.

I have since learned that this moment was my last earthly chance to correct what was wrong. I replay it in the eternal dustiness of the afterlife—the decision that defined me as a weak, foolish man. Instead of turning to go home, I pushed my guilt to the back of my mind and focused instead on my eternal search for insects.

I spotted a praying mantis eating a moth, turning the hapless victim in the manner a human would eat a cob of corn. The mantis glanced at me as I passed, as if to ask for salt—a female in the height of mating season. I passed by her and stumbled up the path, looking for the tell-tale black wings of the beetles, listening for the click-click-click of their claws as they fought for dominance in the trees.

When I was a child, scores of them lived in the forest behind our house. After I became sick, my mother paid my schoolmates one *sen* apiece to capture them for her invalid son. I spent hours observing them in my room, watching them in the big glass tank my father managed to procure from a retired biology teacher. Their world became more real to me than the one to which I clung with my shallow breath and feverish dreams. "You must thank the *kabuto mushi* when you recover," advised my grandmother, holding me steady in her square-faced gaze. "As surely as I sit here, they have saved your life by giving you a way to live through them." And in many ways, my dedication to their research was done in gratitude to the horned beetles, though I only came to understand that after my death. Our intertwined history, myself and the insects, the rise and fall of our prominence, our place in the world.

In time, it became difficult to find good specimens to observe as golf courses built on Japan's mountaintops carpeted their habitat with bright green grass. The pesticides that leaked into the rivers tainted the water and air, killing off whole populations of insects and amphibians. By the time I retired from the university, I was giving youngsters in the neighborhood 10,000 *yen* for each one of the helmeted black bugs they found—the same amount I spent on our annual anniversary dinner at the Sonay Jazz Club in Sannomiya.

"Forty-five years, Kenzaburo."

The scene of our dinner together was again before me. I saw my beautiful wife as she shook her head and smiled. In the dim light of the club, her face moved through the different ages it had known, shifting from childhood to womanhood and back again. She pulled a lock of silver hair at the nape of her neck, as she always did when she was nervous or embarrassed, and concentrated on the bassist. He reminded me of my brother, how he looked before the war—hair slicked back except for a piece that fell across his forehead.

"He looks like Zaemon when he was a student at Osaka University," I remarked, watching her reaction over my menu.

Eyes downcast, Satsuki opened her menu as if it were a rare book.

"Doctor Ishikawa, what did he tell you today?" she said, changing the subject.

"Not a thing. He said you are keeping me in fine condition."

Satsuki tilted her head, as if considering my words. She knew I was lying even then, I am certain. There are times when I believe she knew better than I how little time I had left among the living.

An hour before I died, I pressed on, reciting more mindless facts about insects to keep my mind from slipping further. By 7:00 a.m., I had reached the pool under the Mt. Rokko waterfall. This was where Zaemon and I played as children, in the days before the polio came, before the weeks and months I spent sweating on white cotton hospital sheets in my childhood bedroom, my grandmother reciting sutras next to me on the tatami mats at all hours of the day and night

I paused a moment to shake the memory from my head and inhale the cool, dank air, hands on my knees, glad for the chance to catch my breath. Pink crayfish scrambled around the side of the waterfall's basin and small fish darted back and forth in the water a few feet from where the pool emptied into another smaller waterfall that carried the water downriver. Dragonflies hovered over the water to mate, their wings red and green prisms in the morning light.

The sound of splashing and shouting came to me as clearly as if the empty pool was filled with children. I leaned down and dunked my face in the cold water. Before the polio, Zaemon and I had played here together with the other boys in the neighborhood. The very last time we'd come, he'd dared us to jump from the top of the waterfall into the pool below. Zaemon had been the one to go first, jeering at the four Kikawa brothers and Miura-san, our next-door neighbor, for not plunging into the icy water from the height of a second-floor window. *"Yowamushi yanke!"* He called out, labeling us weak-willed worms. Zaemon liked to use Osaka-dialect because it made him sound tougher, though our mother punished us every time she heard us sliding into its growling vernacular.

One by one, the boys jumped. I waited until the end as I always did, hoping they wouldn't notice and designate me a coward for hesitating to meet my brother's challenge. Always the smaller, skinnier, weaker one, I was forever the butt of all their jokes. As if reading my mind, Miura-san, a rough boy whose father drank sake and beat him, shouted, "Kenzaburo—your turn. Unless you want to be the worm again." He and my brother laughed and pointed until my face turned crimson, which made all the other boys join in. Sweat from my forehead ran into my eyes and I wiped them with the back of my arm, which only made them laugh harder, "Crybaby!" they called, "Mama's boy!"

Taking a deep breath, I climbed the rocks to the top of the falls. From my perch, the pool looked little bigger than our bath tub at home, but I had no choice. Closing my eyes, I held my nose with my fingers and jumped. When I burst to the surface of the water, blood was unspooling around me and I felt the sting almost at once. I hadn't jumped far enough from the edge and had gouged my back and hit my head along the rocks on the way down. When he saw I'd been hurt, Zaemon's eyes grew wide and he ran home, afraid our mother would punish him, but Miura-san stayed to help me down the mountain.

The next day the chills of polio started their slow creep up my spine. In the months that followed, the disease claimed the lives of Miura-san and the youngest Kikawa boy. It was my mother, and not my gentle father, who beat Zaemon and made him apologize, his face and body pressed to the floor for hours, outside my bedroom door. We did not speak again until I left my sick room two years later.

Across Japan, children were forbidden to swim in pools or rivers. No one in our neighborhood was ever allowed to play in the pool under the waterfall again, even after I'd recovered.

I used my kerchief to wipe my face.

"I am here to collect insects for my research," I reminded myself. "Not to ponder over things that happened years ago." Softly, the irrevocable click as a door slid closed behind me.

I hobbled up the path to the right of the waterfall and glimpsed a copse of cedar and oak, an ideal place to find horned beetles. These trees were old, had been there when my grandfather was a child. I examined the leaves at the base of the cedars and spotted a group of black ants trying to carry away a protesting grasshopper.

A clicking sounds above my head made me peer into the green of the oak boughs. I took off my hat and set my cane beneath the tree. I grabbed my binoculars from my bag and raised them to my eyes. The *kabuto mushi*, horns locked, were fighting on a branch overhead.

My delight was erased when I heard the distant hum of shrine drums beating and human voices approaching. With a start, I realized that Obon was beginning in a few days.

What sounded like a throng of devout worshippers surged up the mountain toward me. Another sign I failed to understand—the visiting spirits greeting me in preparation for my journey to the afterlife. Pressing both hands to my ears, I hid behind the tree trunk like a frightened child, but the sound grew strident, until the din hit me in waves. One word was being called in unison: my family name, growing louder each time it was recited.

"*Tsuruda. Tsuruda. Tsuruda.*"

"Not real. Nothing is real except the insects on the branch," I whispered with difficulty, my lips slack and uncooperative. I needed to keep my mind on the insects I was pursuing, not the sounds my mind had tricked me into hearing. I focused on the pair of beetles again, and as I had done so many times before in my life, I imagined I was in their place. This time I was the insect in a complex mating ritual, and the world revolved around the choreography of sex. I was the scent of birth on the wind. I was water, teaming with life, rushing toward its own private destination.

My heart beat in my ears, in my chest, in my groin, in my temples. A kind of wildness took hold of me, a kind of fierceness that only the old possess. In spite of the ache in my legs and the sound of the voices coming toward me, I decided to climb the tree and attempt to catch the insects. A rush of adrenalin flooded through my body, allowing me to pull myself onto a large boulder by the oak tree and ease onto its lower branches. My perch brought me closer to the insects, but they were moving away, just out of my reach. I willed my arms and legs to propel my body higher up the trunk, to reach the next branch. Reaching a good vantage point on a branch of the oak, I sat there watching the beetles fight before they gave in to the push of instinct.

A piece of bark fell into my eye, and I reached into my pocket for a handkerchief to wipe it away. The river moved far below me. "How horrified my mother would be to see me in this tree, an old man of seventy-two years, still chasing bugs," I thought, rather proud of myself. I had never allowed myself the luxury of disobedience, even long after my *okaasan* wasn't there to scold me.

I heard the groaning crack before I felt the wood give way. Before

I fell from my perch and crashed down onto the boulders in the river below, I realized that I was no longer holding onto anything but fistfuls of air. A muddy, sucking sensation pulled at my hands and feet. I tried to draw my fingers toward my body, but instead, felt them lengthening, dissolving. I was spinning through the air again, only this time I moved upward, turning like a feather on the wind.

In the moments before my death, these things I knew:

The wild boar scratched her back with a hairy snout, causing one of her babies to waken and begin nursing.

The ancient snake in our garden slid out of her last skin and went off in search of food.

A vixen in a nearby cave nipped one of her kits in annoyance.

A white crane took flight over the river, circling overhead, casting its shadow on my splayed and bloodied body before heading toward the sea.

My wife opened her eyes and felt the futon beside her where my body had lain.

Haruna opened a small box she kept hidden in her room and took out a packet of tattered letters.

The horned beetles mated.

And at the very instant I died, the cicadas' shrill song began.

6
DIFFICULT WOMEN
HARUNA

"It is not often that you see a crane by herself," Satsuki used to remark when Haruna was in her early twenties. "You're lucky, Haru-chan, because cranes are a symbol of good fortune, happiness, and long life. That is why one often sees them on wedding kimono." But as Haruna grew older, each time Satsuki said this, her voice was smaller and softer, until in the end she did not say it at all.

Haruna attended Kobe University, where her father taught entomology and botany and was known as a strict and demanding professor. Because of this, his classes were small but well-attended. During Haruna's second year of college, her male classmates' hesitation wore off and a few of the braver ones pursued her. She began seeing a boy named Oda-san. He wanted to be an astrophysicist, and they had long discussions into the night about space exploration, quantum physics and the forces at work in the universe. Oda-san was serious and quiet, and Haruna thought for a time that she could love him as her mother loved her father. They even talked of marriage.

"Of course, you will give up your research when we have children," said Oda-san after they had been dating for a year. "It wouldn't be proper for you to continue working, like a man."

"Proper? Why not do both," Haruna said, "like foreign women do?"

Oda-san laughed. "You're funny, Haruna. At first I thought you were serious."

He didn't understand when she broke up with him the following week.

One by one, the other boys in her program approached her when it became known that she was single again. She didn't giggle and flatter or speak in a high-pitched voice; she talked to them about quantum theory, physics, and calculus. Her test scores were at the top of the class. One by one, they stopped walking her across campus or calling to set up study dates. At first, she was disappointed, but as time went by she put away hopes of finding someone who was willing to be married to a woman who wanted to make scientific discoveries and be recognized for her work.

"You are a *muzukashii hito*, Haruna," sputtered a student in her sociology class one day. He had asked her to coffee, and instead of flirting with him, she told him that his theory on the genetic differences between Koreans and Japanese made no sense. "You are a difficult woman," he said. She had no doubt he was right and told him so with a slight bow before saying good-bye.

The truth was that Haruna didn't care if the boys in her class understood her or not. Her goal was to become the first woman astronomy professor at the university, not a bored, docile wife who took tennis lessons with the other professors' wives twice a week.

"Why do you want to waste your time studying physics and getting a graduate degree when you could be married to a fine young man? After all, women attend college to meet a husband and become well-educated mothers," said the head of university admissions when she met to discuss doing graduate work. "I'm sure your father agrees with me." His smile revealed large yellow teeth. The man took her application, but when the acceptance letters arrived for Haruna's male classmates, she didn't receive one.

Haruna went to speak to her father in his study the day her rejection letter came. "Can't you do something, *Otohsan?*" she begged. "You've been at the university for twenty years. My grades are better than most of the boys who were accepted. Surely the admissions director will listen to you."

Kenzaburo read the letter, coughed, and said, "Yes, this must be disappointing for you. I will speak with him, certainly. I am glad you have an interest in science, but I never intended . . . " His voice trailed off and he shifted in his seat. "Perhaps you can concentrate on finding a husband who is a professor or scientist now. Many women have helped their husbands by compiling their notes for them."

"Father, I thought you would understand. You knew that this was what I wanted. I believed you wanted it for me, too," she said, her voice rising.

"Do not speak to me in that tone, young lady. This discussion is over," said her father, his voice sharp around the edges. He picked up his magnifying glass and went back to the specimen on his desk he'd been studying when Haruna walked in: a large blue mourning cloak butterfly pinned onto a thick white card. After some minutes he cleared his throat, signaling that the conversation was over. Haruna left, but the bitterness of her disappointment permeated the air of the house like black smoke.

The admissions director would not meet with her again. She applied to other universities, but the rejection letters came one by one, until Haruna gave up hope.

She didn't tell her parents that she decided she would never marry—they would have worried about her even more than they already did. She simply refused every man who was brought to her. "Too short. Too fat. Too stupid." She checked them off one by one, though she knew some were decent enough men. She did not want to be a slave to the words, *"Meshi. Agaru. Neru*—Food. Bath. Bed." In that order, the nightly command of a Japanese male.

More than one man had asked for her hand over the years. She recalled that a stuttering Mister Sakano had inquired, "W-w-would you do my laundry for the rest of my life?" by way of proposal. Haruna whispered, "I'm sorry," and left him standing in the gardens outside of the New Otani Hotel, where their parents were having dinner together and trying get to know each other better in the hopes of an impending engagement.

When Haruna was twenty-seven, she came upon her Aunt Tetsuko comforting Satsuki. *"Taihen desho.* It's difficult. Haruna is beautiful but she is awkward around people, like Kenzaburo. She would rather sit with her nose in a book all day than go shopping or to a movie like a normal young woman her age," said her aunt.

Haruna's mother nodded. "When she was just a small child, Kenzaburo would take her insect hunting on Mt. Rokko; at night he would set up his telescope in the garden. My daughter is more interested in books than she is in being a mother or housewife," Satsuki replied. Haruna was surprised when she realized that along with her disappointment her parents felt their own.

"Saaa, he gave her an unhealthy interest in science," Tetsuko grumbled before bringing out another list of young men for Haruna to meet. Haruna soon met—and rejected—all of them. Matchmaker after

matchmaker set up meetings with prospective men until the candidates came from as far away as the northernmost island of Hokkaido. After that particular date was over, Haruna told her parents, "I don't want to live so far away from you. And I don't think I'm suited to be a dairy farmer's wife." Her mother left the room without a word and her father nodded and looked out the window. Haruna was twenty-nine and this man was her last prospect.

Privately she was relieved, because this left her free to pursue her research. Though she had resigned herself to the fact that she could not become an astronomy professor, she made up her mind to write articles under a pen name. She became Mr. Hoshikawa, creating a surname out of the *kanji* for "star" and "river." As the years went by, her pieces were published in academic journals. Sometimes editors would contact her to get her opinion on black holes or expanding universe theory.

When the first Russian cosmonaut went into space, Haruna received a call from the *Daily Yomiuri*. "Professor Hoshikawa is out of the country. He is currently in the United States doing consultations for NASA," she said. "I am his wife. If you leave me your questions, I can ask him by phone and call you back." The reporter thanked "Professor Hoshikawa" profusely when she called back when her parents were out, and congratulated Haruna on her ability to remember and explain complex subject matter. "He was honored to help you," she said. She stood in the darkened hallway holding the phone to her chest for a long time after the reporter hung up.

For most of her young life, men dated Haruna for a month or so, and then moved on to someone softer and less interested in debating politics or scientific principles. This was the pattern of her life until the day she met Akihiro, whom she loved but would never marry.

乙
THE WILD BOAR
OBON VISIT
TETSUKO

When Tetsuko arrived at Rokko Station, she hailed a taxi to take her up the steep incline to the Tsuruda family home. As the cab made its way up the mountainside, Tetsuko again wondered about what Satsuki could mean by "something that is hidden." Was it a letter written to Zaemon where Tetsuko had complained about having Satsuki in the house with them during the war? Tetsuko recalled that during those difficult years, complaining about her sister-in-law's presence in the house had been a frequent occurrence. Perhaps Satsuki had intercepted it somehow and kept it hidden all these years? She might be looking for an apology from Tetsuko, especially in light of what she later did for Tetsuko's family when the bomb fell on Hiroshima. Tetsuko flushed red in the cab and fanned herself, causing the driver to grunt and turn the air conditioning up. As they made their way up the steep mountainside, Tetsuko composed an apology to Satsuki in her head—one that, she had to admit, she'd never given her sister-in-law in all the years since the war.

"*Hisashiburi!*" Tetsuko called to her niece as she emerged from the cab, returning Haruna's greeting with a smile and a wave of her lace handkerchief with the embroidered "T" on the corner. Haruna ran up and shouldered her aunt's bags, leaving Tetsuko free to notice the weeds that had sprung up and almost overtaken the stone walkway into the house.

Tetsuko examined her niece's face, which had collected more wrinkles in the year since Kenzaburo's funeral. Silver strands had crept into Haruna's black hair and, in the stifling August heat, it clung in damp tendrils to her neck. Still, Haruna retained the grace of an *Edo* print. She had always been the family beauty, with her wide-set eyes, oval face, and graceful movements. More beautiful, Tetsuko admitted, than her own two daughters. Mayumi and Yuriko were both stocky and square, like all the women in the Uribo family, and their love of chocolate éclairs and castella cakes had filled out their figures more amply than Tetsuko's own. But they had both married well some time ago and were busy raising their own children. Tetsuko glanced away so Haruna could not see the pity in her eyes. She remembered that when Haruna was born, the relatives had all whispered it was a miracle the couple could conceive at all, in light of Kenzaburo's childhood polio. Some believed the birth was a result of Satsuki's offerings to the fox goddess Inari and the influence of her home town of the same name—a place where people still followed the old ways. It was said that Inari's townsfolk were *kurai*—dark of spirit—and followed superstitious practices set in place before Japan became civilized thousands of years ago.

"Auntie, you have come so far. You are so kind to visit us."

Tetsuko shook her head. "*Ie, ie.* No, Haru-chan, I apologize for taking so long to come. My children and grandchildren have been keeping me very busy in the last year." Tetsuko noticed that the hem of her niece's summer blouse was fraying. More worrisome was the fact that the frown line between Haruna's eyebrows had become permanent.

"How is your *okaasan*'s health?" Tetsuko asked, fanning herself in the heat.

"*Maa, ne.* There are good days and bad," said Haruna. She smiled at her aunt. "Come inside. I have *mugi-cha* and cold melon waiting for you."

Before she followed Haruna into the house, Tetsuko turned to view the garden. In the far corner, she noticed that a part of the wall was falling into disrepair. She patted the sweat from her forehead with her kerchief and blinked: a shape seemed to be flickering between the bamboo trees. As she peered at the wall, a mourning dove startled from under the azalea bush, causing Tetsuko to jump and emit a tiny yelp. She looked around to see if anyone had witnessed her foolishness, hurried inside, and pulled the door shut behind her.

Tetsuko and Haruna drank their cold barley tea at the low table in the dining room and exchanged pleasantries. They spoke of the weather, Tetsuko's grandchildren, the trip from Hiroshima. When it was time to check on Satsuki, Haruna said, "Aunt Tetsuko, would you like to visit with *Okaasan* now? She will be so happy to see your face."

They rose, Tetsuko's underarms and thighs still damp with sweat. The older woman had realized when she arrived that there were no air conditioners in the house and frowned. She was growing warmer by the minute. Tetsuko had become used to the comforts of modern living and was distressed by the way in which Haruna and Satsuki scraped by on Kenzaburo's pension and the money Haruna earned tutoring neighborhood children in math and science.

She hovered at the doorway of Satsuki's room when Haruna approached her mother's bed. The smell of urine and baby powder made the air sour. "Aunt Tetsuko is here, Mother." Satsuki's expression did not change, but her breath became labored, as if she was having a bad dream. Haruna placed a clear plastic mask on her mother's gray face and turned on the oxygen tanks. "The doctors say this helps her in the hot weather," said Haruna, her back to Tetsuko.

Tetsuko sank to a small chair by the door, handbag clutched to her body, and watched as Haruna attended to her mother. Satsuki, whom she had cared for and envied in turns, reduced to this. She was alarmed by the color of Satsuki's skin and the blank look on her face. When her breathing was normal again, Haruna lifted the mask from her face.

Satsuki looked up at her daughter and smiled, her face trusting and childlike.

"*Okaasan*, Aunt Tetsuko is here," she said again. "She came all the way from Hiroshima to see us."

Satsuki's gaze traveled the room until she found Tetsuko.

"Did you find it yet?" she whispered.

"Find what, Satsuki-san?"

Satsuki's breathing became shallow again, and Haruna jumped up and slid the mask back on her face.

Tetsuko could not say why, but she felt uncomfortable, as if something was pressing down on her chest. She licked her lips and spoke again, "Haruna, it's a bit hot in here, don't you think? I'll just be out in the hall." She left the room and slid the door closed behind her. Tetsuko sat on a bench for a few moments in the dark hallway, both ashamed and relieved to be out of her sister-in-law's room, and now even more puzzled as to what Satsuki could be referring to.

After some minutes had passed, she blotted her face and stood up.

"This is not how an Uribo behaves," she said to herself. There was no use worrying about what she was unable to do, but there were things that could be done to help her sister-in-law and niece right now. By the time Haruna emerged from her mother's room a half hour later, Tetsuko had washed her hands and reapplied powder and lipstick, the determined look on her face restored.

"*Ne, ne*, Haruna," she said. "I have decided that I will go back to the old house in Hajiyama and check on things when I get home. Perhaps there really is something I should look for—your mother obviously thinks so, and I've always trusted her words. Why should I stop now? It's the least I can do after all she's done for me." Tetsuko brushed off Haruna's thanks with a wave of her hand and continued, "I've also decided that I would like to give a gift to Satsuki-san. Let's go down to the shops today and get an air conditioner for her room." Tetsuko put her handbag over her shoulder, her mind already made up. Before Haruna could protest, she added, "Please allow me to do this, Haruna. I want to give something useful to your mother. It is a very small gift, and one I would very much like to give her."

Haruna refused her aunt three times, as was polite. They both knew that in the end Haruna would bow to Tetsuko's wishes, but nevertheless they went through the customary motions of refusal. In the end, Haruna acquiesced, as they both knew she would. They left the house, Haruna's arm looped through Tetsuko's as they began to walk down the hill to the shops. Tetsuko glanced back at the garden wall and was relieved that she did not see any shapes flickering there amidst the bamboo. She laughed to herself but stopped short of telling Haruna. Her niece would think she was not in her right mind, and besides, Haruna had enough to worry about with Satsuki's care on her slim shoulders.

That night, in spite of the comfortable whirr of the air conditioners,

Tetsuko lay on her futon, unable to sleep. She had overridden Haruna's objections and bought new air conditioning units—complete with remote controls with myriad special functions—for each of the bedrooms, the kitchen, and dining room. Although Haruna expressed surprise at her aunt's ability to persuade the store manager to send someone to install the units during the Obon holiday, Tetsuko expected his cooperation.

"When your mother and I were young, Satsuki often compared me to a wild boar for this very reason, and said, 'Head down, you charge and run, seeing nothing but the object you desire.'" Tetsuko and Haruna had laughed over this memory at dinner, but Tetsuko did not tell her niece why Satsuki said this during the first open argument she and her sister-in-law ever had. At the time it made Tetsuko furious, but now she only felt admiration for her sister-in-law's courage. Besides Zaemon, Satsuki was one of the few people who had the strength to tell her what she thought. Now she wondered if she and her sister-in-law would ever have a real conversation again.

She shifted under the terrycloth sheets of the futon and rolled onto her side. Inches away from the tatami, the clean grassy smell of the woven mats calmed her, brought back more images of the old house in the hills above Hiroshima. She lay in the dark in her cotton nightgown, staring at the wooden ceiling. Her mind wandered back to the war. Lately, memories from that time bubbled to the surface unbidden; she felt powerless to stop them from coming.

In her mind's eye she saw the early autumn day when Kenzaburo and Satsuki first appeared on the road in front of her family's country house in Hajiyama, their bags in hand. She had known as soon as Kenzaburo and his young bride arrived that she would be asked to take them in. She also knew that she would be unable to refuse.

It was September, Tetsuko recalled, and the upper branches of the persimmon tree by the front gate of the country house were laden with the bright amber fruit. Tetsuko and her sisters were forever chasing the neighbor children from the fence, where they would scramble to pick and eat the mouth-puckering *kaki,* sometimes before it had even ripened. Everyone was hungry in those days.

Tetsuko remembered that there was some confusion about a letter. Ah, yes. It came back to her now. The letter Kenzaburo sent asking for Zaemon and Tetsuko's help had been lost in the mail, as so many things were lost during the war.

Hiroshima, where she'd been born and raised, had been destroyed by the American bomb. The emperor had transformed from god to mere mortal. And the hardest loss to bear: her youngest sister Fumiko, a casualty of the war, even though she died six months after it ended. So many years later, and she still could not contain her grief. But these things could not be changed, she told herself as she wiped her eyes on the corner of her pillowcase. "*Shikata ga nai*—it cannot be helped."

Tetsuko went back to the day Kenzaburo brought his young bride to stay with his brother and the Uribo family in Hajiyama. Tetsuko had been beating the futon in the backyard. Her family's country house, which they had evacuated to when the war threatened the safety of most city dwellers around Japan, had a view of the dirt road that led into the village of Hajiyama.

The barking of Kabocha, their Shiba Inu, had split open the still-ness of the late September afternoon. The small orange dog ran back and forth behind the bamboo fence, tail standing out straight when he stopped to sound the alarm.

"Quiet!" Tetsuko commanded. Kabocha, named for the color of bright orange pumpkin flesh, would obey only her. Wiping her hands and smoothing down her hair, she hurried to the front yard to see who was there.

Two people, a woman and man, were making their way up the road to her house. It appeared as if the woman was supporting the man under his elbow. Even from a distance, Tetsuko could tell that he was walking with great effort. She saw that he wore a short, navy blue *happi* coat over loose fitting trousers, while his companion was dressed in a black kimono, as if she was in mourning. They both carried square bundles tied in large kerchiefs. She did not recognize them as members of the village, yet there was something familiar about the man. She frowned in concentration. Where had she seen him before?

As they came closer, she understood. It was Kenzaburo, Zaemon's older brother, and his wife, Satsuki. Pregnant with Ichiro, Tetsuko had been unable to make the long journey to their wedding a few years before, but she had met Kenzaburo during the events surrounding her own.

Before Kenzaburo and his bride reached the gate, she guessed why they had come—and the added burden they would bring her. Tetsuko waited for the two travelers, her lips pressed against her teeth in a measured smile meant to convey duty rather than affection.

Tetsuko remembered how hard she worked to scrape together a dinner for seven that night. Zaemon had been called away to business in Manchuria again. There would now be six adults at the table, including her two unmarried sisters and her elderly mother. There were also her young son Ichiro and infant daughter Mayumi to feed.

Tetsuko had sent a village boy down to the shops to buy a few dried trout and a little extra tofu for the miso soup. Her garden yielded only some early squash and a few shriveled cucumbers, but she decided they would have to do. She could almost taste the war grade rice and over-ripe squash while she lay on the futon in Satsuki's house, miles and decades away from the night she first met her beautiful sister-in-law.

When she finally slept, she dreamed of Satsuki, her face changing into the fox goddess and back again at the garden gate. In the dream, Kabocha ran around Tetsuko's feet in circles while persimmons rained down upon them from the tree. When thunder cracked the sky open, Satsuki looked upward and laughed, and then turned to leave.

Tetsuko shouted, "Wait! Don't go—please talk to me!"

"When you go to Hajiyama, look inside the house," Satsuki called over her shoulder. She looked back toward Tetsuko one last time before changing into a white fox and disappearing into the forest.

8

FOX GODDESS
SATSUKI
DECEMBER 1944

It is the morning of Kenzaburo's twenty-eighth birthday. I think of him and wonder when I will see him next. I conjure up his face and go through my ritual of remembrance.

From the first, he made me laugh. We met in the munitions factory in Kobe, nothing more than a local high school converted into an arms production plant. All day long, young boys and the men who couldn't fight sat at long tables assembling weapons for the Japanese Imperial Army. I worked with the women, trudging up the hill every day with food and tea for the workers break at noon. We woke at 4:00 a.m. and made rice balls and soup, fried tempura vegetables and grilled fish. The other girls and I bought fruit at the market and took the bento boxes up to the factory to sell. I was just eighteen years old.

I noticed Kenzaburo the first day. He was smaller than the other men and had the face of someone who would always look young. He wore spectacles. When Maeda-san snapped at me as we passed out food, he winked and imitated her, with her pinched-up face and sour plum lips. I laughed out loud and covered my mouth. He smiled at me before he turned back to his work.

Each noontime, I saw him. On the day the cherry blossoms were at their peak, he bought his lunch box from me and handed me a letter. Once I had finished my tasks, I ran out of the building and opened it. I was only able to read part of what he'd written, and asked my friend, Ogawa-san to read it to me. "I'm saving up for glasses," I said by way of explanation. Round-faced Ogawa-san was from South Osaka. She hoped to become a school teacher after the war and loved secrets and romance. She was more than happy to oblige.

"*Dear Kitsune-san,*" she said. "*Forgive me for my intrusion. I have heard others saying your name, so I have taken the liberty of addressing you.*"

Ogawa-san stopped reading. "Oh, Satsuki-san. He is a real gentleman." Her eyes grew filmy and moist. I nodded, waiting for her to go on.

"*My name is Tsuruda Kenzaburo. I was wondering if you might join me by the Shukugawa River this evening, so we might stroll amongst the cherry blossoms.*" Ogawa-san stopped again. "Sa-chan, he's asking you for a rendezvous! *Ii, na!* Oh, how I envy you." She continued, "*I will be at the train station at 5:00 p.m. I hope I have not offended by asking you to accompany me.*'

"And then, he says here at the bottom of the page, '*Seeing you each day has made everything bearable.*'" Ogawa-san was overcome and removed a handkerchief from her sleeve to blow her nose. "Oh, Satsuki, this is so romantic. You will marry him and become a great lady of Kobe."

I thanked her, my face warm with embarrassment. "Ogawa-san,

he only asked me to walk with him. A stroll is not a proposal. And besides, what if I don't like him?" I spoke with confidence, but inside I was thinking, *An educated man from Kobe would never marry the adopted daughter of poor farmers from Inari. Especially an ignorant girl who cannot read and write.*

I almost didn't meet him at the assigned time and place. But then I remembered his warm smile, his kindness to me and the other women from the bento service. I decided there was no harm in taking a walk together, and it was a lovely night for cherry-blossom viewing. Although it was not proper for us to go without a chaperone—I, an unmarried young girl, and he, a single gentleman—this may have been part of the reason I went. Perhaps I just wanted an evening to be a young woman and not think about the war, the money I needed to send my parents that month, and the air raid drills that had become a horrible part of our daily lives.

It was while we were strolling that I noticed how pronounced Kenzaburo's limp was. He was nearly always seated at the factory, so I hadn't been aware of the difficulty he had in moving. When he wasn't looking, I watched his gait. His left foot twisted in at an odd angle, as if someone had attached it the wrong way. Kenzaburo's courage in asking me to go for a walk surprised me—few men would be willing to show their weakness in such a way. My mother, who was forever scolding me for bringing home orphaned kittens and birds with broken wings, came to mind. "Just because the bird's wing isn't working properly now doesn't mean he won't fly again someday," I always replied.

That first night, Kenzaburo said, "We are all made from star dust—think of it, the very same elements that make up the stars are found inside our bodies, and inside these cherry blossoms and the rocks at the bottom of the Shukugawa River." His voice grew louder as he talked, which made two soldiers patrolling the river stop and watch us. I covered my mouth and giggled as if he'd told me a joke until they looked away, convinced we were just another pair of lovers strolling along the river, taking advantage of the lull in bombings to enjoy the night air.

"In Inari we believe in the power of the fox goddess," I said after they'd moved on. "That we are all made up of star dust—I believe that, Tsuruda-san. But your science cannot explain everything. You will see."

From that time forward, we took every opportunity to meet and talk. At the munitions factory, no one knew about us except my friend Ogawa-san. She and the other girls helped me dodge our boss Maeda-san's probing questions and sharp eye, which allowed me to be the one to give Kenzaburo his lunch each day. She continued to read his letters to me each night. After a while, she stopped telling me to get a pair of glasses because she was drawn into her role as matchmaker.

"It won't be long now, Sa-chan," she whispered to me one night in spring after lights out. "The Bento Girls," as we called ourselves, shared a small apartment by the train station. "You will become a great lady of Kobe, just as I predicted," said Ogawa-san, her voice filled with awe. I did not argue with her but stared out the window up at the stars instead, my arms resting behind my head, my body rocked by the passing trains. Ogawa-san squeezed my hand in the dark until hers grew limp and little snoring sounds emerged from her throat.

That night, I stayed up to watch the moon rise high and bright in the sky. For the first time, I allowed myself to believe that love between a poor girl and a man from an upper-class family was possible. I thought of my father's nickname for me, "Kaguya-hime," the fairytale princess born on the moon and adopted by elderly farmers. The legend said that her beauty was so great that she was courted by the emperor of Japan. Unlike the princess in the fable, my father and mother found me wrapped in a cloth on a path by the rice fields one spring. I never learned who my real mother was, but my father said two foxes were nearby in the field protecting me, a powerful sign that Inari was watching over me and would bless the family who took me in.

Three months after our first walk by the river, Kenzaburo paused by the bridge and produced a small stick from his satchel. He seemed nervous and cleared his throat a few times before speaking. He would not look me in the eye as he said, "When a male crane is courting the female, he offers her a stick. If she accepts, they will use it to create a nest together. Satsuki-san, will you share a nest with me?"

My hand flew to my mouth. "*Ehh,*" I said, my eyes filling. "Yes, I will share a nest with you, Tsuruda Kenzaburo." I took the small stick and held it to my chest. I did not tell him that I worried I was not good enough for him, that I was sure his family would not accept me, that everything inside me said that he would regret his choice in a mate. I did not say these words because my body leaned into his when he kissed me. That night, we did not care that the soldiers saw us touch hands beneath a maple tree before we boarded the train.

The next week, we traveled by train to my parents' house to ask their permission to wed. "Why must we keep with tradition when we know we love each other," asked Kenzaburo. "We don't need a formal agreement between our parents. This is our life; our fate." Unlike most people at the time, we did not have a matchmaker to broker the engagement, and our families did not meet to approve of the match beforehand. "Old ways," said Kenzaburo and shook his head. Later, I understood why he did not tell his mother about me.

My mother-in-law, Reiko, would have never agreed to such a match for her son, and only accepted our marriage when the legal documents were shown to her. Reiko could not bear to lose Kenzaburo—not after Zaemon had left for adoption into Tetsuko's family in Hiroshima. To Kobe society, Reiko pretended to have known about our match, and called us a "modern couple." When she spoke to me, anger lay beneath the surface of her papery skin: bared teeth, red lips, bitter breath.

But on the day Kenzaburo and I set off for Inari, I did not know any of this. I only knew that my heart was full, and I had good news—the best kind of news—for my parents. It was the end of the rainy season in early July, and the landscape was green and verdant against the backdrop of a soft, yielding sky. Our faces looked back at us in the glass of the train windows, and clouds appeared to float over our heads in our reflection.

"The color of the sea in winter," I whispered to Kenzaburo as the train lumbered down the tracks, making its way through Osaka, then on to Kyoto.

"Pigeon feathers," he whispered back, playing the game we'd invented. The object was to describe something without using its name: to win, one had to guess the object and answer the first person with another description that matched. On this day, Kenzaburo had correctly guessed that I had chosen the sky.

"An old man's beard," I said, arching my eyebrows.

"A luna moth," laughed Kenzaburo, sure that he had won this round.

I smiled and brought my hand up to touch his chin but stopped myself when I noticed a middle-aged woman in a heavy blue kimono staring at us. Her glance said that I was standing too close to Kenzaburo, that I had no business being with such a man. I dropped my hand to my side and looked away.

We stopped in Kyoto to shop for food for my parents. Armed soldiers were everywhere in their brown uniforms and flat-topped hats, some laughing and lounging in the station, others walking in formation. Kenzaburo avoided looking at them. I wondered if he felt ashamed of his infirmity. I thanked the gods that he was spared military service. Lately, the Japanese military had started to accept boys as young as fourteen, though children even younger had been known to lie to get in.

A full five hours after leaving Kobe, we arrived at Inari Station. We walked through the village to my parents' house, past the Inari Shrine with its tunnel of arching red *torii* gates and the forest of fox statues that protected it. Even in lean times, worshippers brought offerings to place before the stone figures, in hopes of a good harvest and prosperity for their families and the town.

At first the scenery did not appear to be touched by the war. As we walked, I noticed more and more people living on the streets, begging for food. Many were old or lame. Small children sat crying in doorways from hunger. "They must have come here from the surrounding countryside, hoping for food," I said to Kenzaburo. I gave the children some of the sweet *manju* bean cakes and fried tofu I'd bought in Kyoto. They thanked me and held onto my kimono, begging for more until Kenzaburo pulled me away.

"Your parents," he said, with an apologetic smile. "We are here to see them."

We made our way through the village that was sheltered by Mt. Inari. I was pleased to see Kenzaburo stop and take in the site of the thousands of red torii gates marching up the mountainside to the shrine. To the east were a series of terraced rice fields my father planted and harvested for Noguchi-san, the rich landowner in the area.

I spied the bobbing heads of our neighbors' children in the field above the village houses before we reached my parents' home. They stopped and stared, then swooped toward us like seagulls, dropping their sticks and tools in unison. Kenzaburo laughed, his mouth wide and generous, as six children of varying sizes jumped up and grabbed my kimono sleeves, and told me about their adventures the past year, asked about my life in the city.

Seven-year-old Yurie, the daughter of the Higuchis who lived down the lane from my parents, eyed Kenzaburo and whispered, "Is he your husband?" The other children put their hands over their mouths and laughed.

Tsuyoshi, Yurie's older brother, snapped, "Yu-chan, you know better than to be so impolite." Yurie hugged me tighter and Tsuyoshi gave Kenzaburo an apologetic smile and bowed. I noticed that Tsuyoshi had grown several centimeters taller since I'd been gone, too, and his voice was no longer that of a child's. Soon he would be joining the imperial army, following behind all the other young men in our village. Something in my stomach twisted tight and hard to think of Tsuyoshi in this way, a boy whom I'd helped bathe as an infant.

We said good-bye to the children before we reached my parents' door. My family home was smaller than I remembered it, and in grave disrepair. The tin roof was rusted through in places and seemed as if it were sliding off the building altogether. I felt embarrassed to show Kenzaburo where I'd grown up, and ashamed that I felt that way.

Kenzaburo smiled at me. "Are you going to let me stand here in the rain or will you introduce me to your parents, Satsuki-san?" I smiled up at him and walked through the door of the small frame building and said, "*Tadaima!*" calling out "I'm home" just as I had each time I'd made my way down from the fields at the end of the day.

Kenzaburo followed me, bowing before he entered my family home. It was dark inside and damp-smelling, like smoke and sickness and overturned earth. My mother was stooped over the fire making soup with old cabbage and turnip tops. The floor was hard dirt, the walls were covered with soot. *Okaasan* dropped the large chopsticks she was using to stir the pot and came to me with a startled cry. We greeted each other, bowing and smiling, and I introduced Kenzaburo, who also bowed to my mother.

"*Okaasan*, forgive this unannounced visit," the words tumbled out of my mouth like vegetables out of an overturned cart. "I tried to call Noguchi-san to ask his daughter to get a message to you, but the line wasn't working," I paused and took a breath. "I'm forgetting my manners—please allow me to introduce Tsuruda Kenzaburo-san."

Kenzaburo and my mother bowed to each other again, my mother more deeply. She waited until Kenzaburo rose before she stood. When she spoke, she used the same respectful language she used with Noguchi-san, the only land-owner in our village. I understood the look that passed over her face. She was wondering what this man in fine, expensive clothes would want with her daughter, a girl adopted by a poor family in the countryside. Remembering herself, she called to my father.

"*Otohsan?*"

My father was sitting in the furthest corner of the room, propped up on a futon in the dark. I nearly cried out when I saw him. My *otohsan*'s open cotton kimono revealed a bony chest laced with red marks. Slack flesh hung under his chin. A dry, wheezing cough wracked his frame, and he held his handkerchief to his mouth. A red flower blossomed on the white cloth where he spit.

"Father, what has happened? Have you not been receiving the money I've been sending? Why aren't you eating?" I touched his arm, his forehead, his sunken cheeks. His skin felt dry and feverish to the touch. He smiled at me. "My princess is back from the moon," he whispered, and the shared joke made me laugh. I looked to the ceiling to prevent my eyes from spilling over.

Behind me, my mother said in a low whisper, "We are very grateful for your assistance, Sa-chan. Your father eats when he can, but he is so rarely hungry these days. He has refused to see a doctor. Even if he agreed, it is hard to find one in Inari. What are we to do? I try to take care of him, but . . . "

"*Okaasan*," my father rasped to my mother. "We have a guest here, and our daughter is home after a year away. *Ocha, onegai shimasu.*" His request that we drink tea together stopped our conversation, and we began at once to prepare the mid-day meal.

Kenzaburo went over to my father and bowed, only rising when my *Otohsan* gave him permission. They drank tea and talked in low voices. I could see Kenzaburo taking in all my father's symptoms. I did not want to hear what conclusions he'd made.

Guilt knotted my insides. The last time I'd visited had been six months ago, and though not robust, my father had been upright and able to perform his tasks for Noguchi-san in the rice fields. My father sent two letters since then in his childish hand, using only the Hiragana alphabet he'd taught me. He had only spoken of weather and neighbors and revealed nothing of his condition. Each time he said, "Do not worry. We are fine. Thank you for your hard work." I was so intent on making money to send to my parents—and meeting Kenzaburo on my days off—that I hadn't had time to come to see them again.

I suspected that the money I'd sent had gone to pay Noguchi-san rent, and what was left over was used for food. The Japanese government had taken the farmland back during the war bit by bit, calling it "repatriation for the war effort," including the land my father had managed to save for and buy during his lifetime. Since my departure, he'd been reduced to sharecropping for Noguchi-san again.

Now my mother began taking the food Kenzaburo and I had brought out of our bags, protesting at each new delicacy, her eyes lighting up with delight. We began at once to make soup while Kenzaburo talked with my father. My mother and I chopped carrots and straw mushrooms, cabbage and sweet green scallions and threw them all into the large pot that hung from a hook in the ceiling over the *irori* open fire pit. We dropped pieces of chicken into the iron *nabe* pot, as well, along with some eggs and *mochi*—hard pounded rice cakes that expanded like sponges into the soup as the water boiled. Soon the smells in the house made all of our mouths water.

There was enough to feed everyone three times over. My *okaasan* called to the neighbor children and asked them to join us. Yurie, her siblings, and parents came to our door, bowing until my mother swatted their shoulders with her large-brimmed hat and pushed them through. Everyone ate their fill. For dessert, we had the rest of the steamed *manju* I'd bought from a vendor in Kyoto station. "*O-Manju!*" cried Yurie and squealed. "May I make the tea?"

My mother smiled at her and nodded. I wondered how many months since they'd had sweets—or any real food at all?

We watched as Yurie placed the metal pot on the hook over the *irori,* measured the green leaves into a cracked teapot while the water boiled, and served us all as we sat around the open fire pit on a straw mat in the center of the small house. It is one of my fondest memories, even now—the sound of the last rain of the season on the roof, the smoke twisting and turning its way out of the hole in my parents' roof, and Kenzaburo talking and laughing with my parents and the neighbors. I already felt like the Fox Goddess had blessed our marriage with good fortune. I did not know then that, as with every gift Inari gave, the fortune would be a mixed one.

After we'd all gotten our tea and eaten some *manju*, I noticed a familiar look in my father's eyes and guessed that he was preparing to tell a story. He cleared his throat, and we all leaned forward in expectation.

"Tonight, I will share with you, Tsuruda-san, the tale of Inari." The younger children hugged their legs in anticipation. All the children of Inari loved hearing this story because it was about our town and the capricious deity that ruled over us. My father was well known in our village and beyond for his ability to spin a tale.

"As everyone knows, Inari is the God of Rice," he began, "but it was not always so. In the beginning, his wife Uke-mochi was the Goddess of the Harvest, until the Storm God, Susano-wo, killed her for giving him food that was not to his liking." He raised his eyebrows and looked at my mother, and his expression was so comical that she laughed and slapped her thigh.

My father's voice, though weakened by illness, was low and rich. People in the village said he had the skill of the professional *rakugo-ka,* storytellers who competed in tournaments all over the country. In the heat of the fire, his burnished face looked as if it was carved from Pawlonia wood. He sat upright on his cushion, hands gesturing as he spoke. In the glow of the soft orange light, I almost forgot his illness.

"After his wife's death, Inari became the God of Rice and Abundant Harvest, bringing prosperity to all of his loyal worshippers." *Otohsan* leaned forward on his cushion, moistening his lips. Everyone drew closer to him.

I looked over at Kenzaburo, who was listening with an amused smile on his face. I felt proud of my father and my family and the warmth and affection that filled the little house, despite its dirt floor and the cracks in the walls.

My father continued. "You may think of the god Inari as an old bearded man who blesses weddings and holidays, sitting on his sacks of rice, but he also appears in the female form, as a beautiful young maiden with long flowing hair. She has been known to enchant unsuspecting farmers and marry them, even bearing them children. If you see the maiden Inari, you will know her because she is always accompanied by two foxes. In fact, she lives in the mountains right above our village, and the creatures are her messengers. I saw a pair of them last night behind our bamboo fence and I asked them to give our best wishes to the goddess." His voice lowered in a confidential whisper. "One of the foxes told me Inari was planning a plentiful harvest for the fall." He looked over at us, a slight smile playing on his lips.

"She really said so?" Yurie asked, her mouth a perfect "o."

Otohsan had long ago convinced the neighborhood children that he could speak to animals. In truth, he had a way with creatures of all kinds, and seemed to understand their meanderings and behavior—a skill, I realized at that moment, my father and husband-to-be shared.

"Inari also can appear in the form of a fox. That is why we see so many statues of foxes by each shrine in our village," he said to Kenzaburo, and pointed in the direction of the red pillars of the shrines we had passed on our way up the mountain. The tunnel of red *torii* gates that led up Mt. Inari to the main shrine had been part of the village landscape forever. As a small child, my friends and I had dared each other to walk through them at night, all the way to the top. I had sealed my fame by being the only one who could make it all the way by myself. Unlike the others, I wasn't afraid of the mountain at night—the presence of the fox goddess was comforting to me rather than frightening.

"People have also seen a large white fox with blazing yellow eyes sitting amongst the altars on the mountain. It can only be Inari. I myself saw her once when I was Yurie's age."

"What did you do?" whispered Yurie.

"*Saaa,* I bowed down on the ground and immediately gave her an offering—as I recall, it was a rice ball my mother had made for my lunch. Inari rewarded me by telling me that I would have a fine daughter someday. So, you see, she is a benevolent goddess." He looked over at me and nodded, eyes closing. With dismay, I watched his face age before me again, until he was the sickly version of my father we greeted when we arrived. I hid my sorrow inside a hollow laugh, saying, "*Ie, ie.* No, it is I who am fortunate to be your daughter."

My father cleared his throat. A wracking cough shook his body, and my mother said, "*Sumimasen,*" and attended to him.

Our neighbors and the children bowed and prepared to leave. My mother packed up the remaining bean cakes, two for each family, and we said good-bye to the children.

In the lull that followed, Kenzaburo produced a bottle of fine Rokko sake from his satchel and poured it for my father and himself. Kenzaburo seemed nervous, and he cleared his throat.

"Kitsune-san, may I talk with you about an important matter?" he asked my parents.

"*Hai,* please go ahead," said my father, a dignified look on his face as he gave Kenzaburo permission to speak. I was certain that he had guessed at the reason for our visit from the start.

"We have come here today so I can ask your permission to marry your daughter. I apologize for my rudeness in coming without a formal introduction. However, I would be honored if you would accept me as your son-in-law."

My father hesitated. His dark eyes took in everything as Kenzaburo spoke.

Kenzaburo continued by telling my parents what his goals and ambitions were, and how he planned to take care of me and the family he hoped we'd have one day. He was humble in his explanation of his interest in science and his ideas about going to university and becoming a professor.

After he was finished, my father asked, "And what of your parents, Tsuruda-san? Do they approve?"

He watched Kenzaburo as he stammered, "They do not yet know, but I am sure they will see what a good wife Satsuki will be, and what a devoted daughter-in-law to them."

My father nodded, saying, "I will think the matter over carefully." I felt my heart lighten, seeing my father and future husband together, and hoped that our lack of adherence to tradition had not upset my parents so much that they would not grant us permission to marry. Kenzaburo had impressed them with his humility, his devotion to me. They knew he had the means to give me a good life at a time when we'd heard of parents in Japan who were so poor they had been forced to sell their daughters. If they noticed Kenzaburo's crippled leg, they never mentioned it, and for that I believe my future husband was also grateful.

Soon talk turned to other subjects. Although they had not formally agreed to our match, I could tell by my father and mother's faces that they approved of my choice. I also knew that the *jisankin* money that Kenzaburo brought as the dowry paid to the bride's family would sustain my family for the next year. They would be able to buy some medicine and perhaps be able to afford a bit of meat or fish.

One by one, all of my worries dissipated as we sat by the fire, talking and laughing until my father grew too tired to speak. When it was time for bed, I saw that my parents had given us their best futons on which to sleep. They laid them out on opposite sides of our house and slept between us, as was proper. I whispered good night to Kenzaburo over my parents' sleeping heads.

The next morning, I sat in the corner of the house with my father and watched my mother as she stood sweeping the floor. In the half-light of the doorway, the lines in her face were illuminated by weak sunlight. The wrinkles under her eyes were cross-hatched, her skin the color of the dried tobacco leaves that hung from the bamboo poles that spanned the ceiling.

"We are growing old," my father said with a laugh that turned into a cough. My mother shushed him and helped me prop him up on his futon. "Everything is different now, Sa-chan," he said. "This war has turned earth and heaven upside-down. In this respect I agree with your future husband. You must make your own life now." I bowed, my cheeks wet, knowing that this was his way of telling me that he approved of my match, that we could go ahead with our plans to marry.

Kenzaburo and I walked through the village to the train station making plans for our future. That day, I forever journeyed away from the terraced green hills of my childhood, the security of my parents' house, and a benevolent rice god who could turn himself into a beautiful maiden or a white fox at will.

We were married that August in Inari—my parents, Ogawa-san, and our neighbors all in attendance. The white cranes that flew across the red kimono I wore that day flashed in the sun. My hair was piled high and sleek on my head, decorated with long combs from which little paper flowers hung. Ogawa-san cried as she made up my face with white powder and painted a tiny red mouth onto my lips, small and red as an umeboshi plum on a bed of rice. I felt beautiful.

No one from Kenzaburo's family came to our wedding. Their absence was louder than the sound of the war planes that flew overhead toward Osaka during the ceremony.

Kenzaburo stood in his black silk kimono while the Shinto priest performed the sacred rites for our marriage, for my sake acquiescing to a traditional wedding at Inari Shrine. Kenzaburo had simply wanted to sign a paper at City Hall in Kobe, but I would not hear of it. In this one matter, at least, I would have my way, even though weddings were customarily held in the groom's hometown.

My family drank *amazake* together inside the shrine as the priest intoned the sacred vows. Kenzaburo and I sipped the sweet sake from little golden cups. The syrupy liquid trickled down my throat, and I felt as if I were floating above the crowd inside the compound of Inari Shrine, looking down on the heads of everyone assembled. That day, I saw that our lives had become a circle drawn with a soft black brush onto clean white paper.

We celebrated afterward in one of the open halls of the shrine, with more sake and food than could be eaten or drunk. Everyone from the village was invited. Kenzaburo laughed with my parents and teased the neighborhood children. They came to him all day with their treasures—origami cranes, a bamboo flute, and a small field mouse that Yurie kept in her pocket and presented to Kenzaburo. He took it from her with great care and released it back into the rice field when Yurie wasn't looking.

At the end of the day, my father spoke. In a quavering voice, he drew himself up and told the story of the moon princess *Kaguyahime*, laughing when he warned Kenzaburo not to anger me lest I return to my home in the night sky. He talked about my childhood, what a good daughter I had been, how I was under the protection of Inari. Tears streamed down his and my mother's faces when he said how happy he was that I was now leaving to have a family of my own. I hung on Kenzaburo's sleeve and wept like a child.

It would be the last time I saw my parents alive. Two months after our wedding, my father passed away in his sleep. My mother followed him to the afterlife just one week later. The phone crackled as Tsuyoshi told me the news on a day my husband and new in-laws were out of the house. "Everyone here has cholera, Satsuki-san," he rasped. His young man's voice had aged ten years in the months since I'd seen him. "So many have died. I've just been able to get up from my futon today. Mother was worried and did not want me to walk to Noguchi-san's to call you, but I insisted." He spoke quickly, his breath fast and shallow. In two months, he would be sent to the Philippines to fight, and in three years, he would arrive home with a blank look on his face, his right arm left behind in the jungle.

"Thank you, Tsuyoshi-san," I whispered now. "You were good to call me. Thank you for watching over my parents." I stood holding the phone, my body aching with grief and homesickness. "And your mother is right. Please go home. I will come as soon as I can to make preparations for my parents' funeral."

"Satsuki-san, that is what I wanted to tell you. I am so sorry. It's already over. The military doctor ordered it. They were cremated with the rest."

I let the phone drop and slid to the floor, unable to breathe or speak. Kenzaburo found me there hours later, hunched in the corner with my arms around my knees.

"We must light a candle for them," I whispered. "To guide them to the afterlife. We may not be able to give them a funeral, but we must help get them to the next world." Kenzaburo did not argue with me. He took my shaking hand in his, and together, we lit the long white candle.

九
MOTHER-IN-LAW
SATSUKI AND REIKO (1942)

In Kobe, our bedroom is invaded by my mother-in-law's presence, by her poking and peering. When I come home from the market, my chest of drawers, Kenzaburo's books, the brushes and combs my mother presented to me on my wedding day, have all been rearranged on the shelf. Always, Reiko's smell is in the room: green tea, rose perfume, and something bitter and burnt that was part of her own scent.

My mother-in-law is tall for a woman. Her hair is dyed a bluish black and is pulled into a tight bun on top of her head. The strands at the base of her skull resemble tiny lines and look as if they have been painted onto her neck. Reiko's cheekbones protrude, and were once, she tells me, her "beauty point," along with skin the color of rice paper. Her mouth is small and puckered, and she wears vermillion lipstick that bleeds around the edges. She never ceases to compare my brown skin to her lighter complexion. I do not think her color is beautiful.

To me, the hue is gray and unkind, the killing frost on the flowers of late autumn.

"Might we have a house of our own some day?" I hear the pleading in my voice when I talk with my husband, although I am trying to sound light.

"But why," he asks, shaking his head. "We are comfortable here. My parents think of you as their own daughter." He stumbles on this last sentence, because even he knows it's not true. When I tell Kenzaburo that his mother has been going through our things when we aren't home, Kenzaburo turns away from me. The truth in my words makes him uncomfortable.

"Perhaps she is poking about. Isn't that what mothers do?" I realize that he is afraid of her, too, and that marrying me was the one time in his life that he risked his mother's disapproval.

The memory of the day Kenzaburo brought me home and introduced me as his wife is as fresh as the bite of a sharp stone on the sole of my foot. "Tell her to wait outside," Reiko said, lips barely moving. She did not address me or look in my direction.

Kenzaburo walked me to the door of the traditional sitting room and motioned to a bench in the hall. The room was hung with bold calligraphy scrolls and a large painting of a dragon, teeth bared. A gold vase held an *ikebana* flower arrangement of dark branches and a single red flower. The effect of the room was intimidating rather than welcoming.

I heard low voices murmur in the room, now soft, now strident. I shifted in my seat. The sun had traveled from the front of the house to the back. I wondered how long I was going to be made to wait here. I worried that my mother- and father-in-law would reject our marriage and send me away. I moved closer to the sliding door and put my ear to the green and white paper in an attempt to hear what was being said.

After a few moments, I heard the sound of something cracking open, as if a stone had split in two. Puzzled, I lingered there a moment too long and was forced to jump back just as Reiko emerged. She tilted her head and surveyed me without expression, as if contemplating what to do next. I could not help but be reminded of the large black horned beetle Kenzaburo had pointed out to me on a recent walk, pincers clasping its prey as the smaller insect struggled.

Reiko did not address me, but stared as if I was a curiosity, an obstacle that needed to be removed. "My foolish son may have married you," she whispered, jaw clenched, "but that does not make you any better than what you are, *country bumpkin*." She turned away from me and called into the inner rooms of the house, "Doi-san! My head is aching. Bring me a cold cloth immediately." When the family servant appeared, Reiko swept down the hall without another word.

Kenzaburo appeared and told me not to worry, "*Daijobu*," he whispered, but his shoulders slumped like a child who has been beaten for stealing. He did not look at me when he said, almost to himself, "M-Mother will be fine after she gets used to the idea."

I looked into the room to see what made the sound I'd heard before. On the floor, a stone lay in two pieces beneath the solid beam of the *tokonoma* alcove. It was the sculpture of the Inari Fox Goddess I'd brought my husband's family as a present. I had used the rest of my savings from the Bento shop to buy it. I cried out and ran over to the two pieces that lay on the ground. Kenzaburo came to help me pick them up. I tied them up in a cloth and promised the fox goddess that I would take the pieces to the closest shrine the first chance I could get.

When Reiko dismissed Doi-san a week later, the maid took me aside and said, "Beware of that woman, Satsuki-san. She will try to break you if she can. I have been with this family since your husband was a child, but she thinks nothing of sending me away because she has a new servant in you, her daughter-in-law from Inari." Looking around to see if anyone was near, she whispered the story of Reiko's marriage to my father-in-law. "She lords her rank over your father-in-law, and brags that she has a better family name, but I've never believed her claims. Says she, her family, the Kitadas, have ties to noble families in Kyoto," she sniffed, "but I'm not so sure."

According to Doi-san, my mother-in-law's family was once powerful in Kyoto and Kobe, but their fortunes had been dwindling for more than a century. At the time of Reiko's marriage to Kenzaburo's father Osamu, my mother-in-law was living with her parents in a decaying house, wearing threadbare kimono, and her family was trading on their last drops of supposed aristocratic blood. Reiko's beauty was all they had to turn around their fortunes, and her marriage to Osamu was arranged when he was twenty-nine and she was just fourteen. The Tsurudas were wealthy upper-middle-class merchants with no nobility in their bloodline, and they needed to marry off their eldest son, who was thought to be simpleminded.

"All this time and she's still bitter about not marrying a more impressive suitor," said Doi-san with a laugh that sounded more like a bark. "I heard from her family's elderly servant that they found your mother-in-law trying to run away with her cousin the night before her wedding to Tsuruda-san. Her *cousin*, can you imagine? But they caught her before she got too far. He ran away out of shame and died soon after—malaria. She's never forgiven Tsuruda-san for it—any of it. Thought she should have had a better match, I suppose." Doi-san's words gripped my stomach and twisted. I wondered if Reiko would ever allow an adopted farm girl from Inari to be her eldest son's wife, or if she was already planning to remove me from the house.

Doi-san picked up her bundle, tied with a large blue kerchief into a knot. She would carry it to her unmarried sister's house, she said, where she would stay until she found employment. "This house is *kurai*," she whispered before leaving. "There is a darkness here, Satsuki-san. *Ki wo tsukete*." After she left, I thought of her parting words again and their true meaning: "Take care of your spirit."

As the weeks and months went by in the Tsuruda family home, I saw that Doi-san spoke the truth. Reiko demarcated the line that ran through her household, Kitada against Tsuruda. The rule was simple and devastating: all things Kitada were important and worthy of praise; all things Tsuruda were somehow inferior and false. "You take after my family. You are a Kitada," Reiko said to my husband one night as I served dinner. Her tone hardened when she added, "Your brother Zaemon is a Tsuruda." My father-in-law bowed his head and ate the last grains of rice in his bowl without a word. Reiko stroked the rings on her left hand, her mouth making a flat line, a dead fish across the white butcher's paper of her face.

Like his father, Kenzaburo bent his head and continued eating. I realized that a part of him enjoyed her attention, even at the expense of his brother. I could not look at him when I saw this.

Reiko's bullying began in earnest when Doi-san was no longer in the house. If a dish was broken or the rice burned, it was my fault. The soup was either too salty or too thin, the tea never brewed to perfection. There were times when I wondered how Reiko managed to feed her hatred so thoroughly. I imagined fat black slivers of anger and bitterness devoured by her yellowing teeth each morning upon waking.

At first, I worked to change her mind by being the perfect daughter-in-law. I did this for my husband's sake, but soon saw it was no use. On the days when we were alone in the house, she drew back from me when I passed, holding her kimono away from me so as not to be dirtied by touching me. The simple truth was that Kenzaburo did not pick a woman who had his mother's approval—he did not choose a woman from an established upper-class family in Kansai to be his wife. Reiko wanted him to marry into a family with noble lineage to continue improving the Tsuruda name. She had arranged many meetings with prospective brides for him through the years, but he refused all of them.

"None of the women the matchmaker brought to our house had curiosity about life, about nature. They did not talk, Satsuki, they just sat stiffly like statues, heads bowed." He smiled and held my chin with his forefinger, "Not like my goddess of the rice paddies."

In Kenzaburo's mother, this nickname would be something to hurt, to insult. From my husband's lips, it was reverent and kind. I believe his gentle spirit came from his father, and from the time he spent observing insects and animals. When I was a girl, my father said, "It's difficult not to be influenced by the god in all things when you spend time in nature," and I saw the truth of his words in my gentle husband.

My mother-in-law was the opposite. She was like a crow who lined her nest with shiny objects. In the back storeroom of the house were combs, shoes, unworn kimono, fans, gloves, hats, jewelry, umbrellas, stockings, packets of seeds, unopened boxes of sweets, and a gramophone with hundreds of shiny black jazz records in crinkly paper. This was strange to me, because in public she acted as if she hated anything Western.

Since the government labeled hoarding a crime, Reiko kept her goods under lock and key. She tried to be secretive about it, but I knew that she visited her storeroom every day like a shrine. There were nights I went by the door and heard her counting and recounting her supplies, as if she was about to wage a battle and would need to dress an army of women and throw a lavish party beforehand.

Reiko's habits were strange. She did not leave the house for weeks at a time, then she would ask me to air out her best kimono. On these days she swept her hair up into an elaborate bun, completed with mother-of-pearl combs and ornaments, and visited with her circle of friends. Like much in Reiko's life, it was a performance meant to impress Kobe society, and nothing else.

When she invited her acquaintances to her home for tea, it was my job to wait on them as if I was a servant. My mother-in-law did not introduce me to them. I was not certain if they knew that I was Kenzaburo's wife—or even that he was married.

Reiko's friend Namba-san, who was plump and wore a series of elaborate wigs to disguise her balding head, bent to whisper in my mother-in-law's ear when I was in the room. One day I overheard her telling Reiko and her guests the rumors about women from Inari—"They are demons disguised as beautiful women. Their only goal is to bewitch a man into marrying them," she said, but stopped talking when I opened the door with more tea.

She covered her words, pretending the women were having a different conversation. "Reiko-san, you are so amusing! Tell us about the train conductor with the lisp!" Namba-san was frightened of me. Reiko glanced at me before she began, her face almost radiant with victory. I wondered if she thought I would be so easily removed from her son's life. She clapped her hands at the start of her story as I served the four women tea in the traditional sitting room of the house.

My mother-in-law soon had the other women laughing, their soft hands over their mouths to cover their teeth. Reiko was a gifted mimic. She found the weakness in people, the soft unprotected spots, and turned their misfortune into entertainment for her friends. The only person who she did not mock was Kenzaburo, which was how I knew she loved him above all others.

My father-in-law, Osamu, spent his days in the garden, looking up only when he saw a bird's shadow gliding over the grass. He was attentive to animals, to plants, to weather. Some saw him as the simpleminded son of a wealthy family, the weak one who had to be taken care of, but I saw something else. He hid behind his plants and trees like a shy animal that has learned how to survive in a hostile climate. Both Kenzaburo and his father understood the natural world better than the human one.

"I am a scientist first," said Kenzaburo at dinner one night, "and Japanese second." His mother and I both shushed him in unison, for fear our neighbors would overhear and report him to the authorities for unpatriotic speech. Reiko and I agreed upon one thing alone—the need to protect Kenzaburo from his own carelessness. I believed the fierce way I watched over him made her able to endure my presence. Even so, she made me pay for my marriage to her son each moment I drew breath in her home.

When Reiko shrunk back from me, afraid my kimono would brush against hers, I wondered if she believed what Namba-san said about me—that I was a servant of the fox goddess, come to enthrall her son.

Reiko ordered me about the house and started all her instructions with words like, "You probably won't have any idea what I'm talking about," or "I'm sure they don't have such things in Inari." When others in her social circle were around, she spoke to me in slow, exaggerated sentences, like one might speak to a child or the very old. But when we were alone in the house, she barked at me, yelling, "Clumsy! Can't you walk without thudding on the floors like a cow?"

To the side of the house behind the kitchen window, Osamu kept his most prized possessions: ten perfect *bonsai* trees, clipped and pruned to stunted perfection. Sometimes I came to watch him, and his eyes twinkled when he saw me. He told me how to pare the branches so they would grow the right way. "Not too soon, or you will

kill the plant. Too late, and you will not be able to control the growth."
Whenever Reiko saw us together, she scowled until I returned to my
chores.

I told myself that I was living this way for Kenzaburo, for the nights
we ventured up the mountain after his parents had fallen asleep. We
lay by the waterfall and watched the stars together or searched for
nocturnal insects. When he was not looking, I released them from
their mesh cages back into the night. I could not help but imagine
their mates waiting for them on the surrounding branches, praying
for their return.

One day I returned from a visit with my friend Ogawa-san to find
my mother-in-law in our bedroom on the second floor of the house.
The letters I'd received from Kenzaburo when we were courting were
fanned across my dressing table. Reiko was sitting on a cushion beside
it, reading the last one he sent before his proposal. Angry red splotches
appeared on her cheeks underneath the white powder of her make-up.

"Those are my private things," I said, my heart beating hard in my
ribcage. "Please put them down."

"It is clear to me now that you have bewitched my son," Reiko said,
her voice high and strange. "But I know a priest who will rid my house
of the fox who has taken up residence here." She stood unsteadily and
dropped the letter she was holding. I watched it slip to the floor.

My tongue was stiff and dry in my mouth, but I forced myself to
speak. "I am doing my duty by you and your husband. I take care of
your son and this family."

Reiko licked her lips. It occurred to me that she wanted to leave the
room but was unsure how to pass by without touching me.

"Duty? A daughter-in-law's duty is to take care of her husband's
parents and provide children and grandchildren," she said, edging
along the wall. "I wonder why you have not gotten pregnant yet. But

maybe it is because you are not a woman at all, but a fox spirit sent here to harm our family and to rob us of our treasures." Reiko's eyes darted from my face to the door.

"Don't be foolish," I blurted out before I could stop myself. "It's the polio. The doctor said it's made it impossible for us to have children." I should have stopped then, but all the words I'd been keeping inside clawed their way to the surface. "I know what happened with your cousin, before you married Osamu-san," I continued. "I am sorry you weren't able to have the love match you wanted, but please don't punish us because we did."

I covered my mouth, but it was too late. My mother-in-law's expression changed from an angry mask to something hard and cold. She moved so close to me that I could smell the sour *gobo* root and carrot she ate for lunch.

"How dare you," she hissed. "How dare you spread lies about me, or suggest that your failure to have a child has anything to do with my son, *my* family," she said, her eyes narrowing. "You are replaceable, *bumpkin*. I can easily arrange to ship you back to your dirty little hole in Inari." Then she smiled, smoothed her kimono. "You will tell no one else what you have just told me. *Wa. Ka. Ri. Ma. Sen. ka?*" She spoke slowly, her teeth clenched. "Do. You. Understand?"

I held Reiko's gaze but knew she was right—if she wanted to get rid of me, she could do it. I bowed my head and stepped aside as she walked out of the room, hiding my shaking hands in the sleeves of my kimono. Closing the door, I sank down to the tatami mats on my knees. No sounds emerged from my throat; I did not want Reiko to know that she had wounded me.

When I was able to stand, the room seemed to be at odd angles. I leaned on the windowsill and looked out over the foothills of Mt. Rokko to the rooftops of Kobe. I wanted to leave, go back to my parents' house in Inari. Even though they weren't there any longer, I knew the village and our neighbors would welcome me home. I wondered if Kenzaburo would come looking for me if I left. I was not certain if he would have the strength to choose me over his mother.

The nightingale in the garden sang her song as a stray breeze blew through the open window and washed over my face. My father-in-law was standing by his *bonsai* trees in the garden watching me, hat in hand, shaking his head, fingers to his lips. "Don't speak," he seemed to say. "Let Reiko have her way and the storm will pass."

When I bowed my head, my eyes rested on the small statue of the Inari fox my mother had given us on our wedding day; a smaller version of the one Reiko had broken in half. I heard my mother's voice say, "Remember who you are, daughter. *Gaman shite.* You must be patient in your husband's house . . . and you must keep going."

Leaning on the windowsill, I closed my eyes and breathed in the April air. Although I was a day's train ride from my village, I could smell the first green rice seedlings of spring, the dank path leading through the tunnel of red *torri* gates to the top of Mt. Inari, and the familiar smells of earth, food, and smoke in my parents' house. Then I thought of Kenzaburo's smiling face, and the words in his very first letter to me: "Your presence has made everything bearable." When I opened my eyes, Osamu was still standing under my window, waiting for my answer. I nodded, and he smiled and went back to clipping his *bonsai.*

I would not let a grudging old crow get the better of me.

"You could outwit the gods," my father used to say with a laugh.

Reiko was no god.

10
FUNERAL
KENZABURO

I remember my daughter's tears and the broken face of my wife when I died. I remember my funeral. I remember the moment when the door of the crematorium vault shut, the sadness that held me as I watched my body burn.

This is what happened:

At 1:15 p.m. the day I fell, I was pronounced dead by a perspiring young Dr. Miyazaki.

"Where is my doctor?" I asked the nurses standing next to him. "Call Dr. Ishikawa immediately."

This other doctor, this stranger, did not respond to me, and neither did the women standing next to him in their pink nurse's uniforms. He was young, nervous, pulling out a kerchief to wipe his glistening forehead as he examined me. "H. M." was embroidered on the bottom left corner of the white cloth. I heard the nurses giggling about him when he left the room, saying that his mother hand-delivered his *obento* lunchboxes every day. *"Amaenbo,"* they whispered behind cupped hands. "Mama's boy."

The nurses also talked about me. I heard them describe in low tones how a group of children had found my body crumpled on the rocks by the river. I wanted to tell them that an hour before the rescue team came, I watched as a plump boy with bruised knees and a priest's haircut prodded my belly with a stick when no one was looking, as if I was a dead crow.

I stood in Dr. Miyazaki's office and listened to him debate with the nurses over what they should tell my family. The taller, thin nurse finally called my wife at 2:00 p.m., saying "Mr. Tsuruda has been seriously injured. Please come at once." Satsuki and my daughter Haruna arrived at Kaisei Hospital within ten minutes, both disheveled and wide-eyed. Relieved, I got up and ran to them.

"Satsuki, it's me! I'm fine. There's been some kind of mistake, but no one will speak to me." I turned to my daughter. "Haruna, tell them. It's your *otohsan*." I waved my arms in front of their faces. My wife and daughter did not respond or even look in my direction.

"From the bag we discovered with his body, it appears that he was . . . hunting for insects?" asked Dr. Miyazaki. "Is that an activity in which your husband frequently engaged?" Satsuki nodded and sank to the pink plastic cushions of the waiting room benches, Haruna's arms around her elbows. The young doctor cleared his throat. "He fell from a tree onto a boulder in the river. His death was instant. He would have felt no pain. I am sorry for your loss."

My wife's body seemed to fold inward while I watched. I knelt in front of her, reaching to touch her hand. "Satsuki," I pleaded, "look at me. They don't know what they're talking about. I'm right here. *Sa-chan*, it's me."

"Kenzaburo?" she said, her eyes focusing on me for an instant. I moved to embrace her, but instead lost my balance and fell forward as if I had stumbled into an open doorway.

"I think my *okaasan* believes she sees my father. Doctor, can you do something?" asked Haruna, panic rising in her voice.

"Kenzaburo?" my wife whispered again. "*Ikanai de*. Don't go. I'm not ready for this, for you to leave."

"I won't leave you, Satsuki. I'm right here," I said. "Tell the doctors."

"My husband is here with us," said Satsuki, her voice quavering. When no one responded, she said again, "My husband. He is here with us. He wants to know why you are ignoring him."

Haruna motioned to the doctor and he gave Satsuki a sedative in the form of a shot. My daughter sat stroking my wife's arm until she was calm. Within minutes, Satsuki's eyes had glazed over, and she stopped speaking, even though I was sitting on the other side of her in the waiting room, begging her to talk to me. "*Sa-chan*, I am here. Don't worry," I said. "Don't listen to them, please."

An hour later, the nurses took my daughter to a room where a body lay in a hospital bed, a white sheet pulled over its head. An orderly lifted the sheet and pulled it down. Bloated and gray, the flesh was bruised and ashen. My face, my body, lay on the table like some damaged wooden doll, a caricature of who I was. This could not be death, I thought. Death was eternal blackness, a return to the soil. Death was the end, not the keen awareness I now felt. "I must be in some kind of coma," I reasoned, "and should wake up at any moment."

"Yes, that is my father," said Haruna, and covered her face.

"Haruna, please listen to me," I whispered in her ear. "This is not what you think. Tell them to check my pulse again. They must have made some kind of mistake."

"What is next?" asked Haruna in a dull voice, and I thought she was talking to me until a nurse answered her.

"We are waiting for a space to open in the morgue," answered the woman. She added, "I am sorry for your loss."

My daughter returned her bow and asked for a candle and some water. "My mother will want a candle lit for my father, to help him find his way to the next world," she said. I walked beside her, pleading, "Haruna, it's me. Please, do not believe these idiots. I've simply lost consciousness. Tell them!"

She hesitated, then moved forward. "Are you . . . are you certain he is dead?" she asked the nurse.

The nurse looked startled, and then stammered, "Yes, we are very sure, Tsuruda-san. Your father's heart stopped beating before he arrived at the hospital. There was nothing we could do." She bowed and added, "I'm very sorry."

"Haruna, don't listen to her. I'm here," I said. "Please answer me."

Moving closer to my body, I examined my silent gray twin. My body lay inert on the table with a blank expression on its face. Cold fingers. Dead lips. I tried to embrace its stiff shoulders, climb inside the husk that had been my body, but it would not receive me.

Haruna lit the long white ceremonial candle the nurses brought. "Forgive me, *Otohsan*," I heard her say. Much later I was able to admit that my daughter possessed wisdom where I did not. She understood that the rituals we perform for the dead are also for the living. She moistened the lips of my corpse with the water a young nurse brought. "*Otohsan*, I am giving you the *matsugo-no-mizu*, the water of the last moment," she whispered. My daughter did not brush away the tears that fell from her face to mine. All of these rituals she performed for me and for my wife, while Satsuki sat in a sedated stupor in the waiting room of the hospital, unable to move.

When they brought my body home to lie in state the next day, Haruna and Satsuki sat next to it on the tatami mats. My corpse looked pale and foreign in the room, its sharp angles the color of aba-lone shells, my mouth frozen into a permanent "O."

"*Otohsan* will lie here for three days. The candle must be kept lit for another thirty-six," Satsuki whispered, her voice low but determined. "He has forty-five days to leave our world and go on to the next one. This light will guide him to the spirit world." She covered the shrine in our house with white paper and placed a table next to my body decorated with flowers, incense, and the lit death candle. That night, she rested a knife on my chest. "Ken-chan, you didn't believe in an afterlife, so I'm here to help you. This knife will help you drive away evil spirits as you travel to the next world," she whispered in my ear.

"Satsuki, I don't need these things," I said, sitting beside her. "I don't need magician's props; I need you to see me, to hear me." Satsuki bowed over my corpse. With eyes closed she recited the sutras one chants to prepare the dead for their journey to the afterlife. "Don't send me away," I said, my voice cracking. "I am here with you. Please let me stay."

A calligraphy scroll hung in the alcove next to my body, its black pictographs on paper stark and white as bone. I can conjure up the char-acters even now. They shimmer and shift above me, materializing out of memory. My wife had selected my favorite scroll, the one by the master poet Issa. Silent as the pause before one's last breath, the words read,

Oh Cricket!
Act as a grave keeper
After I am gone.

I sat against the far wall reading the haiku on the scroll, puzzled to think how death could be so different from what I imagined it to be. The gray lips and sunken cheeks of my body angered me. That inanimate thing could not represent a life, could not possibly be the sum of my years. There were no instructions for this moment, no research to rely upon. I had no way of knowing that my time with my family was drawing to a close; that from now on I would only be allowed a short visit with them once a year during the Obon holiday.

For three days, Satsuki and Haruna cried, avoiding each other's eyes, and for three days I tried to speak to them without success. Whatever connection Satsuki and I had in the hospital seemed to be broken and gone. Visitors came and went. I caught snatches of their thoughts, heard whispers of ideas around me. Blame, guilt, and reproach all simmered together in the stale air.

I had time to consider my wife and daughter in that room. In many ways, it was the beginning of my understanding. I recalled the time when Satsuki and I first married, how she made me sit and listen to the stillness around us, to the sounds of plants breathing and blooming on cool summer nights in the walled garden under the moon. For hours we sat by the riverbank on top of Mt. Rokko while I did my research on nocturnal insects for the university. Each time we arrived, Satsuki would undress and jump into the shallow pool below the waterfall. Many times, my work was abandoned in favor of swimming with my young wife.

Satsuki married me even though she understood we might never be able to have children.

"The polio makes it unlikely that I will be able to produce any offspring," I told Satsuki with difficulty before she introduced me to her parents. I had researched my disease and knew that our chances of ever having a child were slim.

"*Ie*, Ken-chan, you will see," she said. "The Goddess of Inari will send us a child." And in the fall after the war ended, Satsuki told me she was pregnant.

"You see?" she said. She was crying, and her arms were folded around her chest. "The trip to Inari and prayers to the goddess have been successful."

I had laughed and hugged her. I saw the look on her face, and for once I did not mock her superstitions.

Our daughter Haruna was born the next year. Watching her now, I see the women of my family pass across the surface of her features. My spring child, born in April when the cherry blossoms were in full bloom. I wanted to name her Haruko, "child of spring," but Satsuki held firm.

"Let's name her Haruna, 'spring green.' That way, she'll have the strength of trees in her back, the sway of sea grass in her walk."

Haruna was pure Tsuruda, except for the fact that her eyes were the same large, gold-flecked almonds of her mother's. When she was born, our daughter's face was as pale and round as her mother's was brown and angular. Haruna loved to read as a child and listened wide-eyed while I described the creatures of Mt. Rokko and beyond: the cicada nymph, who lies buried for up to seventeen years before hatching and mating, the red dragonflies who could fly as fast as a car speeding down the highway, and the brilliance of the Atlas moths of the Sumatran jungle, whose wing span could stretch further than my two hands placed beside each other. When she was a child, it seemed as if everything I said entranced my daughter. Haruna sat for hours curled up in my study, dusty bookshelves forming a protective wall around us. She spent so much time with me that Satsuki worried that she wouldn't know how to speak to other children.

When she was thirteen, Haruna said she wanted to be a scientist like me. I felt a growing sense of worry; I knew that women did not fare well in the scientific community in Japan. I saw my daughter as a small bird flapping her wings, pushing her slight frame against a window that would not open.

When she was sixteen, she said, "*Otohsan*, I do not like Japan. My science teacher laughed at me for wanting to become a professor because I am a girl. I want to study the stars in the desert, and work in America or Australia. Must I become a mother and wife, like all the other women in this country?" It was 1962, well before the time women were allowed to join the ranks of academics and scientists in earnest, though a handful of persistent women had managed to do so. They were odd and lived alone. They wore pants like men and were not accepted so much as tolerated. They did not have husbands or families. I did not say the words out loud to her, but it was not the life I wanted for my daughter.

Satsuki had overheard our conversation, and called out, "And what is wrong with becoming a wife and mother?" She was paring carrots in sharp movements over the sink and bustling around the kitchen. The tantalizing smells from the stovetop had drawn us out of the study and lured us to the table.

"Nothing, *Okaasan*." Haruna replied turning scarlet, head bowing under Satsuki's glare. Our daughter jumped up and began to set the table, knocking over a brown vase full of plum branches. On the floor, a swirling pattern of pink buds and dirty water. I see the petals again in my mind's eye, and I know that they hold part of the answer to what I am supposed to understand about my wife, my daughter, our lives. Something that I was supposed to have been for them but wasn't.

In truth, I could have helped my daughter in her career, but instead decided that she should marry a young professor or scientist. I saw her as the helpmate to a brilliant man, an able partner in his studies. That is what I envisioned for her—not the life of a lonely spinster living alone in a shabby apartment, with fickle students for comfort instead of children. But nothing of what I'd hoped for her had come to pass.

These were the thoughts that plagued me as I lingered in my home for three days while my body lay in state.

The night before the wake, Satsuki and Haruna held the Otsuya ceremony to say farewell. They burned candles and incense and stayed awake all night. My wife paid a Buddhist monk to pray over me and give me my Buddhist name for use in the afterlife.

The wake was held the following day. In attendance were relatives I had not seen in years, each placing their envelopes of 30,000 yen in the box at the front of the hall, some more reluctantly than others. "I am happy to help Satsuki-san and her daughter pay for the funeral, even if the amount is more than my plane ticket from Tokyo," my second cousin Junichiro Kitada announced in his booming politician's voice.

Various family members came—my brother's widow, Tetsuko Uribo, from Hiroshima, whose eyes were small and red in her blotchy face. Her son and two daughters, stocky and self-important Uribos to the core, came in their designer clothes and looked at their watches.

My body lay on dry ice at the front of the room, head pointed north, the direction of good fortune. A white kimono, a pair of sandals, and six coins were placed in the casket with me, along with my father's pocket watch. The coins were money for berth across the *Sanzu no kawa*, the river it was believed I would cross in the afterlife. These details made me cross my arms and sigh as I watched the proceedings from the corner of the room.

The throng of dark suits and kimono amidst the black and white striped death banners surprised and pleased me, even though I did not yet believe I was truly dead. At least two hundred people had come to pay their respects, sitting on folding chairs in that pale green room. Perhaps the manner of my death drew them. "Fell from a tree . . . " they whispered. "Collecting beetles at his age? He always was rather *okashii* . . ." The word "strange" was repeated and spread through the crowd. The mourners moved like reeds in the wind and were as lasting. It was no love for me, but the supposed eccentricity of my life which had brought most of them.

My former colleagues shared green tea and condolences with my wife and eyed my daughter under faces heavy-lidded with mourning. Jealous Okabe-san with his triangular face and cupped ears sat in the front row. He had relied on copying his colleagues' work for the duration of his career and had never risen to the heights he imagined for himself. At the university he was servile and evasive, bowing and clinging to the wall when he passed me in the corridors.

"This is a sad day, indeed," I heard him say to Haruna, fingering his business cards as he bowed. Next came Mori-sensei, the dean of my department, scanning the room for faces he knew. "Your father was a brilliant scientist. He will be missed in the academic community," he said, and moved on to speak to a professor from Kyoto University.

The hired priest rode up on his motorbike minutes before the funeral was to begin. He entered the rented hall, purposeful and businesslike in flapping gray robes, bald head shining under the florescent lights. In a dull monotone he recited his sutras, banging on a small gourd drum with his mallet and shaking a copper bell at regular intervals. Haruna steadied Satsuki as she lit sticks of incense and placed them in the urn that stood before my casket.

After the priest finished, my wife sat pale and silent in her black kimono, accepting condolences from family members. She leaned on Tetsuko as they left the building. I rushed to her side, saying, "Satsuki, don't you see? None of this is real. I'm here with you, *Sa-chan*. I'm not leaving." She paused for a moment and looked through me, then clutched Tetsuko's arm and continued walking with my brother's widow to her waiting car.

Haruna stood in the genkan just beyond the line of the doorway, handing out the *orei* gifts to mourners. I had been with my wife and daughter when they met with the funeral director. His pockmarked skin reflected pale green walls. With small black eyes at once sympathetic and mercenary, he suggested they give canisters filled with small packets of sugar, each in an individual paper wrapping. They looked for all the world like the straw candy that turned children's tongues bright blue or red. "These are very popular this year," he said with a studied smile. Haruna look at her mother, whose face was drained and pale. My daughter responded to the funeral director's question with a quick nod, then stood up to take Satsuki back home.

At the funeral the next day there was more chanting and offerings of incense. Guests placed flowers around my body in the coffin, and Satsuki and Haruna wept as they nailed it shut with stones. I watched as if it were another body being loaded into the small wooden shrine built onto the back of the black hearse.

They cremated me the next day. I watched my body as it crumbled and shivered in the fire, becoming nothing. Ash and smoke and bits of curled skin flew like blackened paper up the chimney, swallows chasing each other in a playful, unending spiral. It was the first time I allowed myself to grieve what had been taken.

The following day my wife and daughter returned to the crematorium. They sat next to my remains, each holding a pair of large iron chopsticks. They picked through my ashes to find my voice box, my "Buddha's bone," the *nodobotoke*. Haruna uncovered it first. Lifting it out of the gray ash, she passed it to Satsuki, who took it with her chopsticks and, with the delicacy of a praying mantis, put it down it in a small urn. It made a clicking sound as it touched the dish.

The moment my daughter grasped my voice box, I experienced a phantom sense, like the amputee veterans from the war whose fingers itched even though their limbs had been lost years before. I could not breathe. Helpless, I flailed and gasped, clawing at my throat.

What finally stilled me was the sound of a dry, sputtering laugh that seemed to come from across the room.

"Who's there?" I yelled, my voice hoarse. "Who is laughing?"

Satsuki closed her eyes and gripped both hands in her lap, but she did not look in my direction.

My question hung in the air as my wife and daughter rose and left the crematorium, the urn containing my ashes clutched in Satsuki's hands.

That night, paper lanterns decorated every wall in our neighborhood, forming an illuminated line down the mountain to the sea. The small river beside our house reflected the light of the lanterns that bobbed along its surface. Fireflies blinked and sparked in the night air. Other lanterns seemed to float down the street, carried by unseen hands.

I hurried toward the last one in the procession, calling out, "*Sumimasen.* Excuse me! What is happening? Where is everyone going?"

"Don't you know?" An old woman's voice by my elbow startled me. "It's the last night of Obon when our families light the lanterns to help guide us on our journey back. It is the night we spirits must leave the living world." My candle illuminated a tiny, bent woman with a white kerchief on her head; she looked to be over one hundred years old, with a wrinkled walnut for a face. She saw my puzzled expression in the low light and laughed. "*Asoka.* Your first time? *Daijobu, yo.* It's all right. Always hard to leave, but you'll get used to it. And of course, there's always next year."

She hurried off and left me standing in the street, the flame from her lantern blinking and flickering until I could no longer see it. I stood there immobile, watching the lights traveling down the mountain, convinced that this must be—had to be—a dream, no matter how convincing the memory of my funeral had been. I hesitated. I'd spent decades at the university lecturing students, but now I felt like my twelve-year-old self leaving my sickbed for the first time, unsure of my next step. My rational mind told me to return to the house, but I could not control my curiosity—nor could I shake the powerful instinct that compelled me to follow.

The procession thinned until I found myself in near-darkness, save for the candle I'd brought with me and the lanterns perched on garden walls. This was the first time the instincts of the spirit world took over—something told me to follow, an insistent push as sure and shrill as hunger in the belly. I took one last look behind me toward the dark forest of the mountaintop. There were no animal sounds, no breezes blowing through the leaves; only the still air that closed in around me like a second skin. Nervous now, I hurried to catch up with the others and got in line behind the last spirit, a thin boy with a shaggy head of hair and poor posture. He looked to be about twenty.

"*Sumimasen.* Excuse me, young man. Where is everyone going?" I asked, panting. He kept walking, his long, anxious face staring straight ahead as if I had never spoken. He seemed to be talking to himself, and I strained to hear his words.

"*Sensei*, please. I will try harder next semester. I will write an additional paper, do extra work for you. Please don't fail me."

A half-memory hovered near my ear like a buzzing mosquito. I knew this voice. I held my candle up to get a better view of his face.

"Ando-kun? Can it be you?" The boy had been a student of mine some twenty years past. He didn't answer, but I knew it was him now, for certain. Ando had a very distinctive mole on his left cheek that resembled a turtle. For that reason, the other students had nicknamed him "The Tortoise," which made him blush and duck his head, laughing with them in a way that made me think he had no other defense.

"Ando-san, it *is* you," I said, overjoyed. "Don't worry, my boy. Yes, you can do extra work for me, that is a grand idea. You will pass my class this time."

But Ando continued to beg and plead, his voice taking on a dull, gray tone, as if he had already accepted what was to come. "I cannot fail. *Otohsan* will disown me."

"*Hai, hai,* I hear you," I repeated, trying to make my voice sound jovial as I attempted to reassure him. "You will pass my class. Just please don't do anything rash. You gave us all quite a scare, you know." He didn't reply, so I asked again, "Ando, my boy, do you have any idea where we are?"

Ando's request came as if I had never spoken. "*Sensei*, please. I will try harder next semester. I will write an extra report, do work for you. Please don't fail me." And then, "I cannot fail. *Otohsan* will disown me."

"Ando-san," I said, getting annoyed now, "Aren't you listening? I'm telling you I won't fail you."

The morning I heard the news about what the boy had done at Mukogawa Bridge, I was drinking tea in my office at the university, reading the paper. Professor Shohara came to tell me. "Upset over his poor grades this semester. His father was a councilman for the Liberal Democratic Party, had big things in store for him," was all Shohara said, but I could feel his disapproval. It was rare for a professor to fail a student from such a prestigious a family, and my colleagues had criticized me for it behind my back, I was sure.

But I did not tell him that I regretted how strict I'd been. Ando was not a bad sort—I could have let him work to pass my class, but I chose to be stern because of a conversation I chanced to overhear in the college library a few weeks earlier. The students did not know I was there, tucked away doing research behind the stacks in a dusty carrel. "As long as you pretend to be interested in bugs, he'll give you a good mark," I heard one student say with a laugh, unaware that I was listening. Another boasted, "He wouldn't dare fail me. My dad would have that cripple's job." For the next few weeks, I scanned my classes, listening for the offending voices, but never discovered who they were. By the time Ando came to me with his plea, my pride had already made up my mind for me.

How many times have I wished to change that small bit of history?

I tried again. "Please Ando-kun," I continued. "I will let you do some extra work for me this time. Just please, don't do this thing you are planning."

But his words came again in the same dull tone. "*Sensei*, please. I will try harder next semester. I will write an extra report, do more work for you. I cannot fail. My father will disown me."

My shoulders slumped in defeat. Cold and silent, we snaked down the narrow lanes and neighborhoods of Mt. Rokko, passing over the towns of Mikage and Sannomiya until we reached the sea. Along the way, many more travelers joined us from the houses we passed in the night, until hundreds of candles lit the darkness. I heard voices lamenting around me, whispering in my ear, pushing me forward. "It's time," they said. "*Jikan da yo.*"

We arrived at Suma Beach just as the sky lightened from black to purple. People murmured to each other or stared straight ahead as if in a daze. I realized with a start that I had become separated from Ando-san, and I scanned the crowd for his face in vain. The crowd gathering on the beach, all dressed in white kimono, seemed to sway over the sand. "Our feet connect us to the ground, to the earth. That is why they fade away after we die," my grandmother had told me one night during the Obon when I was ten. I'd woken up from a night-mare where I saw my parents mourning at my graveside. "Do you still have your feet, Kenzaburo?" My *obaachan* asked, wiping my tears away with a cold cloth. I nodded. "*Yokatta*," she said, smiling. "Then I can assure you that you are still very much alive."

"*Asoka*," I said, raising my finger. "I am dreaming of *Obaachan* and her stories," A woman next to me clucked and moved away just as the sun began its slow crawl over the horizon, until the shoreline was awash in pinks and yellows. Suma Beach had changed; or rather, it looked as it had when I was a child—as if Japan had never gone through the changes it experienced after the war. No cargo slips were apparent when I looked eastward toward the city of Kobe, no great metal cranes stood in the water ready to remove freight containers from foreign ships. And on the beach, no high-rise apartments or concession stands marred the view, no sounds of cars honking or construction work filled the early morning. Instead, pine trees rose around the edge of white sand and water lapped against the shore.

"Yes, this must all be a dream," I said, convincing myself again that the fall from the tree had never happened. "I am lying unconscious somewhere, at home or even in the hospital, about to wake." I stood on the shore prepared to awaken, but no comforting hand shook me from my slumber, no whispered greeting compelled my eyes to open.

┼11┼
WAITING/HAJIYAMA
SATSUKI
NOVEMBER 1944

I have lived with the Uribo family in Hajiyama for three months. They let me know every moment I am here how grateful I should be. Tetsuko, who is the wife of my husband's brother Zaemon, is the firstborn and the most imperious. Her sisters, Atsuko and Fumiko, whisper behind my back. They imitate my country dialect and old-fashioned manners. I do not say much to any of them. I bow and remain polite. Sometimes I fear I will break in half with the effort.

I am starting to forget what it means to be treated with kindness.

Kenzaburo left me here three days after we arrived at Tetsuko's country home outside of Hiroshima. When Tetsuko greeted us, the first thing she said was that Zaemon was not home. "Your brother is in Manchu-kuo on government business," said Tetsuko to Kenzaburo, puffing up like a bullfrog who thinks itself lord of the rice paddy. As she talked, she took every opportunity to tell us about her husband's success. This is how we learned that the small exporting company Zaemon inherited from Tetsuko's father had expanded to include shipping contracts for the military. Kenzaburo complimented Tetsuko's home and chubby-legged son. For the three days he was there, my husband's body remained in a permanent bowing position. He was not used to begging and I was not used to seeing him that way. I wondered how it came to him so naturally.

When Kenzaburo told me it was time for him to return to Kobe to take care of his mother and go back to work at the munitions factory, I pleaded with him to take me home. I didn't want to stay with these arrogant Uribo women in their second house one moment longer.

"Satsuki, listen to me. Kobe is under attack. Half the city is gone. I've lost my father—I can't lose you, too. It doesn't make sense to go back."

The morning Kenzaburo's father died, the sky was heavy and gray. I watched my father-in-law leave the house in his shuffling, stoop-backed way. I remember that I waved to him when he paused at the corner of our street. It was his habit to check the sky and hold his finger to the wind before leaving the house. I stood in the bedroom window watching as he hurried down the mountain to the train which would take him to Sannomiya. If he had turned and seen me, I would have called out for him to come back; I would have told him that something felt wrong about this day, this cloudless sky. But he did not so much as glance over his shoulder at his beloved house or garden.

Later that day, Reiko and I stood silently watching the bombs in the distance, heard the sirens and explosions from our home several kilometers away, pillars of fire and smoke blossoming in the distance. I believe we both knew my timid father-in-law would not return.

I remember the weeks that followed, the hollow feeling in my chest, my shallow breath as I searched makeshift hospital beds around the city, but found no trace of the kind, quiet man who had been my only ally in the Tsuruda family except for Kenzaburo.

I cursed this war that had sent so many to the afterlife with no funeral candle to light their paths, no sutras chanted to ease their passage to the next world. My parents' bodies burned on a hillside in Inari without me there to mourn them; and now my father-in-law, his flesh reduced to ash in the firebombing.

"Please, don't send me to Hajiyama," I'd begged my husband one night in the dark of our bedroom when he'd told me his plan. "In my dreams, your brother's house is filled with hungry ghosts who shriek with pain. Their bodies turn black and shrivel up in front of me. I am afraid to sleep for fear of seeing them."

"Don't you understand, Sa-chan? I cannot keep you safe here any longer," whispered Kenzaburo. "It has already been decided that you will go to the countryside and stay with Tetsuko's family. My brother Zaemon will be there; he will protect you and the women of Tetsuko's family. I wrote them weeks ago to tell them we would be coming."

But when we arrived, we learned the letter had never been delivered. That first night, the Uribo's welcome was as meager as the rice they gave us, as sour as the old *daikon* radish Tetsuko served. Kenzaburo did not meet my eyes when he left a few days later. "I will write to you," he whispered. "When the war is over, everything will be as it should be again. You will see."

Before he left, Kenzaburo said that the war could not last much longer, that they were running out of materials with which to build ships and bombs, that Japan was slowly being depleted of steel and iron. The ships from Manchuria were having difficulty getting through with supplies. I wondered if Tetsuko knew, and if she worried about her husband like I worried about mine.

Since the bombing in the part of Sannomiya City that took his father's life, we were all afraid, hiding in the house like timid rabbits. My mother-in-law stopped seeing her circle of social acquaintances altogether. When I gardened or hung laundry out to dry behind the kitchen window, I searched the skies for war planes. Kenzaburo no longer went hunting for his beloved insects on Mt. Rokko.

My husband would come home at the end of each day, discouraged after working at the defense factory. I cooked his mother's meal early and served it without speaking, except to apologize when the criticism came. This was how I had learned to live in peace under Reiko's roof. After my father-in-law was killed, we formed an uneasy alliance for Kenzaburo's sake. I waited for my husband to come home and served his dinner first, sitting on the tatami with him and listening to his stories.

My shy husband's gift for mimicry—of insects, animals and humans—was something most people did not know about him. In the role of his twitching supervisor, Horiguchi-san, Kenzaburo stuttered and brushed his shoulders compulsively. The poor man was afflicted with a case of dandruff so plentiful it formed little white heaps on his shoulders each day. Next Kenzaburo would shift character and move about the table like a puffed-up rooster, barking orders and crowing like the strutting military commander Major Jomon, who was in charge of the factory.

I knew Kenzaburo's performances were intended to make me laugh, to remove the worry from my face. I believe they also gave him courage. One night before he brought me to Tetsuko's country house in Hajiyama, he came home angry, his eyes bloodshot and tired, his limp more pronounced.

"Satsuki, they are so foolish. These military commanders of ours actually think we are descendants of the Sun Goddess, and that the emperor is in the direct line of divinity. They turn away from scientific fact to worship whatever they believe will bring them more power. Their need to feel superior is too great—they cling to the belief that we are better than the Chinese, the Koreans, the rest of Asia, and deny that we come from the Asian continent ourselves."

His voice rose as he spoke, and I put my hands over his lips to quiet him, afraid our neighbors would hear and report us for lack of loyalty to the emperor. We were already treated differently because Kenzaburo had been too infirm to be accepted into the army. Because of his limp and history of polio, the military deemed him too weak to be of use, so he was sent instead to the factory in Kobe where we met. For the first year he worked at the tables making bombs and artillery, but because he had a head for numbers and facts, they placed him in the office to write reports, organize supplies, and add figures.

"The Emperor is divine," Kenzaburo read in the newspaper, "we must be willing to give our lives in his name, we must be shields to protect him." Like Kenzaburo, I did not believe this, but for a different reason: to me, the Emperor was no more or less divine than the rocks or the trees, or the birds in our garden.

Kenzaburo searched articles frantically looking for glimmers of rational thought. I asked him to read to me each night as I cleaned up after dinner. "You have such a fine reading voice," I said. I did not tell him the truth—that my reading level was that of a five-year-old because I only knew the Hiragana and Katakana alphabets my father taught me. I'd never been to school or learned to read like an adult. I did not lie to my husband about my inability to read Kanji characters— he never asked. He assumed that I chose to use only the Hiragana alphabet when I wrote anything. I was ashamed, but I encouraged this belief.

"You are like the women of the Heian Court of a thousand years ago, who invented Hiragana and used it to write their love letters and stories," he said. I did not tell him the truth—that my parents needed me to work in the rice paddies from the time I could walk to help support our family. Whatever I learned was taught to me by the light of the fire after the chores were completed at night. And I had been lucky—my father had been thought unusual to take the time to teach me, a girl, to learn to read.

Here in Hajiyama, Tetsuko's youngest sister Fumiko plays her *koto* in the afternoons when the children are napping, her fingers flying over the strings like tiny birds. I cannot help myself—I am jealous that Tetsuko and her sisters were educated by a string of private tutors in literature, the traditional arts, and music. For generations, Uribo children have grown up eating delicacies and going to the seashore in the summer, with servants whose sole purpose was to keep them from becoming bored.

Unlike Kenzaburo, Tetsuko and her sisters support what the politicians say as they get richer on Zaemon's military contracts. I know to keep my thoughts to myself. I cannot help but feel trapped by the Uribo household, suffocated by their absolute assurance that they are right in all matters.

Today one of Tetsuko's neighbors told me there have been more bombings in Kobe, and that Chinatown was razed during one of the attacks. I am sick with worry and

I want to go home. I don't care if it's dangerous or if Reiko belittles me; I want to be with my husband again. I miss the way his eyebrows furrow when he concentrates, the look on his face when I tell a story, the way his eyes close tightly when he eats too much wasabi. I fear for Kenzaburo's safety, working in a place that is surely a target.

He promised me he would come back before the New Year's holiday, but there has been no word from him since he left in September.

When my chores are finished for the day, I steal up the mountain to the tiny red shrine set amidst the rocks by the waterfall. I saved some of the rice from my breakfast and leave it as an offering in front of the statue of the fox goddess. Ringing the round brass bell, I clap my hands twice, bow my head, and hope the gods are listening.

過去の旅
Journey

12
TETSUKO
1990

Tetsuko's visit with Satsuki and Haruna stayed with her after she returned to Hiroshima. Memories fell into the moist soil of her late summer doldrums, sprouted, and grew. She remembered the lines of exhaustion around Haruna's eyes and mouth. Again, she saw Satsuki's body, curled and twisted in her bed. Again, she heard her sister-in-law's request that she "find what is hidden." Now she wondered if it was something else. Why would Satsuki have hidden something from her all those years ago? And why was she asking her to find it now?

Tetsuko decided to go up to the old thatched cottage in Hajiyama the following week. She felt agitated, almost giddy, and her cheeks were flushed like a school girl's as she prepared for her trip.

"I don't understand why you need to go up there," said her daughter Mayumi, her mouth turned downward in a pout in her powdered, doughy face. "I thought we were going to that new spa on the Japan Sea next week."

"The hotel will still be there when I get back," said Tetsuko. "I want the house in Hajiyama to be a family place again, as it was when I was a child. If we get it ready this year, perhaps we can all go spend time there together next summer." Her daughter Mayumi, who'd never been one for the countryside, murmured a noncommittal answer and checked price tags at a Louis Vuitton luggage display. Tetsuko continued. "It will be good for my grandchildren to be in the mountains," she said. She didn't tell her daughter about what Satsuki had asked her to do. Mayumi was prone to gossip and would surely repeat the news to her brother and sister, probably with a few twists thrown in to heighten the drama.

My children wouldn't understand, thought Tetsuko, *and besides, this 'thing that remains hidden'—if it really is anything—is probably best kept a secret.*

In the days that followed, the journey to the old house in Hajiyama began to excite Tetsuko more than anything had in ages. Besides her desire to look for the object Satsuki wanted her to find, she wanted to clean the house up and bring her grandchildren there to show them what life was like in traditional Japan.

Sometimes she thought of Japan as the fable of Urashima, the fisherman who had fallen in love with the Sea God's daughter and ridden a tortoise to the bottom of the ocean to marry her. When he at last returned to his village, people he met told him that four hundred years had gone by. His family and friends were long gone. Unable to find a way to return to his wife in her undersea dwelling, he lived out the rest of his days in confusion.

Japan was like that in many ways, Tetsuko mused, with its embrace of all things modern. Her family needed to see what the real, traditional Japan looked like. As it was, her grandchildren barely looked up when she came to visit, intent on their *manga* and video games.

Her son, Ichiro, was so busy working and running the family trading company she rarely saw him, and her daughters were more concerned about getting their children into the right cram schools than teaching the girls about traditional Japanese ways.

The truth was that, although Tetsuko had everything she thought she wanted, she felt empty and without purpose these days. Going to the old house and fixing it up for her family would change all of that, she was sure. And while she was there, she would find what Satsuki had lost, if she could, and bring it back to her sister-in-law.

"Satsuki was right," Tetsuko thought, "When she said I was like a wild boar, because I focus on getting what I want in life."

The first time Satsuki had compared her to a wild boar was during their argument over the empty rice barrel in their old storehouse in Hajiyama. The autumn Satsuki came to stay with them, Tetsuko had been puzzled for weeks over the fact that their rations of rice were being depleted so quickly. Tetsuko's cheeks burned when she remembered confronting Satsuki and accusing her of taking more than her share.

"Head down, you charge, seeing only what is in front of you," Satsuki said to Tetsuko that day. "Please learn to look around you more carefully, Uribo-san. I may have grown up poor, but I am no thief." Satsuki left Tetsuko standing in the kitchen, open-mouthed with bright red spots on her cheeks.

The following week, Tetsuko's sister Atsuko found the culprits who had been scampering away with their rice. Atsuko, who was always very excitable, chased the mice out into the snow with a broom, screaming, and collapsed in a heap in Tetsuko's bedroom as she explained what had happened. Atsuko had to rest in a darkened room for the remainder of the day in order to calm her nerves, and Satsuki had completed Atsuko's tasks for her in addition to her own. She was embarrassed to recall that none of them had apologized to Satsuki.

The next day, she boarded a bus bound for Hajiyama mountain. She sat on the edge of her seat, pocketbook on her knees as the orange bus lumbered up the narrow road, stopping every so often to let off passengers and allow other vehicles to pass by. By the time they reached the halfway point on the mountain, Tetsuko was the sole passenger. She tried to engage the bus driver in conversation by commenting on the weather—"What an unusually hot August we're having!"—but he only grunted in reply. On his radio, a man's shrill voice announced the score of the Hiroshima Carp baseball game. *Rude*, thought Tetsuko and sniffed. In an earlier time, a person of lower rank would never have dared to be so impolite. Then again, it had been a good many years since the Uribo family were known in Hajiyama.

Tetsuko looked out the window and let her mind wander to the villagers who had walked the mountain when she was young: There was Wada-san with a huge bag of kindling on his back, sweating and struggling up the incline. She could almost hear him crying, "Bundle of kindling, only one yen today!" A rusted old bicycle leaning up against a tree reminded her of grinning Nakawa-san, who delivered supplies to their house on his bicycle throughout the war. She wouldn't have been surprised if he materialized as they passed, a live chicken squawking in one of his bamboo baskets. And just before she reached her destination, she imagined she glimpsed the Sakurai family with their nine daughters, each one smaller and prettier than the next. They had always reminded Tetsuko of a set of painted Russian nesting dolls with their long eyelashes and red plum mouths.

Tetsuko remembered that the villagers often didn't have shoes during the war, and wore *geta* sandals, even in winter. She could hear the *toka toka* on the pavement even now when she thought of the bustling village in earlier years.

The bus dropped her off in the middle of Hajiyama village. No one stirred in any of the doorways, and in fact, the small post office looked as if it was vacant. What was worse, there was no sign of a taxi anywhere. As Tetsuko walked along the road in the heat, she began to perspire heavily. Tetsuko did not approve of sweating and began to regret her decision to venture back to the country house at the end of August.

She stopped to fan herself and then continued trudging up the mountain road in the heat, pulling her small suitcase behind her. At least she'd had the sense to wear her comfortable low-heeled shoes, though her nylons were making her legs and feet hot and uncomfortable.

As the minutes wore on, Tetsuko started to wonder if she'd taken the wrong road. The vegetation had grown since she was last in Hajiyama—she realized with a shock that it had been at least a decade since she'd ventured up the mountain. Small houses had been overtaken by the woods; the courtyards of the once gracious summer residences of her former neighbors were now home to cedar trees and creeping vines. Tetsuko nearly dropped her bag when a flock of crows began to call in one voice as she walked by, screaming, *"kaaa, kaaaa,"* their beaks thrusting at her like black scissors from the roof of an empty house. She was wondering if she should turn back and look for a taxi again when she saw it—the house her father and grandfather had built at the turn of the century.

All the discomfort and irritation that had gathered within her fell away. Tetsuko remembered coming here with her sisters when they were young, calling each other by their childhood nicknames as they ran through the woods on their way to jump into the cool river. As Tetsuko drew closer to the front gate, she was surprised to realize that their old summer home was smaller and shabbier than she remembered. The dark wood siding was in bad need of staining and the tin roof had rusted in some places, and spindly weeds grew up through the holes. Old thatch peeped out from underneath the scalloped metal edges of the roof.

Tetsuko touched the gate with her hand and felt goose bumps rise on her arm in spite of the stifling heat. The tangible presence of all the memories contained in the house made her suddenly feel uncharacteristically timid. Zaemon. Her sisters and mother. Satsuki and Kenzaburo. And somewhere in the house, a hidden object that her sister-in-law insisted she find.

Tetsuko felt around in her beige handbag until she grasped the key to the front door. She was surprised when it swung easily on its hinges, as if welcoming her back.

The house was cool and dark inside, if slightly musty-smelling. She walked through the great room with its dark wooden floor and down the hall, pausing at every door. Mildew fanned out on the walls, and she thought she heard the skittering of animals overhead. She sneezed loudly when she opened the large wooden shutters on the back of the house, then cracked the sliding glass doors of the veranda to let in some light and air.

The back of their house faced a mountain whose bluish green shoulders sloped gently down into the misty gorge below. How could she have forgotten this, the most extraordinary aspect of the house, and the reason her father had built in Hajiyama in the first place, when he could have purchased land anywhere outside of Hiroshima?

She closed her eyes and breathed in pine, cedar, and moss. Tetsuko felt her entire body relax into the fresh green air. "*Tadaima*," she whispered. "I am home." Stripping off her nylons with a grateful sigh, she remembered the sounds of her sisters playing in the waterfall, her mother's call to the table, her father's low laugh. And later, the gentle cooing of her babies in the adjacent room. She pulled herself away from the veranda and continued her inspection of the house. She opened the shutters in each room to let light in and opened drawers and cabinet drawers, dutifully looking for whatever it was Satsuki was talking about but not finding anything of note. Light from the windows made the wooden crossbeams in the ceiling glow. The long bamboo pole over the open hearth in the great room still had her grandmother's iron pot hanging from the hook on its end.

Tetsuko hugged her arms tight around her chest. She had become more and more certain that she wanted to fix the cottage up and bring her grandchildren here, perhaps as early as October. They needed to exercise outdoors, experience life in the country, she thought. Her youngest grandson, Tomo, her daughter Yuriko's boy, was overweight already and he was only twelve.

"Before I bring them here I'll have to get the place into shape," she said aloud. She decided that she would continue to look for Satsuki's hidden object while she cleaned and tidied up. She changed into some old clothes and got to work hanging futons on the bamboo poles of the second-floor balcony, sweeping the floors, and used a spray bottle of bleach to attack the mildew on the walls before scrubbing them vigorously. She checked every cupboard and old drawer, but nothing turned up except an old pipe of her father's and a small rusty key. In the small room where Satsuki had stayed during the war, she found a dried out *fude* pen in the back of the drawer in the small writing desk, nothing more. Tetsuko pocketed everything she found and kept on cleaning.

Tamura-san stopped by an hour after Tetsuko's arrival, blue-black curls framing her tanned and rounded face. Her hair was styled in a tight, curly permanent wave. Tamura-san's left eye was weeping and red and every few minutes, she dabbed it with a handkerchief. Her whole demeanor reminded Tetsuko of an aging bulldog. Tamura-san did not look Tetsuko in the eye when she opened the door but settled on a spot somewhere on her chin. This was a sign of respect and something people in the city rarely did anymore. Tetsuko smiled at her approvingly. Finally, someone who remembered to do what was proper.

"*Douzo, douzo*—please, come in," insisted Tetsuko.

Tamura-san stepped out of her shoes and walked into the house. Tetsuko was pleased to see that the caretaker had brought cold buckwheat tea and *senbei* crackers, along with a set of freshly washed sheets. Tamura-san was dismayed that Tetsuko had been cleaning—"Please forgive me, Uribo-sama. I would have prepared the house for you, if I had only known you were coming," she protested. "Please do me the favor of allowing me to come tomorrow and do the rest." Tetsuko dismissed her worries with a stiff wave of her right hand, "No, no. You are only hired to inspect the house and sweep it once in a while, after all. And it feels good to do some work."

The cleaning woman began bustling about the house, making sure that everything was in order. Tamura-san lit coils of the heavy green incense that repelled mosquitoes in each room. Tetsuko followed her to the veranda and cleared her throat.

"Tamura-san, one more thing," she said, unsure of how to ask the next question. "My sister-in-law who lived here during the war recently told me she lost something here, asked me to find 'something that was hidden.' She is sickly now and unable to tell me more than that. Have you ever found anything unusual while cleaning the house, by chance? Some small locket, maybe, or a packet of letters?"

Tamura-san thought for a moment and then said, "Saaa, I don't think so Uribo-san. Wait a minute—yes, there was something. Just a moment!"

Tetsuko's heart beat faster and goose bumps rose on her arms as she anticipated whatever it was Tamura-san had found. The cleaning lady hurried back carrying a small silver baby rattle, now tarnished and bent. "I did find this last winter. I'm sorry for not telling you about it—it completely slipped my mind until this minute."

Tamura-san looked so pleased with herself that Tetsuko didn't have the heart to tell her that this was one of her own children's toys, and most certainly not what Satsuki was talking about. Before Tamura-san left, they made plans to go grocery shopping together in the village the next day.

When Tetsuko was alone in the house again, an image of Satsuki came to mind. Tetsuko wished she could talk to her sister-in-law about all the strange thoughts that had been plaguing her of late. Now Tetsuko was sorry that they had rarely spoken about what they'd lived through during the war. They had kept in touch, talking on the phone, taking the occasional vacation with their children, and, as they grew older, she and Satsuki met faithfully once a year in autumn for lunch in Himeji, the halfway point between their two cities. On these occasions, they went to a certain *Shabu-Shabu* restaurant with a view of Himeji Castle. While they dipped thinly sliced beef into boiling water at their table and ate, they talked about their children, their families and everyday events, but rarely about the war or the bomb that fell on Hiroshima. Tetsuko felt the unfamiliar weight of regret creeping over her again. She shook her head and glanced out the front windows.

"Filthy!" she said out loud, and then looked around to see if anyone had heard. Here she was, an old lady in her old house, talking to herself. She laughed and rolled up her sleeves, ready to work.

When evening came, she soaked for a long time in the now-sparkling *ofuro* and then ate the dinner of cold udon noodles and dumplings Tamura-san brought by as the sun was setting. "Uribo-sama, these are undoubtedly not delicious, but please do me the favor of eating them," the cleaning woman had said. Tetsuko was grateful—Tamura-san's specialty was *gyoza* pot stickers. She refused the food three times, as was polite, and then accepted everything with a smile.

When it was time for bed, Tetsuko sank into her futon with a contented sigh, so tired she could barely move. She was sleeping on a futon on the veranda, as she and her sisters had done as children, and left the windows open to let the cool mountain air float in through the pines. Tetsuko looked at the stars until her eyelids became heavy and her body melted into the fresh cotton sheets.

It felt as if only a few seconds had gone by when Tetsuko woke to find Satsuki sitting beside her in the moonlight. Calm and serene, her sister-in-law looked as she had when she first arrived at the house in Hajiyama. The smell of sandalwood and pine filled the room.

Tetsuko sat up. "Satsuki! You're here," she said to her sister-in-law. "Oh, I'm so glad . . ." her voice trailed off when Satsuki didn't say anything, but simply stared at Tetsuko for a long moment.

Tetsuko continued, "I've wanted to speak with you for such a long time. Lately I have been feeling so strange."

Satsuki nodded and tilted her head toward the night sky. After a few minutes, she spoke. "Have you found what is hidden yet, Tetsuko?"

"N-no, not yet. I have looked, but—"

"Tomorrow, you must go into your old bedroom, to the place where your husband had his writing desk. Pick up the tatami mat in the far-left corner. Underneath you will find a small gap in the wooden floor. Look inside, and you will find something that should not be kept secret any longer. Use the key that you found today."

Tetsuko's heart began to pound in her chest. She glanced around the room before whispering, "But what am I supposed to be looking for, Satsuki-san?"

Satsuki did not answer but gazed out over the unkempt garden to the moon. It cut a perfect white circle into the fabric of the night sky. Light cascaded toward her in waves, and Tetsuko was reminded of *Kaguya-hime*, the fabled princess born on the moon. Tetsuko looked at her lap, confused about what her sister-in-law wanted her to find. When she turned back to where Satsuki had been sitting, all that remained was the scent of sandalwood.

Tetsuko awoke with a start, a strangled sound caught in her throat, and sat up on her futon. Sweat trickled down her scalp and her heart was pounding heavily in her chest. The same moon was shining above her, but somehow everything felt different. Satsuki's presence lingered in the room, and so did her words: "You will find something that should not be kept secret any longer."

Cargoless,
Bound heavenward
Ship of the Moon
—Dohaku

13
KENZABURO YAMATO

"Hurry!" called a voice behind us. "The sun is coming up. Those left behind will be sent directly to the River of Three Crossings." A cry went up in the crowd as the people gathered on the beach scrambled to find a berth. Among the waiting boats was one stamped with our family crest—two cranes in flight—and my surname written on it in thick black characters: "Tsuruda." A man with a square face and black sunglasses gestured for me to get in. "What are you waiting for, old man? It is time to depart for Yamato." I wondered why he had used the old name for Japan, but when I turned to ask him, he was gone.

I leapt inside the boat just as the bells started ringing at Suma Temple. Around me, others were sitting in the canoe-like vessels, and on their bows, I made out the names Ito, Nochida, Takagi, Sanda. I studied each one and noticed that they all carried piles of reeds tended by figures in black kimono.

I looked back toward the shore and saw Ando-kun standing on the beach, watching me. I waved and shouted, "Ando-kun, get in this boat immediately!" He held his arms out to me in answer but did not move. I could hear his whispered pleas in my ear again, his broken voice asking me not to deliver the blow that would send him to the Mukogawa Bridge.

"No! It will be different this time, you will see!" I said. As we pulled away from shore, he faded into the gathering fog. I slumped in the bottom of the boat, my head in my hands. If I had been another kind of man, I would have gone back for him. Why was this memory coming to me now, I wondered? What good could it do to think about what could not be changed?

The others in the boats around me did not speak; most sat watching the shoreline as if they were looking for loved ones at the airport, hoping for one last glimpse as the journey began. A young woman near me began to keen until someone shushed her.

And then I saw her—a small girl in a blue cotton kimono stood on the beach holding a white balloon, the other hand brimmed over her eyes. I waved to her, a feeble half gesture. She saw me and raised her hand in answer, losing the balloon to the August wind. I was too far away to see the expression on her face, but I heard her cries— or was it the cry of an angry gull?—as the boat moved farther away from shore.

"*Iya*. I grunted. "What kind of transport service is this?"

From behind me, a low, rumbling laughter. Turning toward the sound, I was surprised to find a man sitting in the bow of my boat, black kimono open to his chest. Swirls of white hair tufted out of it, reaching out to meet a bushy white beard. The man, who seemed almost giant in stature, was smoking a long brown cigarette and appeared to be deep in thought, watching the ocean. The slight breeze that had begun to blow did not touch him. Occasionally he bent to touch the end of his cigarette to the pile of rushes in the belly of the boat.

"Your funeral fire," he said without looking at me.

I saw smoke rising up from the reeds in the boat next to us. The pile in our boat crackled and hissed, but no flames licked its edges.

"*Sumimasen?* Excuse me?" I asked.

Again, the sound of that dry, scraping laughter. "Your funeral fire," he said again. "It must remain lit until we arrive in Yamato. We'll be there soon, Ken-chan." He talked to me in a familiar way, as if he'd known me since I was an infant. The old man pushed us out to sea as the bell at Suma Temple ceased ringing, its black iron struck by the priest whose duty it was to greet the dawn on the morning following Obon's end.

"You must be mistaken. I'm not dead," I said, drawing myself up.

"Correction, Ken-chan. You are choosing to deny the fact that you are dead. But I assure you, it all happened—the fall from the tree, the funeral, your cremation. We are now crossing over to the place where you will spend the afterlife. That is, if you are able to succeed in the task the goddess assigns you."

I didn't like that this strange man talked to me as one would a school boy still in short pants. The boatswain must be some symbol of something in my waking life. I closed my eyes and braced myself. "Go ahead, then—tell me what you are here for. I must remember this," I said, "to tell Professor Kikazawa." He was a Jungian and a well-traveled colleague of mine at the university and I knew he would be fascinated. I made a mental note to call him so that we might go to lunch and discuss it later this week.

The bearded man turned to me, smiled, and bowed.

"I am your great-great-great-great-great Uncle Benkei. And I am taking you to Yamato, the place where spirits reside."

I laughed aloud. "*Asoka!* That explains everything. Your name, Benkei—the legendary warrior monk. My grandmother told me the old stories of your bravery, but every child knows them by heart—you were the soldier who fought and defeated 999 men at the Gojo Bridge, isn't that so? Until you lost to Yoshitsune, the famed warlord's son. My *obaachan* said you pledged loyalty to him until you died defending his honor."

"*Legendary?* Well, perhaps some might have said that about me, but while I may have been named for the Benkei of a thousand years ago, I assure you, Nephew, I lived and breathed in the streets of Kobe as surely as you did. I just came before you by a few centuries."

"*Saaa,*" I said, putting my palms together. "If you're not a character meant to remind me of the old tales, then your presence must have something to do with the article I'm writing." I stopped for a moment to ponder. "*Naru hodo.* Now I see—your kimono is the same color as the horned beetles I study. Perhaps you represent them. Try making a clicking sound with your pincers."

"You think I represent *horned beetles?*" The man who called himself my uncle snorted and then bit down on his long cigarette. When he spoke again, he did not face me, and his voice shook. "You carry the fate of our family line, Nephew. Listen to me: If you cannot complete the task that will be given to you in Yamato, we will all be turned into hungry ghosts—*gaki* doomed to wander the earth for eternity."

"Come, old man. Where are you really taking me?" I said, smiling. The wind ruffled the collar of my white kimono as we moved. All the other boats had disappeared in the haze. No one appeared to be here but myself and this strange old man.

"I will tell you again. I am taking you to Yamato—what you might call the afterlife," he said. "I was the lucky soul given the task of ferrying you across."

"*Naru hodo.*" I paused and drew myself up. "Unfortunately, there's no scientific basis for an afterlife, *Jichan*," I sniffed. I called him "uncle," the way I would address any old man who tended shop or worked at the train station. "How can I possibly be taken to an afterlife in which I do not believe?"

The man looked at me, his eyes narrowing. "Your words are regrettable. I fear that your time in Yamato may be difficult for you, Nephew. You have answers for everything you see, don't you? As the Buddha said, 'A fool who is conscious of his folly is wise; the fool who thinks himself wise is the one to be called a fool.'"

The conversation ended, I faced backward toward the shore, watching as the boat moved out to sea in the pale light. My self-proclaimed "uncle" hummed an off-key tune while he worked, the sound more like the wind whistling through a bamboo grove than any melody I'd heard. Although he used the oar to paddle, the boat seemed to move of its own accord, as if a long rope was pulling us toward open water.

The ocean we were traveling on appeared to be the same one in which my grandfather fished, the same water in which I'd swum with my brother before the polio, the same place my daughter splashed about as a three-year-old. Making a fist, I stretched my fingers over saltwater as harmless as the fluid that cradles a baby before birth. A cluster of seaweed swirled beneath my outstretched hand, looking for all the world like a serpent's tail.

I pulled my hand close to my body and shivered. I'd seen and felt enough of this place, and now I wanted to waken from this dream. Benkei turned and stared at me for a long moment, eyebrows raised. The burning reeds were fast being reduced to ash, which the old man scooped into a flat lacquer box, taking care that none spilled. I had seen boats like this before and strained to remember where.

"The *shoryo-buni* you are thinking of, Nephew. You saw these spirit boats on the last day of the Obon festival with your grandmother when you were twelve. Remember? She told you to watch until the boats moved to the horizon, because as soon as they were out of sight, they would have crossed into the afterlife on their journey to Yamato."

"But how could you know that?" I began to ask, and then stopped. I had forgotten myself. No doubt the emperor's imminent demise had me thinking about the war and my own mortality. I was convinced more than ever that this dream represented some truth that had eluded me, some riddle I needed to solve while my conscious mind slept.

I thought of my grandmother—her tiny, birdlike face and delicate hands, how she liked to tell the old tales. It was my grandmother and not my mother who sat by my futon and brought cool cloths for my forehead when I was feverish and ill, limply hanging onto life on the white cotton sheets of my childhood. This was the same time that my interest in insects began in earnest, in part because if I was fortunate, I was sometimes able to capture them on my windowsill. I would then study them for hours on end.

When I couldn't sleep, I loved listening to my grandmother's *mukashi banashi*, hearing stories of the great blue and red *oni* demons— giants who lived in the mountains clapping boulders together and kidnapping unsuspecting children—and *Momotaro*, the boy who was born from a peach and vanquished them with the help of a dog, a monkey and a pheasant.

Religion and the old tales mixed together in her stories, and when I was a child, I believed every word. But by the time I was eleven and the polio had been with me for a year, I began to reject her ideas. None of the gods had come to my assistance when I was sick, after all, no matter how many sutras my *obaachan* memorized. It was the doctors who cured me: medicine and science. And another memory: One night before I recovered from polio, my grandmother gave me a foul-tasting drink. "It is medicine from your *heso-no-o*, saved since your birth," she whispered. "I mixed this portion of your umbilicus with water from Mt. Rokko. It is the most powerful thing I can give you, but it may be taken only once in your lifetime."

"Uncle, my grandmother told me that to pass into the afterlife, one must ford the *Sanzu no Kawa*—the River of Three Crossings. This proves that we are dreaming. If all the old stories are true, it should be as my *obaachan* said."

"Ah, so you want to argue the particulars of the afterlife now—even though you don't believe it exists? Truly, you are a stubborn spirit," said Benkei. "Eh, Kenzaburo? But listen carefully—Yamato is not always what one expects. Your grandmother was right: some must cross the *Sanzu no Kawa*. Your birth, however, depends upon how you lived your life. Those who amassed good karma may cross over the river by bridge. Others, who were neither very good nor very bad, are able to wade through the shallows—this is the second crossing. Serpents, dragons, and demons lurk in the river, and some even hide in the shallows, waiting to pull spirits down to the darkness. By far the most perilous place to ford the *Sanzu no Kawa* is at the rapids. It is almost impossible to make the third crossing, but some have managed to do so. You can understand why spirits would prefer to avoid that gamble in Yamato. If they are lucky, or have been chosen for a special task, they find their entrance from the sea or in other places the gods have designated."

"Ridiculous," I muttered under my breath.

"You would do well to be a student here, Nephew, and not a teacher. If you can manage it, that is," said Benkei.

The candle I'd brought was still burning in the bow of the boat in front of the funeral pyre. When the sun disappeared into the sea,

Benkei used it to light two lanterns which he hung on either side of the boat. We sailed on into the night, no sound but the rippling tide pushing the boat forward. Voices whispered around us, growing softer, then louder. "Too late?" they seemed to ask, their plaintive question fading into the mist.

When the sun rose the next morning, it was a tiny pink spark on the horizon, igniting into full sunlight within minutes. The ocean became golden silk billowing beneath our boat.

"Yamato," said Benkei. "We are here."

But all I could see was the largest doorway imaginable—a *torii* gate three times taller than Miyajima, built millennia ago in the harbor outside of Hiroshima. The structure before us rose out of the water and towered overhead. It appeared for to be an open doorway attached to nothing, placed in the sea by some giant hand.

The other boats from Suma Beach materialized around us and lined up, waiting to enter Yamato. Most carried solitary passengers like myself, but some appeared to have as many as five or ten people aboard. Waiting with us were businessmen, school children, grandmothers, and one imperious looking priest with the unmistakable *bozu* cut, hair shorn close to his scalp. He alone seemed aware of what was happening but gazed around him with a look of disinterested arrogance, as if he were a king borne to his kingdom.

"Pray that the gods let us pass through the gate," whispered Benkei. "Not everyone is allowed." He leaned into his work, pushing the oar with renewed vigor.

"And what happens then?" I asked.

"*Seiryu* is the name of the sea serpent deity that lives under the islands of Japan. 'The great azure dragon,' some call him. The gods give him the spirits that are not allowed to pass through," said Benkei in a hushed voice. "It's his reward. He's kept satisfied this way."

"Of course," I said, not quite able to keep the mocking tone from my voice. My grandmother had told me about this dragon as a child. How strange that he would appear in my dream as a ghost-eating pet of the gods.

One by one, the boats in line began to pass through the gate. I heard a man's voice shout, "I ordered an ambulance hours ago. I will report you to your superiors!" A woman's voice hushed him. A bride in a boat nearby me wept and called for her mother.

When it was our turn, Benkei bowed and put his hands together. "It would serve you well to pray, Nephew," he murmured.

I nodded. I was certain now that this dream was about my childhood, and so a prayer to the gods made sense. My *obaachan* would have been happy to see me at this moment, and I almost felt her hand rubbing circles on my back. Clapping my hands together, I bowed my head.

"It's time to chant sutras that will allow our entrance. One hopes you will be able to remember some of them," said Benkei with a snort.

Surprised at how the words came back to me, I began to chant. I heard Benkei's voice join mine and the others on the boats nearby, until the hum in the air was as electric and palpable as the drone of swarming bees. Our voices blended together, and we chanted as if from one mouth.

As we passed through the gate, I found myself crying over a memory of my long-departed grandmother. I heard the whispers around me again, and one voice very much like hers that said, "Too late?"

"Who's there?" I asked as we emerged on the other side. Benkei studied me, head tilted to one side. "Perhaps there is hope for us after all. The spirits are worried that you may not be in time to complete the task that will be given to you," he said. "They've been waiting."

I gazed past him to see a mountainous island covered by a halo

of blue mist. One by one, the boats before us moved in toward the
shore. The men and women wearing black kimono at their helms disembarked and pulled their charges to the beach. I tried to move, but
Benkei stopped me. "It is not allowed," he said, and silenced me with
a look. "You may not touch the water here until you've been purified."

As he spoke, we heard a splash and a cry out beyond the giant gate.
The imperious looking priest flailed in the water, his boat and guide
nowhere to be seen. He called for help as he tried to swim toward the
gate. As we watched, a dark shape undulated through the water near
him. The priest struggled for a few moments until all was quiet.

"There are many things you do not yet understand, Nephew," said
Benkei. "Do not forget. The rules are different in Yamato, and scientific reasoning and logic won't assist you here as they did in the living
world."

I crossed my arms on my chest, annoyed by his superior manner.
He continued, "You must rely on that which tells you the most vital
truths, but which you have ignored for fear of appearing weak or
stupid."

Benkei added ashes from the reeds and drops of water to a black
lacquer box, then produced a long calligraphy brush from his robes.
I saw that a small container adorned with a carved fox hung from
Benkei's waist. He took some powder from it and added it to the
mixture.

"It is ready. Please give me your arm," he said. When I sat unmoving,
he sighed and grabbed my hand, pulling my sleeve up to my shoulder.

"I am writing purification sutras on your arms and hands, the
spirit sutras on your legs and feet," he said by way of explanation. "All
spirits new to Yamato must be protected in this way." He took a breath
and spoke as if he were talking to a young child, "This island is protected. If I don't prepare your body with these sutras, the gods will not

allow you to disembark in Yamato. You will turn into a white flame and disappear when you come ashore."

I looked around to see the others being marked in the same way, like the soldiers and monks of long ago who had written protection sutras on their bodies before going into battle. Was I to fight someone here, I wondered?

Benkei answered as if I had spoken aloud.

"In the living world, this is a very powerful protection for those who are about to face death, though you have no need to fear that now." When he laughed the sound came from his belly, low and hoarse. "What you will soon come to understand is that there are things far worse than death." A shadow passed over his face and he continued covering my arms with kanji.

He worked as he talked, in short, fluid strokes. Now he moved down to my legs, his brush leaving black kanji on my body, shiny trails of ink turning to matte on my limbs in a matter of moments. I could not read many of the archaic characters Benkei wrote, but I was able to make out the words, "gods" and "protection." "Crane" flew across my chest in bold strokes, along with the word "Inari," the place where Satsuki had been born. I saw with alarm that my feet seemed to be transparent.

"We lose them after death," said Benkei, following my gaze. "Remember your grandmother's words. Our feet are our last physical connection to the earth. Soon yours will fade away, like all spirits do in time." I looked down and noticed that he seemed to be floating a few centimeters from the ground.

In the boat next to us, three teenage girls were giggling as their arms and faces were painted by an old woman, who smiled at them as if they were her granddaughters. The woman finished and the three left the boat and joined a long line of people moving toward a sandy pink path up the mountain. I realized we were the last to disembark. Again, I found myself last, running to catch up with the others.

"You will need four kanji on your face: one on each cheek, and one on your forehead and chin," he said. "These are more difficult, because I must wait until they come to me before I can write them." He closed his eyes and dipped his brush into the thick black paste he had made. He then took the brush and, eyes half open, he wrote first on my left cheek, then my right, then my chin. He seemed to have the answer he was looking for and wrote something on my forehead.

"What does it say," I asked.

Benkei himself looked surprised.

"It says 'Crane, Fox, Snake, and Boar,'" he said. "I have no idea what it means. But you do, Nephew. These words came from you." He shook his head and said, "Wait—there is one more." He told me to lift my chin, and he drew another black character on my neck with long, fluid strokes. "Dragon." He regarded me as if I had an answer for him. I returned his unasked question with a blank stare. He nodded as if to himself, grabbed the bow of the boat and pulled it onto the beach, and said, "It is time, Nephew. Welcome to Yamato."

In the distance, we heard drums and saw smoke rising from a great fire on the mountainside. The sound of chanting reached our ears. Benkei motioned me toward the procession of souls that meandered up the mountain trail.

I followed, uncertain where we were going. My last physical memory—the hunt for *kabuto mushi,* the crack of the tree bough, my hands clutching air—replayed in my mind. I saw the moment in pieces: a white feather in the sun, a sharp pain in the back of my skull, and a light that spread from my head to my entire body.

I walked behind Benkei as he strode up the mountain in his black kimono, the smoke rising from the bonfire in the distance. Moving forward, I resolved to learn the task ahead. Even if this was a dream, it might somehow deliver me from the state in which I found myself— neither here nor there; neither alive nor dead.

The temple drums continued playing, and their beat grew stronger and more insistent with each step we took.

Now this year goes away
I've kept it hidden from my parents
That my hair is gray.
—Etsujin

GRAY HAIR
HARUNA

Two weeks before my father's death, he found the letter from Akihiro. He never knew that Akihiro was already gone; our affair a memory I kept hidden away in a box in my room. It consisted of three photographs, a few letters, and ticket stub from the Osaka planetarium.

There are times I blame myself for my *otohsan's* death. It is a truth I carry with me; my bones are becoming curved and dry under the weight of my guilt. I should have followed *Otohsan* that day, gone with him up the mountain to hunt insects as we had when I was a child. I was foolish to have thought I would have time to talk with him later.

I have gone over the explanation in my mind many times; the way I would talk to my *otohsan* and explain that Akihiro and I were a true "*ren-ai*"—a love match. I would tell him that Akihiro was planning to divorce his wife, that when I met him I thought I had at last found something as pure and lasting as my father and mother's marriage.

And I would tell him that it was never to be. I met Akihiro the day I turned forty. He left me before I turned forty-one.

On my fortieth birthday, I found my first gray hair and plucked it from its place. I had decided to visit the new planetarium in Osaka to mark the occasion. I wore a blue silk blouse the color of the ocean, twisted my hair into a chignon, and added a tortoiseshell comb to hold it in place. A small pin in the shape of a dragonfly—a birthday present from my father the year before—flew across the lapel of my cream-colored spring coat.

The towns sped by—Ashiya, Shukugawa, Nishinomiya, Juso—as the Hankyu train neared Osaka. The conductor, in his grey uniform and clean white gloves, announced their names as we pulled in and out of each station. I remember his voice purred, trailing off at the end, "Nishinomiyaaaaaa," as if recalling the names of a list of long-dead lovers.

I walked through the park surrounding Osaka Castle on my way to the planetarium, removing my jacket in the warm May air. The trees in the park blossomed yellow, purple, and pink, their brazen colors calling out to passers-by for attention.

When I entered the planetarium, I decided to view the star show that was just beginning. I hurried down the aisle of the auditorium, my eyes not yet adjusted to the dark theatre. "*Sumimasen.* Would you care to sit?" said a voice just behind my ear. I turned to see a man with his arm out, gesturing toward a chair. "*Douzo.* I insist you take this seat," he said. Out of breath, I nodded, thanking him. The lights dimmed, and stars shimmered on the ceiling. I looked up and sank back into the seat, enjoying the sensation of falling into the sky. "*Arigato,*" I whispered to the stranger as the show began.

A sonorous disembodied voice recounted the familiar story of how the universe was created. First the Big Bang, then stars appeared, galaxies formed, solar systems were decorated with planets. Earth was tiny, almost unnoticeable, down in the corner of the universe, and somehow our planet's anonymity comforted me. I heard a long exhalation next to me. The man who'd given me his seat was beside me, our faces only centimeters apart. He ran a hand through dark hair streaked with silver and I smelled the shampoo he used that morning, the soap on his skin. As the planets performed their slow dance around the sun, his face was illuminated, revealing deep creases around his eyes and fine silver stubble on his jaw line. I wanted to kiss him just below his cheekbone, but I folded my hands in my lap instead, embarrassed at the thought.

When the lights came up, I turned to the man once more and bowed a murmured thank you. As I moved toward the door, I heard his voice again:

"*Sumimasen. Eh to.* Forgive me, I don't normally ask people I don't know to have tea with me, but you looked so engrossed in the star show. Would you care to talk about it? I would be honored by your company."

I paused. It had been a long time since I'd been with a man, unless I counted the boys in make-up and furs who followed me and every other woman across Hikakebashi Bridge, trying to entice them to come to their "host clubs." Maybe it was the fact that it was my fortieth birthday and I wanted to do something different to mark the day. I agreed.

We walked through the castle park to a small tea house. The man, who said his name was Akihiro, walked with quick clean strides, as if sure of his destination at all times.

"The *ma-cha* is very good here," he said as we entered the *kissaten*. We were forced to stoop to enter through a low door. Inside the teahouse, rich wooden surfaces and shining bamboo walls welcomed us. Low tables made from slices of ancient oak trees were polished to shine like glass.

The man told me he was a doctor, that he lived in Kyoto. He was interested in astronomy, physics, archaeology. Unlike me, he had lived abroad, in Europe and America. When I told him about my interest in science he did not laugh, but rather nodded and tilted his head when he asked questions.

We talked for hours, until the sun folded under the lip of the horizon. At last, I looked outside and realized it was dark. "*Chotto* . . . My father and mother, I must call them," I said and hurried to the pink pay phone in the middle of the tea house. When I returned, Akihiro had paid the check and was standing to go.

"Haruna-san, this has been most enjoyable," he said with a shy glance. We walked to Yodoyabashi Station together.

"May I escort you to an exhibit next week at the Nara Museum of Art?"

"*Hai*," I said without coyness or hesitation. "I look forward to it." I knew by the band on Akihiro's finger that he was married, but I thought there was no harm in going to a museum with him. There was a part of me that knew what would happen even then, I believe, but I had no way of preventing it. Perhaps I didn't want to.

Before we parted, he leaned close to me and picked a small white flower from my hair. With a half smile he placed the flower in his lapel pocket, turned and walked toward his train.

NEW YEAR
SATSUKI
HAJIYAMA
DECEMBER 1944

It is almost *Oshogatsu*, the new year holiday, and there is still no word from Kenzaburo. Tetsuko is bustling around the house like a swollen ant, getting everything ready for her husband's homecoming. I am not supposed to know that Zaemon has been in Manchu-Kuo with the military for the past eight months, arranging shipments of metal and oil from China to Japan, but I hear them whispering about it. The Uribo women are not as clever as they think.

Tetsuko is radiant. Happiness has changed her appearance. Her eyes sparkle and there is a flush on her pale freckled cheeks. I cannot help myself—I envy her. She will soon see her husband. She has recent word from him that he is alive and well.

Her two sisters, Atsuko and Fumiko, tease her and predict another baby for next September. The fact that I do not have a child yet gives them another reason to whisper behind my back. I came upon them in the storehouse one day and heard them gossiping.

I caught them giggling, and the words " . . . he is so small and lame, the opposite of Zaemon-san. No wonder they can't . . ."

Startled to see me, they stopped their chatter and pretended to look for a bag of rice. Atsuko smirked, but Fumiko, who is the kinder of the two, grew red and bit her lip. She could not look me in the eye for three days afterward.

There are times when I wonder if I will ever go home, if the war will ever end; there are times when I think I have turned into a hungry ghost, wandering the halls of Tetsuko's summer house searching for a peace that will not come.

It is cold up here in the mountains, and there is snow. It is not as mild as Kobe, but the forest is wild and beautiful. The fir trees on the edge of the cliffs by the house are bent and twisted. I call one of them Climbing Man, because he has an angled spine for a trunk and forked root hands that grasp at the side of the rock. He looks as if he is clinging to the side of the mountain by the twin forces of stubbornness and age alone. He reminds me of old Hattori-san back in Inari, sitting on his stool outside his door no matter the season, his face impassive and taut.

I like Tetsuko's mother best, even though from one moment to the next, she does not know where or who she is. *Obaasan* sometimes forgets her daughters' names, or that they are her daughters at all. Like an old creaking cat, she lies and sleeps in a shaft of sunlight all day.

When she sees me, her face becomes bright. She calls me "Hanako" and tells me stories. No one tells me who Hanako is, but I discovered an old photo of two young girls in her room. On the back of the photo from top to bottom on the left side, Hanako is written in tiny, precise hiragana script, and next to it Obaasan's first name, Umeko, "plum child." The date is 1870. The two girls, who appear to be twins, stare at me in their Kimono, solemn-faced and delicate.

I like *Obaasan's* gentle company, and so offered to take care of her when I arrived. At first, Tetsuko and the others were too embarrassed to let me be their mother's nursemaid, but now they allow me to bathe, feed, and clean her. They have grown used to me and most of the time do not even see me. I am an inconvenience they must tolerate until the war ends.

Somewhere in the house the baby is crying, and Tetsuko's disembodied voice tries to lull her back to sleep. Tetsuko's son Ichiro plays in the corner, his fat baby cheeks flushed and round. The Uribos will always have babies with fat cheeks, will always have enough food to eat and warm clothes to wear. They will never know that this is extraordinary good fortune.

My sister-in-law's children make my life here bearable. I do not have much time to play with them, but there are moments during the day when I steal into their room and watch them nap or play games with Ichiro while Tetsuko takes care of the new baby Mayumi. Ichiro comes to me in his grandmother's room on unsteady feet. He loves his *obaasan* and talks to her in gibberish for hours. She nods and smiles, claps her hands in approval. They are both of an age where language is not necessary.

Ichiro is two years old and delights in poking his finger through the fragile paper of the shoji doors. The lower squares of thin white washi have become a net of tiny finger holes. Tetsuko would be furious if she knew, but I let him continue his game. He wets a chubby finger and sticks it through, watches it give way in amazement. *Obaasan* laughs and applauds. Sometimes she joins him from her futon, her long bony finger poking in tandem with his short fat one.

Ichiro, taking after his mother, is plump and round. My face, on the other hand, has grown more pale and thin with each passing day. I try to eat less than my share of food, knowing that I am taking away from the other family member's portions in the household. I bow and step aside when one of the sisters passes me in the hallway and take cover in doorways. I am like an insect that clings to door frames and windows as my benefactors move by, afraid if I get underfoot they might crush me.

Yesterday they fought, Tetsuko against her two younger sisters. Tetsuko won the argument, as I knew she would. She is the dominant one in the pack. In my head, I call them the *Inoshishi shimai*, the "Wild Boar Sisters." To amuse myself, I imagine them with long tusks growing from their faces, their thick bodies waddling through the house, bristling brown hair sticking straight up from their heads. Being penned in together is wearing on their nerves. Today they argued over some petty household matter—who would beat the futon, or clean the *ofuro*, or go to the shops. They did not even notice that I was in the room.

I am becoming invisible. Their inability to see me makes me feel hard and cold and small. It causes my stomach to twist and tighten like a wet cloth on the clothesline in November. Sometimes I see myself as a compressed snowball in the hands of a little boy. He will throw me into a snow bank and I will melt until I am gone.

We have chores today before the new year holiday comes. It is the time of year when the house gets its most thorough cleaning, and we are all enlisted to make it spotless for Zaemon's homecoming. I was given the job of scrubbing the smooth wooden floors of the hallway with water I draw from the well.

The shutters have been opened to let in the fresh winter air, but I am damp with perspiration. On my hands and knees, perspiration drips down the locks of hair that have escaped from the bun at the nape of my neck. By the time the drops of sweat reach my skin, they are cold. They leave wet tracks on my arms. My hands and wrists are scarlet, and my fingernails show bluish white against them like a dead woman's. I finish wiping the wooden floor and dip my rag into the bucket of freezing water that's grown dark and cloudy with dirt. The Uribo floors gleam like polished mahogany.

I kneel there for a moment, too dizzy to rise. A chill creeps into my arms and down the length of my body. For an instant I fear that I am slowly freezing solid and I let the sensation take over. The distant sound of Ichiro wailing downstairs brings me back, and I hug my arms, sliding my wet hands inside the loose sleeves of my kimono.

Shaking my head, I stand up to toss the contents of the murky pail into the snow behind the house. Stretching my hands toward the ceiling, I feel blood flow into the aching muscles in my back and shoulders as I arch my spine and let out a long sigh.

When I turn around, a man in an expensive overcoat with his hands in his pockets is watching me. Only half of his mouth smiles. The other half matches his eyes, blank and calculating.

Zaemon is home.

16
HIDDEN THINGS
TETSUKO
SEPTEMBER 1990

Tetsuko woke at 10:00 a.m. the next morning, four hours later than normal. She laid on her futon looking out the window, the dream of Satsuki still fresh in her mind. She remembered her sister-in-law's words, but the blue sky outside chased away the panic she'd felt the night before. Going back to Hajiyama had simply stirred up recollections of the past, she reasoned. Old memories were bound to appear as naturally as the finches that nested in the roof of the old country house. The reference to the crevice under the tatami mats in the old upstairs bedroom was probably something she had once known about but had long since forgotten, and her brain was simply reminding her through the dream of her sister-in-law.

Even so, she could still hear Satsuki's voice: "Look inside, and you will find something that should not be kept secret any longer." Another thought swimming below the surface of the new morning made Tetsuko shiver: What if she did find something—and what if it was unpleasant? Perhaps things that had been kept hidden should not be disturbed.

More of Satsuki's words followed her into the next room as she folded and put away her futon: "I have been waiting for you to return to this house." Tetsuko closed her eyes, shutting out the idea that somehow the spirit of her sister-in-law really had visited her the night before.

"Crazy old *obahan!*" Tetsuko scolded herself. It was impossible for Satsuki—or anyone, for that matter—to appear to someone in a dream. She would continue to search the house, to be sure, but what could possibly be hidden that she didn't know about? Tetsuko and Zaemon had enjoyed a working partnership; together they had raised three children. They were known in Hiroshima, respected. Articles were written in the newspaper when Zaemon passed away, and a retrospective of his life shown on the evening news. No less than the mayor paid his respects at Zaemon's funeral.

It was ridiculous to think that Zaemon might have kept something from Tetsuko that Satsuki would know about. Her husband and sister-in-law had barely spoken to each other when he was home on his visits during the war. And after the war ended, Satsuki and Kenzaburo always made excuses to avoid seeing Tetsuko when Zaemon would be present. Tetsuko had suspected it was because Zaemon had been so successful in business, while Kenzaburo had been a professor of insects. The brothers, Tetsuko knew, had never gotten along very well, but she'd never known why. She suspected it had something to do with Kenzaburo's illness and the attention he received from their *okaasan*, because Zaemon had always sneered and referred to Kenzaburo as "*amaenbo*" and "my mother's favorite."

Tetsuko smoothed her nightgown with a sniff. While other men might have felt lesser if they were adopted into their wife's family, Zaemon thrived. Tetsuko had always suspected he'd relished the chance to remake himself, to be somebody important in Hiroshima, to leave Kobe—and a childhood where he was always too loud, too brash, and too impatient with his sickly older brother—behind.

Although her family did not have the same pedigree as Zaemon's, Tetsuko was proud of the fact that the Uribos had achieved success through hard work and shrewd business deals. After the war, their family had risen to heights never before imagined.

Her mother-in-law had been quick to remind her of her lack of station each time they met. Tetsuko remembered a visit she'd paid after their wedding. When the tea and manju cakes were served, Reiko had paused before saying, "Strange, you are nothing like the girls my younger son entertained in his university days."

She said the word "girls" as if she was talking about women one might see in the pleasure district at first light—the inhabitants of the so-called floating world. Reiko had paused, her eyes flicking over Tetsuko. "But a plain, loyal wife is an advantage for any man. Zaemon has always been clever, if not too sophisticated in his tastes."

Even now, Tetsuko recalled how her face had burned. Reiko's sharp eyes had taken in the expensive furnishings in the Uribo home before settling on Tetsuko's plump middle. "No doubt you will produce many heirs for the Uribo name." Her mother-in-law sniffed and drew a purple silk handkerchief from her obi, a signal that the meeting was over. Tetsuko felt as if a thief had stolen the words from her mouth. She hastily bowed before Reiko left the room, walking in the short, sliding gait of a woman of the upper classes. She had the feeling her mother-in-law had toted up the value of the entire Uribo estate during her visit to her parents' home. And, as Reiko did each time they met, she had managed to make Tetsuko feel like a barnyard animal, lacking in any beauty or grace.

Fifty years later, and Tetsuko's face grew red again as she remembered Reiko's words. Perhaps reliving this painful memory, along with all the others, was the reason she had avoided coming to the old house for so long. Tetsuko had allowed herself to idealize the past, but the years spent in Hajiyama had been fraught with fear: fear that her husband would not return from one of his many trips to Manchuria during the war, fear that one of her children would fall sick, fear that they would run out of food, fear that the war would never end and that the Americans would invade Japan. In the end, the bomb they dropped was far worse than the temporary invasion of pale, freckled soldiers that followed. *Okagesama de*, thankfully the gods sent Satsuki to her. Without her sister-in-law, Tetsuko wondered if she would have survived.

Tetsuko reconsidered Satsuki's words from the dream. She decided to act on the instructions from the night before, just to clear her head of any silly superstitions that remained. She had just made up her mind when she heard a voice calling to her from the front door.

"Uribo-sama! *Gomen kudasai!*"

Ah, yes, it was Tamura-san come to take her shopping. Tetsuko picked up her watch and squinted at the numbers. 10:30 already. It would not do for Tamura-san to think her lazy. "*Chotto* . . . I will be right there," Tetsuko answered. She hurried to dress and comb her hair and grabbed a feather duster as she came down the stairs.

"Tamura-san, thank you for stopping by," she said, panting. "I was just . . . cleaning the veranda. I'm definitely in need of groceries, but the co-op seems to have closed since my last trip here."

"Ah, you are correct, Uribo-sama," said Tamura-san with a bow. "Not enough customers up here anymore! *Dakedo*, we are fortunate that there is an open-air vegetable market in town today. Although my son's car is not very good, he will drive us there and help us carry your purchases home."

Tetsuko agreed and thanked Tamura-san. Before they left, she dashed into the bathroom to apply lipstick. She splashed water on her face, dried it, and patted on some powder, hoping Tamura-san had not noticed her unkempt appearance. A few minutes later, Tamura-san's son Hiro pulled up in his Nissan Bluebird. Tamura-san insisted Tetsuko get in first. While it was not a new model, the car was spotless inside and out. Like many young men his age, Hiro displayed a collection of stuffed *anime* characters in the rear window. And from the size of his stereo, Tetsuko also suspected that he drove to the nearest big town at night with music blaring, the interior lights of the car glowing purple in the dark.

Hiro turned his baseball cap backward and chewed a large wad of gum. Tetsuko was startled to see that he was watching her in the rear-view mirror.

"All custom made," he said.

"Eh?" asked Tetsuko, unsure of his meaning.

"The car. Everything is custom-made. The seats, the stereo, the lights on the wheels. You can't buy one like this."

"*Asodesuka* . . . is that so?" asked Tetsuko. Her voice must have sounded impressed, because both Hiro and Tamura-san beamed in response.

As they drove, Tetsuko realized just how much the town had changed in the past five years. She saw firsthand what Tamura-san had indicated—people were leaving at a rapid rate, and many stores stood empty. Most of the shoppers at the market were elderly, with a handful of young people Hiro's age.

When he parked the car, Tetsuko glimpsed a woman selling trinkets in a stall near the vegetable farmers and purveyors of candied nuts and dried whole squid at the open-air market. She told Tamura-san she would be with her in a moment and went over to see what the woman was selling. Her wares included trinkets from the local shrine, images of the Buddha, post cards and small fox statues. "Surely, we are far from Inari," Tetsuko commented as she perused the merchandise.

"Not as far as you might think," came the seller's reply. When Tetsuko looked up, she was struck by the young woman's likeness to Satsuki at the same age—quick, delicate, and wild, with large amber-flecked eyes and hair that curled in tendrils at the nape of her neck.

"Eh?" Tetsuko hid her shock and continued to look at the items in the stall. This woman could have been Satsuki's sister.

"The fox goddess is worshipped all along the Japan Sea, and in many forgotten pockets of the countryside. Hajiyama is as forgotten as any place I can think of." Her words were tart and matter-of-fact, but she smiled at Tetsuko. "There's a shrine dedicated to the fox goddess near here, in fact. I have a map if you'd like to see it." Tetsuko nodded, and hastily paid for the map on a whim before hurrying to catch up with Tamura-san.

At the market, they bought daikon radish, *miso* paste, fresh tofu, cabbage, and noodles. Tetsuko did not speak but let Tamura-san prattle on. She was well known in the town and introduced Tetsuko to everyone who stopped to say hello. No one she met looked familiar to Tetsuko—she had come back to Hajiyama after too many years, and now nobody remembered or cared about her or the Uribo family.

Tetsuko bowed and smiled at each villager who came to greet her, but her mind was back in the trinket stall. She remembered how Satsuki had often disappeared for hours at a time when she lived with them during the war, and now she suspected she knew where her sister-in-law had gone. "This is one thing that will no longer be kept hidden," she thought. She promised herself that she would venture up to the fox goddess shrine before she left Hajiyama, and she resolved to write a letter to Haruna and Satsuki and tell them all about her discovery.

When the shopping was done, Hiro brought them home and carried everything into the house in loafers that slapped on the ground before announcing that he had an errand to run in the next town.

"Always busy, that one," said Tamura-san, her face breaking into a grin as Hiro blushed and bowed before leaving. Tetsuko heard Japanese pop music pulsating from the car as he drove away. She was grateful he had spared her the pain of listening to his stereo while she was in the car.

Tamura-san insisted on fixing some cold *soba* noodles for Tetsuko's supper. She waited on her until Tetsuko waved her off, thanking her for her efforts and slipping an envelope with a ten-thousand yen note into her hands for Hiro. She would pay Tamura-san in a lump sum before her departure to Hiroshima. Tamura-san bowed and cleaned up the kitchen before leaving. Tetsuko stood and bowed when Tamura-san announced she was going home and thanked her for her help.

"*Mata Ashita*," Tamura-san called before heading out into the dusk, letting Tetsuko know that she would be back the next day.

As soon as the house was quiet again, the dream Tetsuko had the night before returned full force: the smell of sandalwood, Satsuki's gentle voice. Tetsuko felt foolish, but she couldn't deny it—something pulled at her, made her want to check under the tatami in the room she and her husband had shared in the old country house.

Tetsuko remembered the day when Zaemon lost his ledger. She caught him searching for it frantically in their bedroom. They'd had an argument, Zaemon shouting at her to go from the room and leave him in peace. That night, he'd drunk too much whiskey and left the house while the rest of the family was having dinner. No one spoke. Finally, Tetsuko said, "It is very hard for my husband. The emperor is depending on him to make sure we have enough rubber for our tanks and boats. It is not an easy task." Tetsuko's sisters both agreed with her, saying, "Poor Zaemon. It must be very difficult," until Tetsuko changed the subject. Tetsuko remembered that Satsuki said nothing.

She paused on the veranda to look out at pink evening sky. Again, the smell of sandalwood in the room, and the feeling from the night before.

"Now," she heard Satsuki's voice whisper in her ear. "Go and look now, Te-chan. It is time."

Tetsuko looked around the *engawa*. "Sa-chan?" she asked, and she heard her voice quiver like a child's. On a small table by some floor cushions, she noticed something she hadn't seen before—a drawer was ajar. She opened it and found a small ivory fox *netsuke*. She picked it up to examine it and almost cried out. Satsuki had given it to her after they returned from Hiroshima, the day she and Kenzaburo left Hajiyama for good.

"This is an Inari fox, Tetsuko-san. My mother gave it to me before she died, and now I am giving it to you. I am your friend, and I am with you."

Tears trickled down Tetsuko's cheeks. In their haste to leave Hajiyama when the house in Hiroshima was finally ready for the family again, she had left the *netsuke* behind. Over the years, Tetsuko had looked for it but never been able to find it. She sank to the *zabuton* cushion as if in a trance.

A breeze from the mountains cooled her face. Tetsuko stood up. She was ready to do what Satsuki had asked.

She went upstairs to her old bedroom. The room had no lamp—she had forgotten. She found a candle in a holder sitting on a table near the door with a book of matches beside it. Each room had one because the power went out in Hajiyama on a regular basis. Tetsuko lit the candle and held it high and felt her pulse swell through her body. Tetsuko put her left hand on the table to steady herself, and then walked to the far corner of the room. The light of the candle threw shadows on the wall. She jumped when a large gray moth flew in the open window, attracted by the flame.

"Go to the place where the tatami mat covers a gap in the floor," Satsuki had instructed. Tetsuko got down on her hands and knees, putting her candle down on the floor beside her. The woven grass of the tatami had grown fragile and gray, and it turned to powder when she rubbed it. The dust in the air made Tetsuko wheeze and struggle for breath, but the panel was lighter than she expected, and she was able to lift it easily.

Tetsuko's breath caught in her throat. Just as Satsuki said, there was a gap in the floorboards underneath. "I must remember this hiding place from when I was a girl," she said aloud to the empty room. "Perhaps my sisters and I kept treasures here . . . " Maybe she would find an old key or piece of jewelry, or perhaps some old worthless coins. She lowered the candle into the gap to be sure there were no creatures living down there—Tetsuko could not abide insects or vermin—and, seeing that it was clear, she put her left hand inside.

She felt around and touched something hard and cold. It was a small object that turned out to be another Inari fox, carved in ivory, like the one Satsuki had given her. Curious, she placed it next to the wall and put her hand inside the compartment again. Her fingers next grasped something that felt like a piece of bamboo. She pulled out a *fude* brush pen. Next, she discovered the hard, flat edge of a book. Tetsuko grasped it, pulling it up toward the opening. It slapped back down before she could pull it out, and she felt pages flutter past her fingertips. She went in again and this time managed to pull out a slim black volume with a small lock on it, its leather binding gnawed by mice. There were teeth marks on its top right corner, but it was in otherwise good condition.

Tetsuko recognized it at once as being one of her husband's business ledgers. Zaemon kept copious notes when he was alive, so as not to forget the details of any commercial deal he was engaged in. He must have told her about the hiding place when they lived in Hajiyama, she reasoned, although the hairs on the back of her neck were now standing. In case something happened while he was away in Manchu-kuo, she would know what trade negotiations he was engaged in.

She took the key she'd found the day before from her skirt pocket. It turned in the lock, to her surprise. She opened the ledger and began to read. Just as she thought, each entry detailed her deceased husband's business transactions in precise detail. Tetsuko read through each one, relieved, until she saw a page labeled "New Year's Eve, 1944." She thought back and realized that he had been home that year for the holiday.

The 18th year of the Showa Period, 12th month, 31st day
Oshogatsu Holiday
The Year of the Monkey
Country House, Hajiyama

Military Contracts, December:

Steel shipment to Kobe: 200,000,000 円 (200 million yen)
Steel shipment to Nagoya: 130,000,000 円 (130 million yen)
Steel shipment to Tokyo: 550,000,000 円 (550 million yen)

Rubber from Philippines to Nippon:
2,000 kilograms, October-December
Contact Commander Ushikawa for payment

Hiroshima Warehouse:
Delivery of Munitions, Jan. 5th, via train from Kobe—
14:30 arrival.

Tetsuko continued reading and smiled when she saw an entry mixed in with the others that mentioned their eldest son Ichiro, and the house in Hajiyama. What greater proof did she need that Zaemon was a devoted father and husband?

※ Ichiro: Weight: 8 kilograms, Height: 57 centimeters
※ House: Repairs: Tell Furuda to replace thatch on north side of cottage.

Supplies: Arrange with Nakawa-san for a larger supply of dried fish and rice to be brought up to Hajiyama from Hiroshima.

Tetsuko was touched by her husband's thoroughness. She missed his steady hand, his self-assurance. There were those who had thought him arrogant, but she had always excused it by calling it confidence. Tetsuko remembered how Zaemon would laugh and say, "Humility is for the likes of my father's generation. After all, being humble did not get our company the contract with Mitsubishi."

Her thoughts again turned to Satsuki. What had she meant by "something that is hidden?" Was it the fox *netsuke*? But she'd found that downstairs in drawer of the small table on the veranda. Tetsuko put her hand into the hole under the old tatami mat and continued searching. At the far end of the hiding place, she felt some paper and pulled out a packet of letters. They were dusty and moth-eaten, but still intact. She held them up to the light. They were addressed to Satsuki here in Hajiyama, and the return address was from her brother-in-law Kenzaburo in Kobe. By the postmark, she could see that the letters were written during the war. But why would her husband have kept letters from his brother and sister-in-law in this secret place? It made no sense to Tetsuko, and she frowned. She set the letters aside to send to Satsuki and Haruna later.

Her curiosity piqued even more, she reached in and found the edge of what she thought was another book. She managed to pull it forward with her fingertips until she was able to get a grip on it and remove it from the chamber.

She was surprised to see a book of *mukashi banashi*—Japanese fairy tales. It must have been something that the children had enjoyed and perhaps hidden here. She thumbed through it, the candle flickering over beautiful traditional prints of *Momotaro,* the peach boy, and the Tale of the Bamboo Cutter. Tetsuko smiled to see the illustration of *Urashima* riding the giant sea turtle home from his hundred-year ocean sojourn, his long white beard flapping in the wind.

When Tetsuko came to the tale of *Kaguya-hime,* the moon princess, she was surprised that the paper felt stiff and heavy. Her heart started thudding heavily in her chest again. She turned the page, but instead of a print of *Kaguya-hime,* there was a photo of Satsuki on her wedding day, lovely as the fairy tale princess.

Satsuki stood alone in her white kimono, the bridal hood over her head. Her eyes were large and dark, and her face had the sharp, delicate angles of a wild animal. A sheet of folded rice paper lay folded next to it. Tetsuko wiped her perspiring hands on her skirt and opened the letter. The handwriting was unmistakably Zaemon's, but he'd written the message in hiragana. Why would a man who prided himself on his calligraphy use the alphabet only children knew? At first, Tetsuko thought it must be a note to their children, except for the greeting at the beginning—it was for Satsuki, because he'd addressed it to "Ne-chan"—the endearment for "older sister."

"Ne-chan: A small present for you. I thought you would enjoy these stories. Our weekly instruction will help you, no doubt, as you learn to read kanji. I hope you have enjoyed the time as much as I have."

Tetsuko felt her armpits dampen. Zaemon had been teaching Satsuki to read? And how could she not have been aware that this had happened—or even that Satsuki didn't know how to read kanji when she lived with them? This did not seem possible—after all, Zaemon had made it plain that he detested Satsuki. Tetsuko well remembered how he scowled at her sister-in-law as she moved about the house, his mouth curled downward in disapproval. Tetsuko had always imagined it was because he resented having to take in his brother's wife, and that her husband had seen it as yet another imposition foisted upon him by his "crippled older brother," as he often referred to Kenzaburo.

Tetsuko tried to calm herself, but her pulse continued its hard, marching steps inside her chest. Fear, disgust—the barest slivers of knowledge—grew as she read.

"Tonight, we will read your story—the tale of Kaguya-hime. Think of how surprised Older Brother will be when your ability to read kanji exceeds his!"

Then Zaemon had written, *"Be waiting for me after everyone is sleeping, as usual."* Further down on the page, he'd written something else, but an inkblot from his fountain pen must have ruined the letter. Instead of throwing it away, he'd kept this draft. She grimaced. It was not her husband's way to be sentimental, or so Tetsuko had always thought.

Tetsuko's tears were bitter as burnt tea. The disdain Zaemon had shown Satsuki must have been a show. Or worse, it had arisen from lovers' quarrels they'd had under the roof of the Uribo family home.

A strangled animal sound came from Tetsuko's throat. She, a woman who rarely cried and who never allowed herself to indulge in the pointless act of self-pity. She slumped into a kneeling position. Stray memories came to her, and her mind placed them into this new framework in which she now saw her life.

Everything looked different, meant something different to her. She remembered Zaemon's interest in coming home that last winter before Japan lost the war. Each time her husband arrived that year, he looked more haggard, drank more whiskey, smoked more cigarettes. He was prone to angry outbursts and moody silences. Tetsuko had blamed this on the war, his responsibilities, and in her private moments, had explained his bad temper with the idea that he was concerned about her and the children's safety. His visits had increased until his final trip home in July, just one month before the bomb was dropped on Hiroshima. Her husband had not been able to secure passage home from China until two weeks after the war ended, when Satsuki and Kenzaburo had already left.

Tetsuko's mind circled those months leading up to Japan's surrender. She remembered watching Satsuki as she grew thinner and thinner, becoming nearly invisible at times, disappearing for hours on end. Tetsuko had ascribed her absences to her embarrassment over imposing on the Uribo's good nature. At the time, Tetsuko had thought Satsuki intimidated by her superior rank and wealth—Satsuki had been born in the countryside, after all, and adopted by an older couple shortly after her birth. Now, she wondered if in fact Satsuki had been hiding her shame and guilt from Tetsuko.

Dull certainty filled her, weighed her down as if she was trapped under layers of plaster and stone, like the victims she'd seen after the bombing in Hiroshima. The victims she'd seen with Satsuki, the only one who was brave enough to come with her to search the city for Tetsuko's father.

Was this act, the basis for their friendship of more than four decades, a sacrifice Satsuki had made to pay back Tetsuko in some way?

Now Tetsuko felt weak and empty. The guiding certainties of her life—that her husband had honored and respected her, that Satsuki was her most loyal friend, and that she, Tetsuko, was a most fortunate woman—had all evaporated with the discoveries made in a single night.

Tetsuko's grief turned to anger. She had taken Satsuki in, shared food with her. Tetsuko now imagined Satsuki cornering Zaemon and begging him to teach her to read. Zaemon must have felt sorry for his brother's wife, and started tutoring her out of kindness, Tetsuko thought. Her cunning sister-in-law had slowly endeared herself to her unsuspecting husband until he didn't know what he was doing.

Tetsuko had never been superstitious, but now she wondered if there was some truth to what they said about the women from Inari and their connection to the fox goddess. She and Zaemon both possessed a fox netsuke from Satsuki—was that part of her plan to bewitch both of them into trusting her?

Tetsuko had never expected Zaemon to be faithful to her—what husband was? She suspected Zaemon had his dalliances with women of the Floating World from time to time, as most men did. In turn, most Japanese women turned a blind eye to the red-light district and lived by the proverb, *"If your husband is healthy and out of the house, that is good."*

Tetsuko sat and stared at the book. She forced herself to thumb through the ledger and book of folk tales but found nothing else. Minutes passed. Gradually she became aware of the other sounds around her—an old clock ticking on the wall, the candle flame burning beside her, dancing in the drafts that managed to find their way into the old house, the voice of the wind in the eves saying, "hush, hush."

Defeated, she placed the letters, the ledger, and book of fairy tales back into the gap in the floor, and slid the tatami mat over the top of the hidden recess.

Tetsuko picked up the candle and left the room. She had the odd sensation that she was floating above the ground like a footless ghost, no longer tied to the earth by anything but bitterness and sorrow.

Tetsuko went to her room and began packing. She would not spend one more night in this house. Above all, she would not chance another dream of Satsuki.

When she was finished, she called a taxi to bring her down the mountain to the train station. It would be double the normal price at this time of night, but she didn't care. She left an envelope on the kitchen table with 50,000 yen in it for Tamura-san, with a note saying that she'd been called away on important business. She instructed Tamura-san to close the house up for the winter—her family would not be visiting in the autumn after all.

The taxi zoomed through town, past the point where the woman in the trinket stall told Tetsuko she could find the path to the Fox Goddess shrine. Tetsuko pressed her lips together and stared straight ahead. She would not be paying her respects at that particular shrine now, or ever.

十七

KENZABURO
THE HOUSE OF MY AFTERLIFE
1989

I didn't speak to Benkei as I followed him up the mountain. His wiry hair, now twisted into a silver ponytail, flickered in the moonlight. Sometime in the night, we broke through the forest and I found myself on a familiar street. I spied the roof of my own beloved home in Rokko. There was the pine tree bent in its eternally pained and elegant gesture over the gate, the stone wall of the garden crumbling in one corner, the vent under the roof of the house that had become the entrance for the family of weasels who lived in our attic. For the third time that day and the fourth in my adult life, tears fell from my eyes. I was home.

Before we entered, Benkei stopped me at the gate and said, "Nephew, you need to understand something before you enter. This is indeed your house, where you'll reside in Yamato, but there are a few differences." Silent and reassuring as a monk, he walked with me to the door of my own home. He led me gently, like one might guide a blind man making his first tentative steps on new soil, urging me without words to remember every dip and bump in the road, to memorize this new terrain with every false cell in my absent body.

He paused, allowing me to absorb the disappointment and grief of being home but not home, and then said, "You won't find Satsuki and Haruna here, but we will be going to see them soon, I promise you. Time, if you want to call it that, passes quickly here."

Other spirits passed by on the street, and I noticed Nakawa-san's daughter, who had died during one of the firebombings in Kobe. "*Konnichi wa*, Tsuruda-san" she called.

"Kimiko-san. *Konnichi-wa*. Where are you going?" I asked.

"Why, to the train station, Tsuruda-san. I am to graduate high school today—didn't you know? Mrs. Tsuruda sent flowers to our home. How lovely they are! *Domo, arigatou gozaimasu!*" She bowed low and held it before standing up again and smiling. And then called, "May Japan be victorious!" as she ran back in the direction of her house.

"She does not know she's dead, you see," said Benkei behind me. "Very sad. Spirits get trapped here, unable to go on to their next life and attain Buddhahood, unable to move toward enlightenment. That is where most of the Tsurudas are now—*in between*."

"My mother, my father, my brother—are they here?" I asked, looking around the garden, and expecting to see them at any moment.

"In time, Kenzaburo," said Benkei. "You cannot rush spirits."

I soon learned that he was right. Though I spent my days with Benkei, other spirits came and went from our ancestral home. The older ones—those who died centuries or more before—did not show themselves very often.

"They are tired, Kenzaburo," Benkei explained. "The longer we are here, the more faded our image becomes."

Still, he said that I was a drawing force in our family—what I likened to a type of magnet. Family members gathered and congregated around me. For reasons I could not discern, I was their touch stone.

Of those who appeared in the bodies they wore in life, I most often saw my great uncle Fumihiko, who was my grandfather's younger brother. Doleful, he moved through the garden outside of our house. His long gray hair swung down past thin shoulders. He looked neither to the right nor left as he walked. At the fence, he stopped and stared out toward the place where the ocean disappeared into the sky. At times his mouth gaped open like a koi, corners bent in a down-turned grimace. He left home when he was fourteen to become a sailor, and never returned.

"Drowned," explained Benkei. "Most unfortunate. The ones who die in the waters off Japan often do not regain their wits afterward."

There was a small, slight girl who smiled at us shyly from behind the pink azalea bushes. I recognized her the first time I saw her, from old pictures my father had in his room. She was my aunt Tomoe, his younger sister. She died of *hyaku-nichi zeki*, the hundred days cough, when she was eight. I saw something of Haruna in her, too, with her birdlike movements and wide set eyes.

My uncle Senji and aunt Kimiko, my father's older brother and his wife, appeared on occasion, always together, my aunt walking four steps behind. My uncle was as imperious and proud in death as he was in life. All three of their boys died in the war. My cousin Hiro, their youngest son, was beheaded attempting to desert the army in Korea. We heard from one of his platoon members that he'd fallen in love with a local girl and was attempting to stage his death. He planned to pass as a member of his lover's family. They were executed together in a village square outside of Pusan. He was twenty-one and she just sixteen.

My aunt stopped and made the same inquiry each time, "Ken-chan, *ogenki desuka?* How are you, Nephew? Your studies, are they progressing well?" And, before leaving, she asked, "Have you seen the photos of my boys in the paper?"

When she glanced at me there was a small, twisted smile on her face. "We are honored that all of our sons can serve." This was something she had never failed to lord over my mother, who had one son too infirm to join the army, and another who profited from the war. I was kind to my aunt's spirit because I remembered how she loved my cousins, how she doted on Hiro even after he had grown up and joined the army. I remembered watching my aunt grow more hunched and twisted with each visit they received from the Imperial Army communications officer. She died after the war ended at the age of forty-six.

Benkei never failed to bow and smile at my aunt and uncle, whose eyes focused through him, somewhere in the distance over Kobe City. Before leaving, my aunt always bowed to us and said, "May the emperor live 10,000 years!"

"It would no doubt be rude to tell them that the emperor is here along with us," said Benkei. I looked at him, surprised. "Oh yes. He died the January after you arrived in Yamato. He is here in his ancestral home, too, awaiting his fate in the afterlife just as we are awaiting ours."

I nodded. The emperor's descent into mortality had been complete. I wondered if he grieved his life the way I grieved mine, if his sadness and regret was unbearable.

At separate times I saw her two oldest boys, my cousins Taro and Haruyuki, who died in combat in the Philippines. When they stopped to talk to me, they asked for directions.

"Have you seen the rest of our troop? We were with them a moment ago, before the bomb went off." Each time, I shook my head and bowed, and they moved on.

There were many other spirits whom I did not know. When they saw me, they talked about people I'd never met who shared our family name. Preoccupied with their thoughts, the spirits of my ancestors were like a passing crowd in a train station.

"They are like you were when you first arrived in Yamato," Benkei explained one day. "Most of our family never accepted the fact that they are dead, you see. They act just as they did in life. They haven't learned a thing in Yamato." He glanced at his fingernails. The one on his right pinky he kept long and yellow, and he used it to pick his ear. He shrugged and said, "Old habit."

"But why are all our family members here?" I asked. "Why don't they know that they are spirits?"

"Just like you, they are unable to face the truth, Kenzaburo, and so they are stuck here," Benkei said. "It was not just you, Nephew. The Tsuruda family lost its way generations ago. Now we must work from present to past and try to repair what has been broken."

On the street, a figure clad in gray moved up the hill toward my family home. His gait was slow and deliberate, as if he was experiencing every sight and sound around him for the first time. There was something about the way he walked that was familiar. In an instant, I knew who was approaching.

"*Otohsan?*" I called. I ran down the street until I saw that it was indeed my father coming home. We bowed to each other when I reached him.

"*Otohsan,*" I said, relief washing over me.

"Kenzaburo, good news!" said my father, a smile spreading across his gray features. "*Ika.* I was able to get some squid today at the market in Sannomiya."

I looked behind him down the mountain, confused. *"Nani o? Otohsan*, I don't understand—"

"Perhaps Satsuki-san will make it for dinner tonight. It has been months since we've had squid."

It was at that moment I understood. The day my father died, he had been bound for Sannomiya on a shopping trip for Satsuki and had never returned. Like the others in my family, my *otohsan* was in between, unaware of the fact that he had died.

"Ahh," I said, masking my disappointment. I spoke to him in the way one might speak to a small child. "Yes, that was good of you, Father. Thank you."

My *otohsan* smiled again and bowed slightly. "Please tell her for me, Kenzaburo. Please tell Satsuki. Maybe she will be happy, *darou?*"

I nodded, unable to find words, and stood watching as my father drifted down the street toward the small temple in our neighborhood, a place he'd often gone for refuge from my mother and from the war. I'd come upon him there on more than one occasion as I was returning home from the munitions factory. Most often I'd spy him sitting on a bench by the koi pond, either reading or staring off into the distance. Each time, we'd nodded to each other and continued on our separate paths—mine to see Satsuki, and my timid father to find respite from the chaos and destruction that was our life.

As I watched him disappear into the gray light, Benkei approached. "It is time, Kenzaburo," he said. "You must take the trail up the mountain that you took on the day of your death. We don't have much longer before the next Obon."

With a heart scraped and hollow, I began the familiar walk up the mountain behind our house. Everything was as it had been the day I died, except the trail was overgrown and a roiling, black sky stretched over our heads. The wind picked up as I climbed the path, willing myself to keep moving forward. Benkei followed behind me, encouraging me when I stopped or faltered. When we passed the waterfall, I could almost see myself kneeling there prior to my death, splashing my face with water as I tried to rid myself of the messages that told me I would soon be leaving the living world.

"So much different from my own death walk," Benkei remarked, "through the red-light district in Osaka." He sighed and said, "Come. We are almost there." His tuneless humming was the only sound as we walked through the forest. When we reached the tree from which I'd fallen, I approached and stood under its heavy gray boughs, almost expecting the beetles to still be fighting overhead in the foliage. My death seemed as if it had occurred only moments ago: I remembered the sound of the worshipers coming up the hill chanting my name; the crack of the branch as I fell; the gentle tug that separated my spirit from my body.

A small stone Jizo statue sat beside the boulder I'd fallen on. "He guards travelers in the afterlife," said Benkei. "This statue marks the moment of your death." The statues were everywhere in Yamato, and I realized that each one marked a spirit's last moment on earth.

Benkei handed me a lantern. "You'll need it to climb Mt. Inari," he said. I raised my eyebrows but took the lantern. "Inari is located a hundred kilometers east of Mt. Rokko," I said, but Benkei didn't explain. And just as he had said, around the next bend in the trail, we came upon the tunnel of red gates from my wife's village.

"In Yamato, many things are not as they are in the living world," said Benkei. "Even, and perhaps especially, time and geography. This path of *torii* gates leads to the top of Mt. Inari. I'm sorry, Nephew, but now you must travel alone."

He bowed and turned to leave.

"*J-jichan*, are you certain you can't come with me?" I stammered. The mountain had grown dark under the moonless sky.

"*Ii-e.* I'm afraid not, Ken-chan," said Benkei. "Each spirit must face his death and journey through the afterlife in his own way. This is the way that was chosen for you."

I hesitated, afraid to move forward.

"The Lord Buddha said, 'There are two mistakes one can make along the road to truth: not going all the way, and not starting,'" said Benkei. "It is time you start, Kenzaburo."

I returned his bow and began my ascent of Mt. Inari, holding the lantern high. Each crimson *torii* gate was spaced behind the next by less than half a meter, so the effect was one of traveling up the mountain through a tunnel of red doorways unconnected to any walls. Satsuki once told me that the children in Inari dared each other to make this journey at night, and that she was one of the few brave enough to succeed at making it all the way to the top. I thought of her now and closed my eyes. Reaching into my pocket, I felt the knife and the fox netsuke she'd placed there at my funeral.

"*Ganbate,* Kenzaburo," I heard her saying, as she had during my first trip to Inari. "Keep going—we are almost there."

The stone path wound around the mountain like a dragon's tail, and as I traveled its upward sloping surface I heard the occasional yipping of foxes in the distance. Halfway to the top, I thought I saw the swish of a white tail in front of me on the path. Again, I heard voices around me whispering mournfully, "Too late?"

"Too late for what?" I shouted out. "Who's there? Show yourselves!" As if in answer, my lantern flame flickered and died, leaving me in darkness. I was forced to touch the flat side of the knife I carried from one gate to the next, using the sound to guide my steps. At times it seemed like I heard footsteps scuffling on the path behind me. Again, I saw a white flash ahead of me on the trail. I wondered if it was some kind of trick; if at the top of the mountain I would come face to face with all the hungry ghosts of Yamato, but I had no choice than to keep going.

At long last, I saw a small, flickering light glowing ahead of me and felt the path leveling off. I emerged into a large clearing, at the center of which was a red shrine dedicated to Inari. Two fires burned in braziers on each side of its altar, and large white fox statues with offerings of food and sake placed in front of them monitored my approach with bland marble eyes. The altar was set with candles, flowers and incense, and a sheaf of rice lay on a raised platter at its base.

It had been years since I'd prayed at a shrine, but I dutifully rang the bell, threw in two coins from my kimono sleeve, clapped twice, and bowed my head.

The sound of someone yawning made me open my eyes. Before me sat a woman who appeared to be in the last stages of pregnancy, flanked by two large white panting foxes. She laughed and said, "You can stop praying now, old man." I looked down at my hands, which were still pressed together.

"Come closer," she said, stroking the head of the fox to her right the way one would stroke the furry back of the family dog.

When I hesitated, the woman in front of me laughed, covering her mouth with her hand. In the flickering light, the foxes beside her appeared to smile.

"Tsuruda-san, you are still using your scientist's eyes to see, even after death," she said, scolding me. As she spoke, her face became more angular. I saw that her eyes were like Satsuki's, the same amber color and almond shape.

"My wife, Satsuki, she is from Inari," I said. "She was adopted by the Kitsune family who farmed in the foothills of this mountain."

The woman's voice became cold and shrill. "You know your daughter. What makes you think I don't know mine?" She continued, "Your wife is ill now, and you are hoping to be reunited here in Yamato before the next Obon. Isn't that right, Tsuruda-san?"

Again, I had misread the signs in Yamato. I bowed to the ground and pressed my forehead to the stone path in front of me. I had been looking for the deity of Inari, who traditionally took the shape of a beautiful young woman in a white gossamer kimono, or a rotund man who graced beer hall signs and dispensed rice and sake to his worshippers, but instead I'd been met by a heavily pregnant woman who was none too pleased to see me.

"Please forgive me for not seeing clearly. You—you are not what I expected," I said, still bowing.

"One does not always receive what one asks for in life in the way one expects to receive it," she said, snapping open a fan. "Please remember this as you make your way in Yamato."

"*Hai*," I whispered, ashamed of my ignorance. "I will remember."

"Your uncle did not lie," she continued now. "You have indeed been chosen to save your family line from its fate. You don't have much time before the next Obon comes."

I thought of my gray clothes, my fading feet, my old man's hands. I was a poor specimen indeed, even as a spirit, hardly fit to save myself let alone the rest of the Tsurudas still in Yamato.

"Forgive me," I said, "but why was I chosen? Surely there must be someone more qualified than I?"

"There is no one else," said Inari, and her words echoed through the shrine. "You must correct what is wrong before Haruna joins you here, or she will suffer the same fate as the rest of your family."

I cleared my throat, afraid to ask her the next question. "You are the patron goddess of my wife's village. Why are you helping me, one who never believed in the existence of the gods at all?" I whispered, unable to take my eyes from the ground.

Inari sighed and spoke to me as if I was a small child.

"Satsuki and Haruna are under my protection. Their veins run with the blood of Inari. Satsuki has been a loyal believer, but she will choose to be with you and your daughter, whom she loves above all others, even if it means she becomes a hungry ghost along with you. To save her, I have no other choice than to help you before she arrives in Yamato—and that time is soon approaching." She paused, her tone hardening: "Understand that if not for Satsuki, you and your family would never have been given this chance. I am the one who intervened on your behalf." And then, in a whisper that was a low growl, "You will regret it if you disappoint me."

"But I don't understand. W-why was my family consigned to an eternity as hungry ghosts?"

Inari laughed, but the sound was not warm. "Your family was motivated by greed and ignorance," she said, wringing disgust and bitterness out of each syllable. "Each generation greedier than the last. There was little concern for your fellow human beings unless it suited you."

"Please, I beg you—was I such a failure of a man?" I stammered. "I took care of my wife and daughter. I was *majime*—serious and responsible."

"Do you think the only way to be greedy is to desire what is material?" she hissed, and the fox kit in her lap whimpered. "Your greed was the greed of ignorance, your selfishness evidenced by your unwillingness to see the truth if it meant your life would be disrupted. So afraid were you of change that you made yourself blind to the people who needed you. Rather than face what came with courage, you hid behind gauzy curtains of pride and fear. And that is the reason, Tsuruda Kenzaburo, why you indeed deserve to be a hungry ghost: your unwillingness to see the truth, admit your mistakes or change course for the people you loved if it meant that your life would be made unpleasant."

I bent down, afraid to look at her.

"Stand and approach the altar."

I willed myself to walk toward her.

"Listen to me," she said, her eyes reflecting yellow at me in the fire light. "You will have three Obon holidays in which to complete your task. Since you fell from the oak and first came to Yamato during The Days of the Dead, your first Obon was spent partly in the living world and partly in the afterlife. This is unfortunate, because it gives you less time to complete the task assigned to you, but it can't be helped. You were the fool who insisted on climbing the oak that day, despite every sign you were sent to go home to your wife."

"Your first task is one that requires you to face what happened in your life. You will soon receive a scroll on which you will write everything that you remember from birth until the day you left the living world. Understand that everything must be laid bare. I warn you, any lies you told yourself when you were alive will not be allowed."

I nodded, wondering what value my life story could hold for Inari.

"You must also find your mother and brother," she continued. "They have been in Yamato since each of their deaths. They hold the key to an important truth." She paused and looked away. "You must not fail, Kenzaburo. And although you will want to, you must not hide. Otherwise . . ."

Her voice trailed off, the statement she hadn't finished hanging in the dank air. Otherwise, my parents and their parents, on down to the first Tsuruda, would be forced to wander heaven and earth as hungry ghosts. My wife and daughter, consigned to an eternity of pain and hunger. I alone would be to blame.

"I warn you, if you are unable to do either of these tasks by your third Obon, you will have no more chances to make right what is wrong."

"I understand," I whispered and bowed to her again. My mouth felt small and meek as a child's. I wasn't certain if I could trust Inari, or if she was tricking me in the same way she was said to have fooled and enthralled unsuspecting men for thousands of years. Doubt filled me, coloring in the outline of my weightless form like burnt charcoal.

"Take this and enter the door to my left," she said, setting a lit candle on a table next to the altar and gesturing to a small red door to the left. The moment before she and the two white foxes disappeared into the dark landscape of the mountain, she turned to me and said, "The Buddha said that there is nothing more dreadful than the habit of doubt. Doubt separates people. It is a poison that disintegrates relations, it is a thorn that irritates and hurts, it is a sword that kills. Do not allow fear to fill you, Kenzaburo—you do not have the luxury of the time it will take to overcome it. And you must not squander the time you have left."

When she'd gone, I picked up the candle in its holder, walked to the red door, and opened it. Stepping across the threshold into a narrow, enclosed space, I paused, fearful of any traps Inari might have had laid for me. In that brief moment of hesitation, the door slid closed behind me and would not be moved. When I held up my candle, it illuminated a wooden passageway decorated with scenes of classic Japan. At the far end, a much larger brown door waited for me. I wondered if Inari had imprisoned my mother and brother and intended to do the same with me, but knew I had no choice but to move forward.

I held the candle aloft to examine the pictures on the wall. One showed a man and woman walking by the riverside, cherry blossoms in bloom, and in the next, a wedding ceremony took place on Mt. Inari. On another wall, a man worked in the garden outside of a comfortable-looking house. He was oblivious to the blue dragon flying overhead. In another, a crane bowed low to a white fox.

A growing sense of recognition made me hold my candle higher to see the rest of the paintings more closely. I was startled to see that the next panel depicted a black mushroom cloud hovering over shattered rooftops. Nearby, wild boars ran up the mountainside toward a house encircled by spiral of gray smoke.

Catching my breath, I swung my arm to the opposite wall and saw a man perching high up in a tree. In the next scene, an old woman lay in bed, her daughter attending to her. To the left of them a crane bowed low; on the right, a white fox sat guard by the woman's side. I saw the daughter bending toward her mother, the older woman's arms outstretched and twisted.

"No, no, this cannot be," I whispered, a choking sob caught in my throat. I shouted and pounded on the brown door in front of me. My wife and daughter were waiting for me in our home in Rokko, and everything depended on me.

Unseen hands slid the door open. There before me stood Benkei in the hallway of my family's home.

"Close your mouth, Nephew. Surely you've seen ghosts before?" he commented as he took my candle. Unable to speak, I followed him across the smooth wooden floor of the *genkan*. My great uncle led me to my study, where a blank scroll and a *fude* pen lay on my old wooden roll top desk. Benkei bowed and gestured for me to sit. I sank into the wooden chair and picked up the pen, ready to begin writing.

And these words, not the words of death, but of life, came first:

"My first memory was of water, light, and sound. The river flowing by our house, the light of the sun on the garden wall, and the cicadas calling to each other in the heat of late summer."

My hand felt as heavy as dull gray rock. I forced myself to write the next words, to start the first task assigned to me and face all that I had been hiding from for decades.

"I am Tsuruda Kenzaburo, and this is how my story begins."

18

SATSUKI
THINGS LEFT UNSAID
SPRING AND SUMMER 1945

I don't think Tetsuko has noticed that her husband watches me. Always busy—busy with babies, busy with housework, busy with her mother's meals, busy arranging for things to be moved from one house to the other, balancing books, tending to things. The simple truth is that she loves him. I can tell by the way she watches him, her upturned face like a sunflower following the sun.

Zaemon paces the house, turns on his heels when he comes close to a wall. Where Kenzaburo is hesitant and kind, Zaemon is wide-shouldered, commanding. He moves with startling quickness: lighting cigarettes, throwing on his overcoat, driving his shiny black car.

Zaemon tends my worries like a gardener, cultivates my fears with things left unsaid, watches patiently as they bloom and grow. Dark spiky shoots rise up and green leaves unfurl as my loneliness gives way to uncertainty.

"No word from Older Brother yet?" he asks during his New Year's visit. He cocks his head when I shake my head "No."

"Ah. Is that so . . ." A hint of expectation in his voice. I wonder if he's anticipating that Kenzaburo will leave me here. When he talks, his words find their way inside my head, pushing out my thoughts and replacing them with his.

There are times when the power of Zaemon's certainty takes over. The sheer force of his confidence makes me see everything from his eyes. In my dark moments I think, *Kenzaburo is not coming back. He has been killed. He is sick. His mother convinced him that I'm not a suitable wife. He has found someone else.*

Everyone has heard the whispered stories about men and women who have simply disappeared during the war. They turn up from time to time in far off places: Aomori, Nagano, Tohoku. In cold northern villages or tropical southern ones, they start new lives with a different husband or wife, leaving their first family behind like a set of unwanted dishes riddled with chips and cracks.

I do not believe Kenzaburo would do such a thing. When the worry becomes too much to bear, I steal up the mountain to the small shrine and pray for his safety, his swift return to me. I do not pray for myself but save all my requests for Kenzaburo. Although he is a man, I believe my husband is more fragile and in need of Inari's protection than I.

In our house in Kobe, at night before we slept I loved to trace his cheekbones with my fingertips. I touched his collar bone and ribs with my tongue or with a flatted palm until his face turned toward mine in the dark. I listened to him talk about his insects, the stars, the cold dark universe where he said our planet spins like a blue and green top. He smiled at me when I told him the earth was resting on the back of an immense tortoise.

"You are my amber-eyed fox goddess, and I am under your

spell." He laughed off the rumors his mother whispered to him about women from Inari—that we are magical and not to be trusted. When Kenzaburo and I were alone together, I could feel his eyes leaving the page of whatever dusty book he was reading to train his gaze on me for minutes at a time. I pretended not to notice because I loved to be held there, in his line of sight, as tenderly as a rare butterfly in his cupped palm.

Kenzaburo and his brother share some traits, but these qualities show themselves in different ways. Zaemon moves with grace rather than deliberation. He is like a clever serpent moving through high grass. When I leave the house to get food at the market, I can feel his eyes burning into the back of my head, my shoulders, my neck. I sense him in his room, alert, nose tipped to the air when I walk to the outhouse in the middle of the night. When I enter a room, he is there waiting, still and silent.

"Surely you have gotten a letter from Kenzaburo this month?" he says in March.

I shake my head "no" again, turn away.

The first time he comes to my room, he waits until the middle of the night. I am on the first floor by the kitchen, in the maid's quarters. When he opens my door, I sit up on my futon, thinking that perhaps an air raid has been called. Only we are in the country, and they don't have air raids here. We have been told we are safe.

He is smoking and carries something in his hand. "Satsuki-san. A fashion magazine for you from Shang Hai," he says with a smile and a small bow. "I have friends who are able to get me things." I have no doubt this is true. Zaemon brings Tetsuko perfume and leather gloves. He presents his children with toys from Manchuria, little wooden ships and trains with the Japanese flag painted on them, the sun forever rising. I thank him when he gives me the magazine. When I slide the door closed, I feel as if he is lingering outside, but I can't be certain. I wonder why he has given this to me, and not his wife.

I edge close to the kerosene lamp and page through the magazine, marveling at the styles from China's most cosmopolitan city. I fall asleep wondering what the characters beneath the photos say. That night, I dream that Kenzaburo and I strolling by the Shukugawa River. By my husband's expression I can see that he is warning me about something, but he is speaking in Chinese and I don't understand him. I try to speak, but my tongue lies in my mouth like a stone.

The next morning, Atsuko scolds me for spilling tea. "Clumsy fool! Wasting the food of people whose hospitality you are imposing upon. They must not teach any manners in Inari," she snaps. I am so tired that I bow, apologizing, and wipe up the clear brown puddle on the table.

While I am cleaning up after breakfast, I overhear Atsuko and Fumiko talking in the next room. " . . . he'll be gone for another two weeks. When he gets back, Tetsuko will talk to him about the situation . . . " I busy myself with a rag on the floor as I hear their voices come closer. Atsuko trips over my ankle and says, "Clumsy fool!" again. I realize that is the nickname she has given me. They have taken to talking about me as if I am not in the room. "*She* eats too much." "Let *her* do it." But I don't care. I can breathe again; Zaemon will be leaving soon. The attention he pays me has made me uneasy and unable to sleep.

It is early May when he reappears; he has been away in Manchuria again. The last few cherry blossoms are blooming in the mountains. He hands me a letter from Kenzaburo. "I was in Kobe on business and saw my mother and brother," he says. "My mother has been unwell since my father's death." He stops and looks at me, watching my expression. "She refuses to eat and her mind wanders. I'm worried about her. She whispers about being cursed by a fox. Do you know what that might mean?"

I shake my head "no," frightened anew that Reiko has poisoned Kenzaburo against me.

"Ah, I almost forgot. My older brother asked me to give this to you," said Zaemon, pulling a letter from his valise. I am so happy I forget myself and smile. He smiles back, studying me.

I read the letter as best I can. I have learned a small number of kanji from a child's notebook I found, but I am unable to understand what my husband has said. Something about the cherry blossoms in the beginning, and then a mention of my mother-in-law. No date is listed to tell me when Kenzaburo would next come to Hajiyama—no mention of when he would come to retrieve me from this house. I try not to show how crushed I am.

I look at Zaemon and there is still that slight smile playing on his lips. "Good news?" he asks.

"Yes," I answer. "He is . . . doing well. He is happy that I am safe." I lie to him. "He is coming for me soon." Zaemon nods, as if considering my words. Humoring me. I wonder if he has read the letter.

Tetsuko enters the room as he leaves, a frown on her face when she addresses me. "Have you hung the futons yet? I told you they must be aired out every morning as soon as the children wake." She raises her voice so Zaemon will be sure to hear. I wonder if it gives her comfort to order me around, to be in charge of someone with no power to fight back, and I am reminded of my mother-in-law. It has been so long since I lived in a house where I was wanted that I have forgotten how it feels.

One night before going to sleep, I realize we are out of green tea for the next morning's breakfast. It is not too late, so I run up to Tetsuko's room to see if I might talk with her, afraid that she will scold me if I am unprepared in the morning. It's my job to wake before everyone else and make the tea, the rice gruel, the miso soup.

When I get to the bedroom door, I hear her arguing with Zaemon.

"Must we really let every stray come to stay with us? Zaemon, I am afraid your brother is taking advantage of our generosity. Why can't she stay in Kobe where she belongs, or go back to Inari?"

Zaemon's voice, at first murmuring, soothing. Then sharper. "She will stay, and I will hear no more about it."

I want to shout at the closed door, "I would like nothing more than to go home!" Instead I retreat down the steps and run back to my room, considering how I might buy a train ticket back to Kobe, but I have no means to do so. I'm trapped in this house and have no idea when I will see my husband again.

An hour later, Zaemon is at my door with another book. "Mishima Yukio, do you know him?"

"Eh? Zaemon-san, forgive me. Is there something you need from the kitchen—"

"He is one of Japan's foremost authors," he continues as if I haven't spoken. "I imagine you must like books because you married my bookworm brother." His mouth twists downward at the mention of Kenzaburo. He enters my bedroom and his voice becomes softer. He speaks to me the way someone would speak to a child who has lost her way, all the while moving closer. "*Douzo.* Here—I am giving it to you. Read it and tell me what you think."

He drops the book on my futon, turns on his heel, and is gone. I spend the night with my sheets up to my chin, eyes wide open, staring into the dark, but he does not return.

In my loneliness, I page through the book Zaemon has given me at night. I cannot read the kanji, but there are gruesome photos of Mishima with arrows through his ribcage or nailed to a tree. In another, he is about to commit *hara kiri*. I wonder why Zaemon has given me this book.

Some nights I dream of Zaemon, his body splayed on a tree like Mishima's, arrows in his ribs. In my dream, I am sorry for him. He is my husband's brother. I go to him with water and a cloth to clean his wounds. As I approach, he looks up at me, laughs, wraps himself around me. He holds me so tightly that I cannot breathe, winding upward from my ankles to my neck. I wake, gasping for air.

When Zaemon comes home, he sometimes brings important people with him from the military. When he does, Tetsuko and her sisters put on their finest kimono and fawn over the guests, offer them more sake, more rice, more fish. I work in the kitchen, and act as serving girl. The women of the house eat together after the men have left the table.

On these nights, my dinner is rice gruel. I am one station below Kabocha, who at least receives the table scraps of the Uribo family. I am getting used to being hungry. Sometimes I take the leftovers from the plates of the guests, or the food left by Tetsuko and Zaemon. I eat in secret in the storehouse, or take the scraps back to my room, licking rice from my fingers. I push my bowl away in disgust when I am done.

I never know when Zaemon will be back with another book. When he comes to my room now, I am not surprised. Over the months that follow, something happens. He is the only person in the house who talks to me, who acknowledges my presence. I start to think I have been wrong about him. He wears spectacles like my husband's when we look at books together. Sometimes I see Kenzaburo when Zaemon tilts his head and looks at the ceiling.

He talks about the books he's brought me. I have been able to follow the story by the photos in the book and what he tells me. One night as the first drops of the rainy season fall on the rooftop, I feel brave and confess my secret to him.

"I wish I understood more, *Ototo*." I call Zaemon "*Ototo*" for "younger brother," and as his brother's wife he calls me "*Onechan*" for older sister, even though I am in fact younger than Zaemon by several years. "My father taught me hiragana and katakana," I say, looking down at my hands in my lap, "but that is as far as my education went. Please don't tell Kenzaburo . . . he doesn't know that I cannot read kanji. I-I want to learn and surprise him."

"You can't read characters?" Zaemon asks. "Well, it's settled then. I will help you," he says with a small bow. "My brother need never know."

I thank him with a red face. I don't like keeping secrets from Kenzaburo, but it pleases me that I will finally learn how to read properly.

When Zaemon leaves my room, he asks, "My brother, have you heard from him?" He shakes his head when I say that I have not.

"I am going to Kobe next week, why don't you write to him? I'll take the letter." I am pleased, and my face flushes a deeper shade of red because I am ashamed at having judged Zaemon when we met. Maybe the bad blood between the two brothers is thinning. Perhaps Zaemon is my friend, perhaps he will help me. I smile at him and say, "That would be very kind of you, Zaemon-san."

He nods, "It would be my pleasure." Before he turns to go, he says, "Oh, one thing—do not tell my brother anything that might upset him. The last time I saw him, he was quite anxious about you. I told him, of course that you were in very good hands and that we were caring for you like a member of the family."

"Of course," I say with a bow. "Thank you for telling me." After he slides the door closed behind him, I try not to smile at the fact that my husband has been worried about me.

The next day, I write to Kenzaburo. I use the hiragana alphabet, even though I'm learning kanji, because the characters I attempt to write still look like unsteady and large, like they've been drawn by a child.

"Dear Husband: Rainy season has begun. I am fine here. Tetsuko and her sisters are kind and generous. I am growing fat with all the food they give me. Are you well? I miss you. When will you come to visit next?"

I give the letter to Zaemon after breakfast when the women have gone. We can hear them chattering on the veranda as they watch the rain sluicing down in gray sheets from the sky. The children play with Kabocha at their feet. I think of my father, how he loved the rainy season. *"Tsuyu* is the one time of year when I am able to stop and think," he said. He believed it was the gift we were given before the beginning of the heat of July and August.

Zaemon leaves the next morning while I am still in my bedroom. I watch from behind half-closed shutters. He strides through the mud, Tetsuko following him with a raised red umbrella over his head, sheltering him from the drizzle. She hurries to keep up with his long steps. The shoulders of her blue kimono are darkening with water. They bow to each other before he gets into his car.

Right before he ducks his head, he looks at my window, stretches his mouth into a half smile, and nods. I step back, holding my hand over my chest, wondering if he saw me watching him.

At night, I practice writing kanji by the light of my lantern, copying passages of magazines and books like a schoolgirl. I read the new books Zaemon has given me—they are simple and meant for children. I read between chores; I read when I am hungry; I read at night, candles stolen from the storehouse lighting my page.

The next time Zaemon comes home from Manchuria, it is late July. He brings me a book of fairy tales this time, and there is slip of red paper in the page that begins the story of *Kaguyahime,* the fable of the princess who was born on the moon. When he comes to my room his eyes are red and he smells of alcohol. I remember what Kenzaburo said about his younger brother's college days, how he drank whiskey and played mahjong and didn't come home for days on end.

Zaemon's smiles are pleading now. For a reason I cannot explain, I believe he wants to talk to me about something. Perhaps he is ready to make amends, to tell me why he has so much bitterness for his older brother. I feel badly for him and how difficult it must have been for him to be Reiko's second son. I am prepared to assume the role of older sister—to listen, to give advice, to soothe hurt feelings.

Zaemon comes to me one night after his bath. The only sound in the house is the distant wail of a baby, then the "shush" of a woman's voice.

He opens my door, and I light a candle. I notice Zaemon does not have a book with him. Instead, he has brought me fresh plums. The purple fruit is my favorite. We eat together, and the room is silent except for our mouths working. The sweet sourness of the plums yields against my tongue. I look for a place to spit out my pit, and he reaches his hand up under my chin, delicate as a father to a child. Embarrassed, I spit the large brown seed into his waiting hand.

Zaemon wipes juice from my chin, and with the other hand, he reaches up and strokes my hair, and his touch is softer than the damp breeze coming through the window. Then he loops my hair around his fist and pulls my head back. I am trembling, unsure of what to do. I shake my head slowly from side to side, my eyes filling. I look at the door, then back at his face. Zaemon wraps his arms around me, holds me. I struggle. All of this is done with no sound, no words.

Before he takes me, I see that I have been lulled into trusting him, that he was willing to take months and seasons to do this, that this was his plan from the beginning. He reaches inside my cotton yukata and cups my breast in his hand, kisses my neck, my shoulders, the tears that spill down my cheeks. I feel powerless, tricked by loneliness and my own foolish beliefs.

He puts his arm behind my neck and with the other pulls me down onto the futon beneath him. His hands leave hot marks on my breasts, my back, my stomach. I feel his kisses, his tongue, the hardness pressing into my thighs. I hate how easily I was deceived, and how my body is deceiving me by responding to him. I push his shoulders back and try to roll away, but he holds me down by the collar bone with his left hand, slaps my face twice, slowly and precisely with his right. I can feel red marks rising on my cheek bones.

Even then, I do not make a sound. Not when he grinds my shoulder down with his fist, not when he forces my face toward his, not when he enters me. For a moment I look down upon us in my dark little borrowed room, his huge frame thrusting inside me, my mouth gaping open like a carp in the rain, noiseless sobs wracking my body. I feel myself tearing inside.

When Zaemon is done, he gets up and puts his yukata back on. I curl up into a ball on the side of the futon.

I feel him watching me in the doorway. Finally, he says, "A fox is not so different from other women, after all." He laughs, revealing the sharp teeth he had so carefully hidden behind smiles of brotherly concern.

I listen as he washes himself in the sink down the hall, gargles. He hums a jazz tune as he moves through the house, as if he has just been to a concert or a party. At last, his footsteps tread the stairs up to the bedroom he shares with Tetsuko.

I wait for another hour. I am bleeding inside and unable to get up without difficulty. I take the white sheets from my futon and steal outside the house. Kabocha follows me, sniffing at my heels and whimpering. Barefoot, I walk across pine needles to the stream in the woods behind the house. Sounds that feel as if they belong to someone else emerge from my throat. I hug my cotton *yukata* around me and walk into the cold water. I crouch amidst the pebbles lit by moon and starlight. I scrub the sheets with smooth stones until all the blood is gone, until they are almost clean and white again.

19

HIROSHIMA
KENZABURO
AUGUST 12, 1945

The official radio report on August 7, 1945, said only that Hiroshima had been attacked, that "details were being investigated." The news that filtered into the munitions factory where I worked was grim. I sat dumbstruck with my colleagues in the old principals' office listening to the reports on the radio.

"My cousin said the Americans dropped gasoline on Hiroshima, and it ignited before it hit the city," said Kitada, who sat next to me.

"I heard that magnesium powder was used to blanket the town. It exploded in the air like fireworks," said my supervisor, Major Horiguchi, eyes blinking rapid fire as he brushed dandruff from the shoulders of his uniform.

"What about outlying areas?" I asked, my voice hoarse. "The towns around Hiroshima?" Blank faces stared back. "Has anyone heard?"

Horiguchi and Kitada shook their heads in unison. They knew

where I had taken my wife. Horiguchi-san looked out the window and back at the reports in front of him. Anything to avoid my eyes. He did not look up even when I told him I would be leaving. He pretended that he was granting me time off, not acknowledging what everyone suspected—Japan's surrender would surely be coming any day now. Before I left, he bowed and handed me an envelope.

"*Tsuruda-san . . . ki wo tsukete.*" I wondered if I would see him again, if he and I would pass on the streets in Kobe some years in the future and remember each other, exchange stories, drink sake together, and reminisce. Or would we hurry down the street, hugging our books or groceries to our chests, pretending that none of this had happened, that the man with the limp and the man with the twitch never laid eyes upon each other? These are the odd thoughts that prey on you when life cracks open to reveal a tiny taste, a snake's lick, of death.

About the bomb, the Japanese press did not say more, just this: "Details are being investigated." I threw the newspapers down on the floor in disgust and started packing, taking only the minimum: money, food, a canteen of water, my father's pocket watch. I had no idea how I would get to Hajiyama, if the trains near the city were even running, but I did know that I had to get there.

I left my mother under the care of a neighbor and set out on my journey that afternoon. While I traveled on the train from Kobe, news came that Nagasaki had also been bombed. I learned that many were taking their own lives, some in fear of the invading Americans.

I rode the train as far as it would go before the rail lines were too damaged to carry passengers anymore, then took buses and caught rides on trucks. Very few were going toward Hiroshima. When no trucks came, I walked. It took me four days to get to the country house in Hajiyama.

"Tetsuko and Satsuki-san ventured into the city the day before the attack," said Fumiko, the youngest sister of the clan. "Tetsuko wanted to search for our father. She said she would check on our family house, retrieve some belongings," Fumiko's eyes were dull, unfocused. "Photos, ceramics, my mother's best silk kimonos." She spoke in a hoarse whisper. In the past twelve months, twenty-five-year-old Fumiko had grown frail and distracted.

This is what the war had given us—a woman in her prime who had the air of an ailing grandmother. I knew the moment Hiroshima was bombed that all the men who called for invasions and stirred our country into a boiling pot of hate and fear and patriotic fervor would soon disappear, leaving shells of people's lives in their wake.

"Tsuruda-san, there is something else. "We, Atsuko and I, we didn't want to go with Tetsuko, we were afraid. Satsuki-san, she offered to accompany her." I grimaced, knowing my wife to be the kind of woman who would not let another travel alone. Fumiko brought out a bottle of sake and a small cup for me. Her hands shook as she poured. I insisted she drink some, too.

"Satsuki-san's kindness, we do not deserve what she has done for us," she said before I left. "Please, Tsuruda-san, please find them."

I left a note for Satsuki in case she should return before I found her. Fumiko packed *onigiri* for me, and two blankets. As I traveled, more bedraggled people with bundles of supplies and food tied up in *furoshiki* cloths joined me on the road. It was easy to find Hiroshima—it lay under a thick black cloud, a mountain of dust and ash. The more I walked, the more the feeling of fear inside of me grew, until it was a crow pecking at my insides.

There was no transportation going toward the center of the burned-out city, so I walked. My leg was tired and heavy from the strain of travel. At times, I felt the panic inside of me would pull me from my skin.

In spite of this, I did not let myself imagine that Satsuki was dead. She could not be; it simply was not a possible outcome. I realized I'd said this aloud when a woman walking near me moved away.

As we came closer to the periphery of where Hiroshima once stood, everyone around me stopped talking. The city was no more. Debris was everywhere, as if a giant hand came down and flattened all the houses, trees and buildings. Strangest of all was the lack of sound—no crickets, birds, or animals moved; I felt like we were standing on the edge of a dead planet.

Plumes of smoke could be seen through the haze of particles in the air. Fires blazed unchecked in the neighborhoods I walked through. Walls of flame lapped at the edges of wide fire lanes.

"We dug them by hand over the course of the last few weeks. We thought we would be bombed the way Tokyo was—fire bombings. We weren't expecting this," said one old man on a street corner, skin hanging off his left shoulder. I turned to ask him more questions, but the crowd surged forward and he was gone, making me wonder if I'd imagined him.

The smell of electricity saturated the air and I walked faster, even though my blistered feet were bruised and bleeding. My legs ached as they had when the polio was at its worst, but I didn't care. All I could think of was finding Satsuki. I kept moving forward although I was nearly unable to breathe. Corpses lay in the streets, and people with broken arms and putrefying wounds called out as I passed. I kept my eyes focused forward and did not stop. Satsuki could be in the same condition, calling to me even now.

From the map Tetsuko's sister had drawn for me, I saw that the Uribo home was in the Koi region of Hiroshima, by the Kyo River. I asked people for directions and they stared at me, wide-eyed. Wailing cries could be heard from every direction.

It was hard to get my bearings, but I found the river at last and hobbled toward the Koi district. Breath rasped through my mouth and lungs, raw from the effort. The particles in the air attached themselves to my face, my teeth, my tongue. I stopped to drink some water from the canteen I'd brought with me and pressed my handkerchief to my mouth. It was black when I pulled it away.

A group of soldiers huddled by some bushes on the riverbank. The skin from their faces hung off their bones in melting pieces. A soldier who could not have been more than seventeen returned my stare. He had a small yellow flower stuck through his buttonhole. He approached me, hobbling on a long stick.

"*Omizu*," he begged, tongue lolling out of his mouth. "Please, sir, can you spare some water?"

I looked back at him, startled. About two thirds of my canteen was left, and I needed to save it for Satsuki and Tetsuko. My face hot, I started walking away from him, pretending not to have heard, while his voice called after me, "*Omizu* . . ." I turned, clutching the canteen to my chest. "I'm sorry, I do not have enough," I said, eager to be rid of him.

The soldier kept coming at me, eyes fixed on the water in my hands. He reached out to grab it and I pushed him back with all the force I had left in my body. He fell over a rock and I heard a sharp crack. The cry that emanated from him was something between the sound of a dog yelping and a child's whimper, and then he was silent.

The other soldiers who could walk started coming for me, calling out "Murderer! You killed him!"

"No, no that's not so," I replied, and I limped off quickly when I saw their faces. I did not look back at the crumpled boy in the soldier's uniform in the rubble of a school yard.

Chest burning and out of breath, I arrived at the gate of what was once the Uribo home. Flames licked at the back of the house, fierce fingers of red and orange turning doors and windows black.

"Satsuki?" I cried into the crackling haze. "Satsuki, are you here?" Trees in the garden had been torn up by their roots, windows and doors were scattered everywhere. Fish floated belly up in the small pond. A large portion of the house had collapsed in on itself. I called out to Satsuki and Tetsuko again and was startled when a toothless old man in the garden courtyard answered me.

"They are gone." He giggled. Making his hands into a bird, he watched his fingers as they flapped through the air. He was wearing a *tsuwashi,* nothing more than a long piece of cloth wrapped around his legs and waist. As I moved closer I saw that he was small, of childlike proportions. In this city where everyone was wounded and dying, his skin was as healthy and pink as an infant's.

"Where are they? Where did they go, Ji-chan?" I tried to keep my voice steady.

The hair on his head was soft and downy, and moved with him as he bobbed and smiled at me. I smelled something sour and saw that he had soiled himself. He did not look me in the eye when he spoke but stared somewhere near my chin. Finally, in a low, crestfallen lilt, he said, "Uribo-san is gone. My master vanished in thin air. He is here." He pointed to a shadow in the sidewalk before us and giggled, hand over his mouth.

I shook my head, not comprehending. "And Tetsuko-sama and my wife? Did you see them?

He looked up at the sky for a moment and then back at me. "*A-sa-no,*" he sang, as if it was a song for the Obon dance.

Asano Park—Satsuki was alive. Relief filled me, then anger. I wanted to hurt this man, punish him for his weakness and idiocy and filth.

"And you? Who are you? Why are you here? Why didn't you go with them, help them?"

The old man looked at me, astonished. "I am staying here. This is my home." He smiled at me. "I have worked for Uribo-sama since I was a boy." He repeated, "This is my home," and started walking back into the house, half of which was now ablaze.

"What are you doing? Come out of there, you old fool," I yelled, hesitant to get any closer to the fire. He giggled and ran until he reached the front door. Turning, he bowed and disappeared into the smoking depths of the Uribo home. At the moment he shut the door behind him, the remainder of the roof collapsed. All the anger I'd felt vanished into something cold and small and hard in the pit of my stomach, and I retched on the sidewalk.

"He lost his mind," I told myself. "There was no way I could have helped him."

As I hurried toward Asano Park, I felt as if my skin was pulling away from my body, melting down the sides of my face. I was afraid that soon I would be no more substantial than a puff of smoke or a drop of water, and my shadow would be the only thing that remained, just like the others.

My feet were numb and slippery with blood inside my boots, but I quickened my pace in order to catch up with two men I saw down the river.

"*Sumimasen*, do you know the way to Asano Koen?"

The taller one looked at me. I saw that he had lacerations up and down the right side of his body, and small pieces of glass sparkled from his skin.

"*Genshi Bakudan*, that's what they're calling it," he said, oblivious to my question. "The bomb the Americans dropped on us. It is some new invention, they say. We'd never seen anything like it when it fell—no sound, can you imagine? Just a brilliant arc of light, running from over the city. It lit up the sky like a huge flash bulb going off."

His friend, a small, dark, nervous-looking man with no injuries spoke.

"People just disappeared into vapor. Can you imagine? There is a place near the mill where you can see bodies burned into the sidewalk, like so many shadows . . ." I nodded and backed away from them. I heard them continuing their conversation as if I had never interrupted it. My head swirling with hunger and dizziness, I kept walking. A young woman along the way pointed me in the right direction of the park. "The bomb the Americans dropped was beautiful," she said. "Like a rainbow over the whole city." She smiled at me and nodded, as if encouraging me. "Beautiful. Until the black cloud appeared."

I made my way through the debris-filled streets until I entered Asano Park. Hordes of people had gathered. A thousand or more, I guessed. Some of them were getting sick by the sides of their blankets. A young boy and girl cried for their mother. I became frantic again. How would I possibly find Satsuki?

"Sir, can you help us?" I looked around and saw a man and woman on a boat. The river was aflame in places, and they were not able to get ashore. I stood paralyzed, uncertain what to do until a large man in an army uniform behind me found a rope by the side of the water and I threw it to them, pulling to bring them to the riverbank.

I wandered the perimeter of the park for hours, calling out Satsuki's name.

I found her at twilight. I spied the back of my wife's head first, her long hair in two braids. It was the way she was tilting, the curve of her neck that first told me it was her. She was hunched over and appeared to be stroking Tetsuko's arm.

Satsuki turned to me before I reached them. Her mouth opened and closed as I approached, but no sound emerged. When I reached the blanket, she grabbed me by my forearms. I lifted her up from a kneeling position, and we stood there in the park, holding each other for minutes. Satsuki's body shook in my arms. I had the irrational fear that she would float away if I didn't keep hold of her, that she was a dream image that would dissolve at first light. It wasn't until Tetsuko moaned that Satsuki pulled my arms away from her gently to attend to our sister-in-law.

Tetsuko was lying on a dirty blanket, her eyes staring at the gray sky, her breath coming fast and shallow. I reached to feel her pulse and was alarmed at how weak it was, and how clammy and moist her skin felt to the touch.

"She is in shock, Sa-chan. We have to leave this place as soon as we can."

Tetsuko moaned again and closed her eyes.

"It's her father," said Satsuki. "We have not been able to find him."

I bowed my head and gave Satsuki my water, which she first offered to Tetsuko. I thought of the soldiers I had seen. I remembered the one I pushed, and shame coursed through my body. I did not tell Satsuki. It was not important to talk about the past. What was important was that I had found her. We were together again.

Satsuki's eyes were liquid and bright. "I have seen what was in my dream, Kenzaburo. This is the hell I saw in my dream before we left Kobe. Before you arrived, I worried that I'd died and was sent here as punishment and would never see you again."

"Shhh, shhh," I comforted her. "It's over now. We'll leave in the morning, find a doctor for Tetsuko." She clung to me and I was grateful.

We slept in the park that night. Black dust devils the size of grown men popped up and swirled around us, scattering dust and debris in their wake. The moaning and crying of the injured was almost deafening. My wife cradled Tetsuko's head in her lap through the night. I could only lie on the blanket, mute, watching the two women.

The next morning, I woke first and found a small wooden cart. We lifted Tetsuko into it and managed to pull her to the outskirts of the city, in spite of streets and sidewalks that looked as though an earthquake had chewed them up and spit them out. Tetsuko lapsed in and out of consciousness in the heat.

"How will we get help for her?" I asked, not sure how to proceed.

"We have gold, jewelry that we managed to save from Tetsuko's house," Satsuki told me. "We can pay someone to take us back to Hajiyama. There is a doctor up there who can help Tetsuko."

Vehicles on the road were scarce, but by evening we were able to flag down a truck and negotiate a ride up the mountain. The man, who wore the uniform of the Imperial Navy, waved away our offer of pearls when he dropped us off in front of Tetsuko's country home.

"The emperor is no longer divine, did you hear?" He called out to us before he left. "I will not wish for his health then, but for yours." He laughed as he drove off, revealing several missing teeth.

I watched his truck until it rounded the bend and moved out of sight. The war was over, and the emperor was no longer a god.

I could not stop bowing to the empty road.

Tetsuko's family was waiting when we arrived at the country house. Her sisters fell on us sobbing and thanked me over and over again for bringing Tetsuko and Satsuki home. Tetsuko's children laughed and played at our feet, and her aging mother giggled and clapped her hands in delight, exclaiming, "It is Obon today! Obon is here." Later, Atsuko told us that her mother thought the sound of bombs in the distance was the temple drum being beaten in preparation for the Days of the Dead.

We spent five days at the Uribos'. Doctor Sasa arrived and cared for Tetsuko and Fumiko, examined Satsuki and declared her in perfect health. The doctor was in his seventies, with the healthy skin and open face of a man who had lived his life in the country. He told us that he would head to Hiroshima next, to help the wounded and dying.

"There has never been anything like this," he said. "No one knows exactly what the Americans dropped, but they're saying it was an atomic bomb. Splitting atoms to kill men. What have we gained with all our intelligence, Tsuruda-san, eh? You are wise to study insects— that's what you said you wanted to do now that the war is over, *ne?* Their ways are far less brutal than ours, in spite of their predilection for consuming their mates."

We left as soon as we were able. My brother Zaemon had not yet arrived, but I was worried about my *okaasan* and wanted to return to Kobe. A neighbor had agreed to take care of my mother while I was gone, but I had no idea in what state we'd find her when we arrived.

Before we departed for home, Tetsuko took me aside. "Kenzaburo-san, I will never be able to repay the debt I owe you and Satsuki-san."

I bowed, unable to speak. I could not tell Tetsuko that the shame I felt at that moment—for sending my wife to the very hell on earth she'd had nightmares about—consumed me.

20

HOME
KENZABURO
1945

On our way home through the wreckage of towns that lined the train tracks from Hiroshima to Osaka, we walked and took the odd train or bus that was running. I could still smell the peculiar metallic odor of Hiroshima and felt the ash on my skin.

We accepted rides from strangers. American soldiers crowded the streets, throwing chocolate at the small thin boys in short pants who ran beside their top-heavy green military trucks. The children yelled, *"Gibu- me cho-ko-leto, gibu-me shigaretto"* to the young American men, some of whom were buck-toothed and acne-scarred.

I hated them for their cheerfulness; I hated them for their lack of hunger. I wanted to send them to Hiroshima and see what their bomb had done. I wanted the skin to melt from their bones and their bodies to become shadows in cement.

When I spilled my bitterness to Satsuki on our blankets by the side of a field one night, she was silent. I thought she hadn't heard my words, until she whispered, "They do not see, Kenzaburo. The American soldiers, like the Japanese, they are young men who were fighting for old men. They will go home soon. They do not understand." She shook her head, her hair tickling my chin, the river-shaped curve of her body folding into mine.

"Why did you accompany Tetsuko-san?" I whispered this the way a child whispers a secret in the dark.

The pause that filled the air between us was so long that I feared my wife had drifted off to sleep. When she spoke, her voice was clear and solemn as a monk's.

"How could I let her go alone?"

I nodded in the dark. The open August sky shone back its dazzling stars, as it had for millions of years. The sound of crickets in the field was punctuated by the deep bass of a bullfrog. I held Satsuki and slept.

My wife insisted that we stop at every shrine we passed to pay homage to the gods. "They protected us, Kenzaburo," she said, a solemn look on her face. "We must thank them now. It is our turn to pay our respects to them, in turn for their protection." She left grains of rice, fruit, and flowers we found along the way.

I wanted to ask, "Where were they when the bomb fell on Hiroshima," but I remained silent. My wife was here with me, after all.

As we drew closer to Kansai, we saw more blonde and red-haired soldiers in British and American uniforms. They smoked cigarettes with cherry mouths, the lips of round-faced children.

Some of the Americans flashed money at me, gestured to my wife. They had learned to ask "how much" in Japanese, and would call "*Ikura?*" to me in their loose-mouthed accent. "*Ai shite imasu,*" they shouted out as their trucks sped ahead of us, "I love you." Their laughter was carried back to us on the soot-filled wind.

Some of the soldiers offered us rides in their trucks. They saw that I was lame, and that Satsuki was supporting me. Each time they stopped, I shook my head "no" and waved them off.

In Himeji, an American soldier who reminded me of Horiguchi-san approached us. "Suzuki," he said, and pointed to his nose with his index finger, Japanese-style, to identify himself. He spoke with a Kansai dialect. "My grandfather was from Osaka. I translate for the colonel. Take these," he said, and handed us a tent, some rough green blankets, and tins of fish. "And watch out for thieves on the road. At the end of every war, opportunists flourish." I ignored him, but Satsuki bowed and said, *"Arigatou gozaimashita.* You are very kind to give these supplies to us." The soldier bowed back to Satsuki and moved on.

We stopped for the night in Suma and lay on the beach under the stars. Satsuki rubbed her belly, then rolled over, a spear of grass in her mouth. This is the moment I relive: Her hair falls down over her forehead, loosened from its braid. My need for her, still wrapped and muffled in guilt. We move into the tent, and I find her with my tongue, my hands, my body, until I am inside her.

An August moon hung over our tent like a large lamp as we moved against each other in the dark. We did this to erase our sadness, our loneliness, my guilt. Satsuki kissed me, showered me with small bites around my neck and collar bone, wiped tears from my cheeks that I didn't know had fallen. Still, I did not tell her I was sorry for sending her to Hajiyama. I did not admit she was right, and I, wrong.

"A man does not apologize to his wife. To do so is a sign of weakness. She will not respect you for it, and it is not necessary." This, the advice my mother gave me when I married. I am obeying *Okaasan,* but also my own cowardice. If I say the words, Satsuki will know I was wrong, she will know my secret: that I am a weak, foolish man, not fit to be a husband.

At Suma shrine, Satsuki prayed for an hour, left some of our precious rice and American fish as an offering. "It is for Inari, to ask that she grants us fertility," she said. This time, I did not tease or mock her. I did not try to dissuade her from her certainty that the gods she believed in were all around us. Instead, I watched from a distance as she rang the temple bell, clapped three times, and bowed her head. It surprised me to realize I was envious. Her beliefs comforted her.

On the fifth day after leaving Hajiyama, we finally saw Mt. Rokko as we walked along the seashore toward Sannomiya. Satsuki gripped my arm and nodded. "We are home, Ken-chan" she said. "We are home." She removed our tent and blankets from her back and handed them to a family of four we saw begging by the side of the road. They did not stop bowing to us until we were out of sight.

We walked the last ten kilometers back to Rokko. Construction had already started in Kobe city, and workers told us that China Town was being rebuilt in a different place, "everything new and different." The stench of the open sewer rose to greet us, and many people begged on the streets. Women in loosened kimono and loud make-up walked on the arms of American servicemen. Small Japanese boys played baseball with the soldiers in the streets.

We ran into Tanaka-san on the way home, picking through rice at a stall in Rokko. When she saw us, she exclaimed at how thin and bedraggled we were. "Your mother will be so grateful to have you home, Kenzaburo," she said, and her tone told me that she disapproved of the fact that I'd left *Okaasan*. "I looked in on her this morning. She seems so *frail* lately." She looked at Satsuki and blinked. "But Satsuki-san will take fine care of her, I'm sure," she said. "Reiko will be pleased to have grandchildren running around the house soon, *ne*."

"We are glad to be home," said Satsuki, without answering Tanaka-san's inferred question. "Thank you for taking care of my mother-in-law in my husband's absence." My wife and I bowed to Tanaka-san again. Before she turned to go back to her shopping, she said, "Oh, did you hear the terrible news about the Kobayashis?" We shook our heads, and Tanaka-san took out her handkerchief and dabbed at her eyes. "They're all gone, save their eldest daughter Maiko. And she is to marry an *American*," she said. "Moving to a place called O-hay-o. Can you believe it?" She shook her head. "But that's what the war has done: given everyone a new life, whether they wanted one or not." She shook her head, her lips set in a firm line of disapproval. "Well. I won't keep you any longer," she said, and bowed before going back to her shopping, still shaking her head.

It was noon when we reached home. I was alarmed to see our gate swinging in the breeze and the front door ajar. We hurried into the house calling, "*Okaasan*?" but there was no answer. Satsuki ran upstairs while I checked the back rooms to see if my mother was in her storeroom. As soon as I reached the back bedroom, I heard a soft groaning sound. I finally found my mother on her side in her store room, blood coming from her lower lip.

"They tried to take my things. I wouldn't let them take your books." On the floor beside her were her precious jazz records, strewn about as if a giant had come into her room and thrown them against the wall. Some were broken, others scratched beyond repair. Her gramophone was gone. "Stolen," she said. "They came right after Tanaka-san left. Must have been watching the house."

"Mother, let me help you," I said as Satsuki entered the room.

My mother's eyes glinted when she looked at my wife. "And how was your visit with my second son?" she asked, her eyes narrowing at Satsuki. "To your liking, I expect?" Satsuki looked away and remained silent.

"Mother, be quiet," I said, perspiration gathering on my forehead.

"Try to rest." She smiled up at me like an infant, eyes wide and happy. "You came home," she said, and giggled. "I knew you would come." My mother's dementia had grown worse—she moved from adulthood back to childhood with astonishing speed.

"Help me carry her to the futon," I called out to Satsuki, and she obeyed, running to the closet to pull out a futon mattress, placing it on the tatami. My mother's body felt heavy in my arms. "Get some water. And call the doctor. I think she's had a seizure of some sort," I said. Satsuki did as I asked, then ran to a neighbor's house to see if their phone was working, after trying ours and finding it dead.

My mother's eyes were unfocussed, her pupils dilated. "It is a mother's job to take care of her son," she murmured. "Until the son takes care of the mother."

"*Okaasan*, just rest, please." I opened more windows, hoping in vain for a late August breeze. In the kitchen, the calendar still read August 6. The day of the bomb. The day I left to find Satsuki.

"You left me." My mother's voice again, accusing. "You left me for her." I limped back into my mother's bedroom with an aspirin I'd found in a bathroom drawer.

"Don't try to speak, mother. Just rest," I said. "You are not well."

She persisted, "What did she ever do for you?"

I felt my mother's forehead. Her skin was chilly, in spite of the August heat. "Here, take this." I held her head up and placed the pills on her tongue. She sipped some water and swallowed with difficulty. Some dribbled out of her mouth.

"She is not good enough for you, son. But I have accepted it. A mother does these things for her child." A light film settled on her eyes, making them dull and grey. My mother began refusing to dye her hair at the start of the summer, and gray roots had grown in around her face. I bent down and felt her forehead again, clammy against my palm. Vermillion lipstick made a trail from her mouth to her chin, and I took a handkerchief and wiped it away. Now she beckoned me toward her and said, "She will never sacrifice for you as I have."

Satsuki stood in the doorway, head unbowed, a piece of paper in her hand. "The doctor said he will come as soon as he can. He said to keep *Okaasan* in bed."

My wife turned and left the room. I wondered how much of my mother's foolish words she heard, and I became angry. "Y-you are wrong, mother," I stammered into her ear. "She is better than I deserve." I watched a tear slide from my mother's eye down to her chin, as she shook her head.

The doctor came and prescribed more bed rest. "She is very weak, Tsuruda-san. The war creates casualties that we never hear about."

That evening, as the nightingale called to his mate in our garden, my mother died. I was sitting beside her, staring out the window as I listened to her shallow breath. When she stopped breathing, her eyes remained open, staring at me.

I felt at once adrift and weighed down by the loss of both my parents, suffocated inside the house, as if unseen hands were holding me down, pushing the breath out of me.

The crematorium was booked for nine days solid, and we kept my mother's body with us until the Buddhist priest came to recite the proper sutras and take her away.

In the months that followed, I heard Satsuki on the phone whispering with Tetsuko. Tetsuko's sister Fumiko had gone into Hiroshima to sort through the wreckage of their house in the weeks after the bomb was dropped. She came down with the illness people were calling *Hiroshima-byo*. The disease took hundreds of people daily and left others unable to do anything but lie in bed while their loved ones applied new bandages to their wounds every hour.

Tetsuko told Satsuki this, how Fumiko would only drink water, how she was getting smaller and weaker each day. Tetsuko's youngest sister would not live to see her twenty-sixth birthday.

I wanted things to go back to the way they had been before Hiroshima, but my wife had changed. Satsuki had become prone to startling when I emerged from my study. After my mother's funeral, she was more pensive than before and given to long silences. I watched her as she stared at the hem of her brown kimono sleeve for minutes at a time, her thin fingers working the cuff. She smoothed it down and looked away when she caught me observing her. In her expression was worry, awkwardness. *This is what the war has done,* I thought, *it has robbed us all of peace.*

The faces of the men and women who asked for help in Hiroshima visited me in dreams. I knew they were dead, that they had perhaps hours to live when I saw them, but that thought offered me no comfort, no salve to my conscience.

I fretted over Satsuki's health, and rejoiced over the fact that she seemed to be regaining her vigor. She was near the epicenter of the American bomb, but her hair did not fall out, red sores did not appear on her arms and legs, she did not get dizzy or have fainting spells. Instead, her body grew full and round and her appetite increased until I was afraid I couldn't give her all the food she needed.

Behind my locked study door, I wrote letters to the university, in-quiring about their biology and zoology department. In the privacy of that room, I began to congratulate myself on saving Satsuki. I com-posed speeches for her benefit, washing my guilt away. I imagined her face smiling and nodding in agreement, but I never spoke the words to her.

In December, Satsuki's appetite had increased to such a degree that I smiled and teased, "All the food we have now is making you plump." In truth, I loved to see the fullness in her cheeks. She did not laugh in answer to my teasing. Instead she replied, "Soon we will need much more food in our home, that is true." At first, I didn't understand her meaning, until she looked at me. "It was the offering we left to the Fox Goddess," she said with tears in her eyes. "You are going to be a father, Kenzaburo."

The following spring, Haruna was born.

So you must persist
in asking where my heart goes
all the long, cold night.
Like following trails left by birds
who vanished with yesterday's sky.

—-Kouho Kennichi

— 21 —
SILVER FISH
HARUNA
1990

At first, we met at museums. Each time we saw each other, my attraction to him grew. I could not stop the way my heart flew into my mouth each time I saw him. When I talked to Akihiro, it felt like water falling over stone, splashing and burbling without care. He listened with stillness.

Akihiro and I were seeing each other so often that I told my parents the first lie: that I had joined a water color club.

Akihiro and I had avoided meeting in Kyoto, where his wife and children lived. He told me he had two sons: Sosuke, who was studying to be a doctor, and Takeshi, who was a graphic designer living in Osaka. I only knew one thing about his wife, Mariko: she wanted to be a professional tennis player when she was young. He did not speak of them often, and I did not ask him to.

After we met six times, Akihiro had asked, "Haruna-san, would you do me the honor of accompanying me to Kamakura next month?" I acquiesced, turning so he could not see me blush in the cool rainy season air of June. I wondered if he was an expert in finding women to flatter and seduce. I knew it was a possibility, but I agreed to go with him, anyway.

The morning I left for Kamakura, I told my parents the next lie: that I was going to visit an old college friend.

"*Tanoshinde, ne.* Have fun with your friend, Haru-chan," said my mother. "What was her name? I don't think I remember her."

"M-Masayo." I stammered. "Higuchi Masayo. I met her at in my third year at the university."

My parents said good-bye as I left the house in a taxi. They stood smiling and waving at me from the garden gate. I felt a momentary wave of nausea. *Guilt,* I thought. I forced myself to smile back as the taxi pulled away.

We turned down the narrow road toward the train station, and I hunched into the corner of the seat. I gathered my purse in my lap, ready to tell the driver to turn around. "I am not feeling well," I would say, "take me back home."

And then I thought of Akihiro, the way his eyes closed when he ate wasabi, how he imitated the stray dogs that came up to us on the path by Osaka Jo Castle. I sat back against the white lace cover on the seat and exhaled.

"*Daijobu yo,*" I whispered to myself. It would be fine. Everything would be fine.

He met me at the station in Osaka, where we purchased our tickets for the bullet train. We rode the long escalator up to the platform in silence. The train sat on the track, its snub nose smooth and white. We boarded and went to our seats. Since it was a weekday morning and past the time of rush hour, the car was almost empty. Akihiro was wearing his glasses, and he brought a book about cave paintings with him. He read excerpts to me as the train began to move.

"The paintings were discovered by some boys in France. They were down in the caves exploring and discovered a mystery that had been buried for a millennium."

I smiled, willing to be amazed with him, able to imagine the boys' faces, full of wonder when they found the pictures created thousands of years ago.

Even though the train was going at full velocity, it felt as if we were moving at a leisurely pace. The only thing that gave away our speed was the rapidity with which we overtook objects, which first appeared as tiny dots in the distance, then became houses, or buildings, or a stand of trees which passed by in a blur.

I thought, *My life has been like this. I have fixed my sight on objects, thinking they were what I desired, only to see them move by me in a blur, unreachable, unobtainable.* I looked from the window to Akihiro and was glad that I had come.

We went first to see the statue of Buddha in Kamakura, which was out in the open air and had been for centuries. The wooden sculpture was painted with gold that was fading over time. I wondered if our gaze made the color diminish, our eyes like cameras taking in the swooping curves of the Buddha's gown.

We visited the Incan Gold in Kamakura, far away from our families. "All this gold, found at the bottom of a lake, sacrificed to Incan gods centuries ago. So much beauty waiting to be discovered." I remember Akihiro peering at resurrected treasures in the backlit exhibit cases. It was our first trip together away from Kansai. His face was open, the lines in it soft. I shivered next to him in the darkened room.

Akihiro turned and lifted both of my hands to his chest, cupping his fingers around mine. I was certain he could feel my pulse beating.

My heart was a bird throwing itself against the inside of my ribcage. I was afraid my need for him was as clear and obvious as an x-ray, a waterfall, a grasshopper's wing.

Akihiro's eyes made tiny fans at the edges as he smiled. He lifted my hand and kissed it. "I saw men in Europe do this," he said, and it came out like an apology. We stopped in front of an exhibit from Egypt and stood beside a mummy whose wrapping was askew. One eye socket stared blankly at us.

"Soon Sosuke will finish his medical training and take over the family hospital," Akihiro said. "When that happens, I will be able to retire and not worry about every small detail there. It will be my son's responsibility, and for that I am glad. I will have more time to spend doing what I want to do."

I avoided his insinuated meaning with a question. "Will you miss your work?" I asked. In addition to curiosity, I felt irritation. I was annoyed with him for taking his good fortune for granted. What I wouldn't have given for the opportunity to study and travel, and have a successful career devoted to science.

"The clinic was built by my father, Haruna-san. I became a doctor for my parents. It did not matter whether or not it was what I wanted. My path was decided for me before I was born."

He saw the look on my face and softened. "*Dakedo*, it has not been a bad existence. I hope that I have helped a few people, and not hurt too many. As an artist, for example, who knows if I would have saved any lives?"

I was silent, wondering if that was what he had wished to be as a young man. He moved toward the center of the museum, where lush green plants grew under a skylight, like kelp moving toward the surface of the ocean. He turned back toward me, and I saw every line and shadow in his face.

"I worry about Sosuke. I fear his mother has pressured him into taking over the hospital, and that he may have wanted other things . . . but it is too late for him to change his mind now, I suppose."

In the times I had seen Akihiro, he had rarely spoken of his wife; I never asked about her. But on that day, perhaps because we were far away from Kansai, he was in the mood to talk.

"*Omiai*," he explained, as if I had asked him the question. "Like most people, we had an arranged marriage. Mariko is intelligent, a caring mother. She ran the house and managed the office of the hospital for years. She even did some of the cooking there. A patient once told me that he chose to have me do his surgery because he had heard about my wife's miso soup." Akihiro smiled and scratched his head, remembering.

"Mariko made patients feel welcome and kept everything running smoothly, from the ordering of supplies to dealing with pharmaceutical salesmen. She has been a good business partner. But the truth is, when it comes to the two of us, she prefers to play tennis with her friends and I prefer this." He held out his hand, gesturing to the paintings on the wall of the museum.

"We are very different, but I do not wish her to be sad. My wife has been very loyal to my family and to the hospital. I cannot fault her." He sighed. "I would be wrong to wish for a different destiny. I am fortunate to be here now, with you. That is enough," he said.

At that moment I wanted nothing more than to be in his arms, my nose pressed against his neck. Instead, I said, "I do not believe in destiny, Akihiro-san. It does not make scientific sense to me."

Akihiro threw his head back and laughed. "Truly, Haruna-san, truly you are the most unusual woman I have ever met." His voice echoed in the hallway of the museum.

People standing nearby looked at us and turned away. There were moments with Akihiro when I realized how foreign he was as a result of living abroad, how like a *gaijin* he behaved at times. I often have wondered since if this was part of what attracted me to him—his not quite being Japanese.

That night, we went to a sushi restaurant Akihiro read about. We drank hot sake and ate eel, squid, Hamachi, and toro. By nine o'clock we were finished, and we took a taxi back to our hotel. Akihiro talked about the next day's plans. Overwhelmed by the day of travel and uncertain emotions, I nodded every once in a while, my eyelids heavy, my thoughts wrapped in sticky white gauze.

Once in our room, I went to the *furoba* to take a bath. The room was slick and modern, with a deep, sunken marble *ofuro*. I sat on the small wooden stool and showered first, washing away the stiffness of travel. The water in the tub was almost scalding hot, and I eased myself in, joint by joint. I sank back against the marble, submerged up to my chin.

The coolness of the stone on my bare neck calmed me.

I heard the door of the *furoba* slide open. Akihiro had decided to join me. "*Ii desuka?*" he asked my permission. "*Hai . . . douzo,*" I answered. I watched him as he showered. His body was lean, and the bright white zig zag of an old scar ran along his left side.

When he was done showering, he eased himself into the *ofuro* facing me, and I felt his leg brush against mine. He rested his hand on my calf. I reached out to trace the scar on his side with my right index finger.

"It was an accident," he said. "My father was driving. We lost my younger brother, Nobu. I was twelve. He was nine." He looked away, his eyes reddening.

I nodded and moved close to him, rested my head on his shoulder. We sat in silence, listening to the drip of the water, hot steam swirling around us. Small silver bubbles clung to my legs on their journey to the surface of the bath, then broke free and rose to meet the air.

When I stepped out of the bath, Akihiro followed. He wrapped me in a plush white towel and patted each part of my body dry as gently as a mother would her child. He leaned close to me, his lips merging with my shoulder, then my neck, my mouth. He watched me put on my cotton yukata, his deep set brown eyes taking in every part of me. I moved slowly, unhurried, and went into the next room and lay down. I felt as if I melted into the futon and became part of it.

Akihiro lay down next to me, and then pulled my yukata from my shoulders as if trying to remove a spider web from a branch without breaking any silken threads. His lips found my cheek, my collar bone, my navel.

He did not close his eyes once, not even the moment he entered me. I was embarrassed until he said, "*Wasurenai you ni*. So I will never forget." His smile contained hope and regret in equal measure.

That night I held three images with me as I dreamed: a smiling Buddha, Akihiro's silver scar, and the memory of forgotten gold lying at the bottom of a faraway mountain lake.

We met as often as we could after our trip to Kamakura. We sat in the hot springs of Hakone and visited the famed *torii* gate of Miyajima, the surrounding islands appearing to float above the water like a deep blue-green mirage. We read books together, went to movies and plays. Akihiro loved opera and took me to see *Turandot* in Tokyo. I found myself humming the tune to "Nessun Dorma" all week afterward.

In the early fall, my parents started asking more questions.

"Haru-chan, you look so different these days. As if there is a fire beneath your skin," remarked my mother one day. She was taking laundry down from the poles in the back yard, so I could not see her face. "Do you have a fever?"

"I haven't been feeling well, that is probably it," I said, and put my hand to my cheek.

I did not want them to know about Akihiro. I did not want to share or explain. I was like a greedy child huddled over a piece of cake, licking frosting from my fingers behind a locked door.

It was with utter astonishment a month after this exchange with my mother that I realized I was pregnant. Forty, unmarried, in love with a man who was fifteen years my senior and who already had a wife and two grown sons.

After I took the pregnancy test, I was not sure what I would do about this child, this tiny mass of cells dividing and growing inside my body. There were moments when I wanted to keep the baby and raise it, and fantasized about being with Akihiro, going abroad to live with him and our child. I decided to tell him.

The day I met Akihiro at Osaka-Jō Koen Park to tell him was the day he told me his news—that we were not going to be together for very much longer. There was another life inside of him, as well: a tumor. "The doctors said the cancer was in remission, but now it is back," he said. "I should have told you, Haru-chan, that I had cancer before. The truth is, I did not want to worry you. They do not tell you when you are about to die, but I am a doctor. I forced them to give me the information. They said I have five months left, maybe nine."

I grasped his hands in mine on the park bench, tears streaming down my face. I did not care what people thought; I did not care who saw me or what they would whisper behind cupped palms.

I opened my mouth to tell him about our child, and then closed it. In that moment, I knew that this baby would never be born. If I told Akihiro, he would not be able to die with peace, he would worry because he was unable to take care of us. I did not even consider what my parents might say if I went through with the pregnancy. I pressed my lips together and turned away, careful not to let Akihiro see my face.

"Haruna, I understand if you no longer wish to see me. What reason could you have for being with a dying man?"

A sound escaped from my throat. I pushed my face into his chest. I clung to him like a child clings to her father as they walk into the ocean for the first time in the summer. He stroked my hair.

"Shhh, shhhhh. *Daijobu. Daijobu,* it's all right, it's all right, Haruna. I am a fortunate man to have spent time with you over these past nine months. You may think me a fool for saying this, but I feel as if we were attached by the *'akai ito,'* the tiny red threads that bound us from the moment we were born. I am a lucky man, Haruna. Perhaps if we have been good enough in this life, we will be born at the right time to spend our lives together in the next."

"The doctors might be wrong, they make mistakes all the time," I said.

"*Saa,*" he said and shook his head, that little smile on his lips. "This time they are correct." When he saw the look on my face, he whispered, "It has been my experience that people never tell you how much a part of life dying really is. Death is all part of it, Haru-chan. Even mine."

I pulled away from him. Before meeting him at the park that day, I'd wanted more than anything to tell Akihiro, "I am pregnant with your child," but my lips were sewn shut. I wiped my face with my handkerchief and looked up at him, tried to smile.

"We must make this time mean something," I said. "We must do all the things you have wished you could do but were not able, go to all the places you wished to go."

Akihiro laughed. "There is no place I would rather be than with you. I do not need to be in Egypt or Australia to know that."

We met as often as we could. Akihiro did not seem to care who saw us anymore. "I do not want to hurt my wife; this is not her fault. But I don't want to waste time by not spending it with you, Haru-chan," he said.

I saw that the doctors were right. His healthy frame began to deteriorate. He was not able to walk very far without tiring, and as the weeks went by, food held no pleasure for him.

One and a half months after his admission, I still had not made a decision about the baby. This life that Akihiro and I had created, how could I kill it? It was the finest part of both of us. I could not do it because I dreamed our son's face, saw him wherever I went. "This boy is a bright spirit," I would whisper to myself in the bath, holding my belly. "His name should be Akira, the same character for 'akarui,' because he is full of light."

I thought of my father helping me with my kanji homework when I was nine and a fourth-year student in grammar school.

"Look, Haruna, this is the character for *akarui*." He sat down and drew the kanji with his horsehair calligraphy brush, dipping it into the wetted sumi ink stone.

"What do you see?" he asked me, after he was finished.

I looked at the page and pressed my lips together, not wanting to disappoint him. "I see a sun on the right, and a small moon on the left," I said, sure of my answer.

"Aha! A large sweeping sun on the right, and a tiny moon on the left. At least that is what most people will tell you. But if you look closely, you will see something quite different."

He reached up to the highest shelf in his study and brought down a book with a binding the thickness of my leg, entitled, *The Origins of Chinese Characters*. In second grade, we had used the book to look up "*kame*," and I had seen a small tortoise drawn as it would have been in the mind of its creator. In third grade, I saw how "*taberu*" was a hand eating some rice. The book held the key to every word known.

In the index he looked up "*akarui*," trailing his forefinger down a page as thin as tissue. Characters marched like trails of ants up the paper, black spindly legs and antennae curling affectionately around each word.

At last he found what he was looking for. "*Hora*. Look here, Haruna. The characters for *akarui*. What do you see now?"

I saw that the large pictograph on the right was actually the moon, and on the left, a tiny window drawn in the upper corner.

"The meaning is this," he read, "*akarui*: the moon rises, and its light shines through the window, illuminating everything that has not yet been seen."

Akarui, the same character as Akira. My luminous child, who has brought all of the feeling I have for Akihiro into the light.

I was stealing away almost every day now to visit Akihiro. He tried to walk as much as possible, ate seaweed because he heard it rid the body of toxins. He had not yet told his family the news.

As I turned to wave good-bye to my father one day on my way to visit Akihiro, I caught a strange look on my *otohsan*'s face, as if he were puzzling through something. He saw me and wiped the expression away.

He knows, I thought. He knows that I am not going to meet friends, he knows it's a man. Then I brushed the thought away. Of course, he didn't know. How could he? I had been careful never say Akihiro's name, or mention that I was seeing anyone.

At night I dreamed our son's face. I saw the clean clear curve of his forehead, smelled the down at the back of his neck. Our boy. Still, I did not tell Akihiro. I was now twenty-four-weeks pregnant, according to my calculations, and I could not make a decision. I hid my pregnancy from my parents and Akihiro by wearing loose-fitting clothing. As the weeks went by and Akihiro became more haggard and bent, I grew ripe and full. My cheeks blossomed with color and my hair hung thick and shiny.

At twenty-eight weeks, I was surprised to hear the voice of Akihiro's wife on the telephone. "Akihiro-san wanted me to tell you. Please come to the hospital now." She hung up without saying good-bye. I was shaking as I put on my skirt, blouse, and shoes. On the train to Osaka, the sky was low with haze and soot. The suburbs of Kobe gave way to factories and smokestacks that lined the train's journey into the city.

Akihiro's wife and two sons stood in the corridor outside of his room when I arrived. I had taken so much of his time from them. His wife said nothing as I walked in. One of her boys, whom I guessed was Takeshi, held her arm and glared at me, but she shushed him with a look. Softly as a fallen feather, I whispered, "Thank you." Out of the corner of my eye, I perceived slight downward tilt of her chin. It was nothing like a bow. I walked into Akihiro's room, shutting the door behind me.

Akihiro lay on the bed, his bones making peaks and valleys under his hospital sheet. Tiny mountains and hills whose lines I used to trace in hotels and inns on Sunday mornings as he traced lines between the freckles on my skin.

This morning, our last, I forced my mouth into a smile and held his hand, no heavier than a child's. It was fleshless and weak, a bird's claw in my palm. His pallor was gray, and dark splotches spread across his skin. A purple chrysanthemum on his bedside table molted petals.

"Haruna," he whispered. "Forgive me for asking Mariko to call you." He smiled, his old sheepishness and sparkle lying under the veil of illness. I felt as if a curtain already separated us, knew that he was no longer on the living, breathing side of the world.

"After all of our careful maneuverings," he said, "she knew about you. She said she could tell because I was so happy." He paused and motioned to a plastic pitcher filled with water beside him. "Haru-chan, thank you. And I am sorry, so sorry for leaving you this way. I am so sorry that I was a coward and didn't take the risk I knew I should take to ask you to be my wife."

I shook my head and ran my hand along his arm, quieting him like a child.

"Some things recently have made me wonder . . . I have seen my mother's face, my uncle's, as they looked when they were alive. They have been talking to me, comforting me. My only regret is that I cannot take some small piece of you with me, if I am indeed going somewhere." His gentle laugh turned into a hoarse, wracking cough.

A soft knock on the door, and I knew my time, as a woman of no status, was up. I lost myself for a moment and hugged Akihiro around the neck and wept. I opened my mouth to tell him the truth and then shut it again. I could not bring myself to divulge the truth about the child he would never see. He stroked my hair until his hand stopped moving.

Another knock, louder this time, and the door opened. "You must go now. It is no longer your time to be with him." Akihiro's older son Sosuke, his voice sharp, stooped over me as he spoke. The sound of a match striking and the scent of burning wax. Mariko lighting the death candles as I left the room.

Nobody said good-bye or even nodded at my departure. It was as if I had never come.

I did not attend the funeral, but stayed at home in my room, unable to sleep or eat.

On the third day after Akihiro's death, the blood started between

my legs. I stood under the shower next to the *ofuro* as cramps con-
vulsed my pelvis, bending me into a squatting position. I felt hot, then
cold, as I watched the blood, my child, leaving my body. Red fell to
the tile floor and curled around the drain like an eel. I reached out
to touch it before it swam down into the gutter. My son. Akihiro's
baby. My only child. I clenched my fist into a ball and jammed it into
my mouth so my parents would not hear me cry out. When I could
move, I called Tae-chan, who took me to the hospital for a D&C. "I
never knew," she said. "Why didn't you tell me, Haru-chan? Why did
you insist on bearing this alone?" I did not have an answer for her. I
could not tell her that my inability to bring an end to the life growing
inside of me for twenty-eight weeks had, in fact, been hope disguised
as indecision.

That night, I dreamed that my boy was a silver fish, a baby carp
swimming through water, until he reached the mouth of a large river
and tumbled into the ocean. I swam after him, stretching out slippery
hands that refused to grasp the small wriggling body in front of me.
I swallowed ocean and seaweed, watching helplessly as he picked up
speed, tail moving like a pendulum.

In my dream, a wave threw me back onto the beach. From the
shore I saw his scales flashing in the sun, his tender spine curving like
a bow when he jumped into the air.

I stood on the beach gulping air, my body hollow and aching, and
watched my child as he sped out to sea and away from me.

22
KENZABURO
THE FINAL OBON

My *obaachan* was the first to warn me of hungry ghosts when I was nine.

"Be careful, Ken-chan. They will try to trick you, so they can inhabit your body, for they have lost their own," my grandmother said as she sat painting faces on the wooden dolls she created. "Never believe them, never trust them. *Wakarimasuka?*" She asked, pausing and watching my face until I nodded "yes" to show that I'd understood the gravity of her words.

My *obaachan* kept hundreds of *kokeshi* dolls in her room. As a boy, I looked at the floor whenever I visited, sure that the miniature figures were watching me and could see every weakness I possessed.

I sat in the house of my afterlife recording this memory with a crooked smile, my pen scratching over the surface of the scroll. I had already begun to think of my grandmother's beliefs as mere superstitious myths as I grew into adolescence and embraced the world of scientific fact. My *obaachan's* tales became something to be indulged. Like Satsuki, my grandmother had been wise where I had been foolish and vain.

"Where is my *obaachan*? Why isn't she in Yamato?" I'd asked Benkei when I first arrived. He sucked his teeth and looked at the ceiling before saying, "Ahhh, yes. Your grandmother. She was a wise woman, family name of Oh, I believe. She has gone on to the next life, Kenzaburo, and achieved *satori*—what is sometimes called 'enlightenment.'" He said that Yamato was a holding pen of sorts, a place for spirits who had yet to understand the connection between the spiritual world and the physical. The lost, the stubborn, and the confused lingered here, and I regretted that I counted myself among them.

Sitting at my desk in my study, I forgot where I was at times. I wrote of my fascination with the insect world as a child, of my years at the university. What Inari told me had been true—the scroll possessed its own will. When I attempted to pass over a memory that embarrassed or pained me, the scroll refused to unfurl. It was for this reason that I was finally forced to write about Ando-kun. I tried one sentence five different ways, but the ink did not show until I put down these words: "I believe my decision to fail Ando-kun caused him to take his own life." The scroll would not allow me to keep writing until I added, "This was a decision I made out of arrogance and pride." As soon as I had written the words, I dropped my pen as if it burned my skin, left my desk, and moved downstairs into the garden.

I was annoyed to see that the stranger who I'd first noticed during my second Obon had begun visiting my house in Yamato as well. Still, he did not speak, but stared in my direction, spectacles shielding his eyes.

"What do you want?" I shouted, and my voice echoed against the hills, startling a group of spirits moving down the road beside our house. They were middle-aged women in kimono, and they began whispering to each other behind their hands.

The spirit turned and disappeared in the other direction, heading toward the ravine near our house. I ran to follow him but when I arrived at the riverbank, there was no sign of him. His visitations were increasing in frequency. Every time he appeared it left me feeling uneasy and troubled, unable to write.

"You must not leave anything out," cautioned Benkei. "Do not take too long to finish. The Tsurudas no longer have the luxury of time." I believed him, but I struggled to write and often found myself empty and numb, devoid of words or ideas.

"All must be laid bare," Inari had said. "Do not let fear overcome you." I forced myself to follow her advice. I had no choice if I wanted Satsuki and Haruna to join me in Yamato. So much we'd kept from each other in one small house. The weight of regret filled my mouth like rough black stones.

When too many dark memories crowded my head, shouting and clamoring for attention, I set down my pen and left my study. Sometimes I sought out Benkei. Other days, I wandered through the neighborhood looking for my mother and brother. I asked passing spirits if they'd seen them, but none ever had. There were times I glimpsed what looked like hungry ghosts in the distance, with their long, stalk-thin necks, bloated torsos, and large heads. As time crept toward the next Obon, their numbers seemed to increase, and they dared come closer to our house. Now the stranger was at the garden wall every day, watching me. Benkei grumbled, but underneath his irritability I detected something that I realized with surprise was fear.

"Why is he here?" I asked. "What could he possibly want from me? I've never seen the man before in my life."

"*Wakarahen*," Benkei said with an annoyed sigh. "I don't know. But I do know that Obon is coming soon. Are you making progress on the scroll?" I nodded but wondered if I was doing enough. I still hadn't found my mother and brother, and I was afraid to tell him that the scroll was only half-finished. Inari had instructed me to write until it was filled, but I was afraid I had nothing more to say.

As I looked out over the garden wall, a ten-year-old boy in a white *happi* coat, matching short pants, and *maki* around his head ran by with a small drum in one hand. He grinned at me as he passed, looking for all the world like he was on his way to the summer fireworks display.

"Pardon me, young man," I shouted, chasing after him. "Wait, I want to talk to you."

The boy stopped, jumped over a crack in the road, and spun around.

"*Hai!*" He said, with mock seriousness, and saluted as if I was an army sergeant. The boy had the vague look of a child with one Japanese and one *gaijin* parent, what people had taken to calling "*ha-fu.*" His hair was straight and black, but his eyes, while almond-shaped, were as green as some of the American soldiers Satsuki and I had seen after the war. I wondered if he was the boy from the foreign school whose death had preceded mine by a year. There had been a car accident near Canadian Academy, the hundred-year-old international school whose Tudor style buildings dotted the side of Mt. Rokko, but I didn't ask the boy about it for fear of upsetting him. Most spirits didn't like to dwell on their demise but preferred to talk instead about the years when they were alive.

"Young man, I have a question for you," I stammered, afraid he would run off again before I could get the words out. "I am looking for my mother and brother and haven't been able to find them. You look like a clever boy. Where can you imagine a spirit might hide in Yamato?"

"*Saa*," said the boy, a frown line forming between his eyebrows. "*Jichan*, have you tried the Jizo yet? His temple is down the mountain a bit, across the river. He might know."

I stared at him, dumbfounded. Why was he the first to mention the Jizo's name to me in Yamato? Thanking him, I rushed back to the house to tell Benkei, whose eyes grew wide when he heard what I had to say. He pulled on his beard and said, "*Asoka*. The Jizo . . . *ehh*, the boy might be right, Kenzaburo."

As we left the house, two hungry ghosts stood swaying outside our front gate. Holding their thin hands out to us like beggars, they gazed at me and whispered, "*O-mizu.*" When I paused, Benkei said, "It is no use, Kenzaburo. Even if we gave them water, it would turn to ash as soon as it touched their lips. Now come, we must hurry. We are getting closer to August and the first day of Obon. We don't have much time left before we go back to the living world."

Small patches of fog hung over the water and near the trees, but we could still make out an old temple on the far riverbank standing under an oak with a rope tied around it. As the fog dissipated, we saw a thin man with a shaven head in a grey monk's habit tending to some children. It appeared he was using a long stick to draw in the dirt, and from time to time we heard snatches of what sounded like a lesson from across the water. Vast piles of stones surrounded the temple. Nearby the outdoor classroom, small, bright spirits were carrying the stones and laying them one on top of the other, creating towers that reached to the treetops. The Jizo stopped to minister to each spirit, occasionally bending to touch their heads gently with his staff.

"He relieves them of the punishment of building the towers—it is not their fault they haven't been able to build up karma in their lifetimes, so he forgives them of that debt," said Benkei. "It is said that he renounced his own Buddhahood in order to stay here in Yamato and take care of the spirits of children and travelers."

As we got closer, the gathering of children erupted in laughter. A gong sounded from somewhere within the temple, and they stood up as one and ran inside.

"This is the *Sanzu no Kawa*—the River of Three Crossings, the place most spirits cross over into Yamato," whispered Benkei. "We are at the *Sai no Kawara* riverbank, where the Jizo protects the spirits of children from demons and hungry ghosts."

An immense stack of wooden *kokeshi* dolls sat next to a tall gray stone tower on the far side of the riverbank. All at once I recalled my grandmother drawing the delicate features onto the dolls' round wooden faces and cylindrical bodies. "The *kokeshi* are wedding gifts for the deceased," she told me when I was a child. "Parents offer them to the Jizo for their children who died, so that they may find a family in Yamato." She paused and looked up from what she was doing, her soft, wrinkled face focusing on my own thin twelve-year-old one. "They will never grow up and find husbands or wives of their own, you see, so we must help them, Ken-chan."

Her words, spoken more than sixty years before this moment, were as clear as if she'd just whispered them in my ear as I stood in the spirit world on the riverbank of the *Sanzu no Kawa. "Yosho.* It is time. Let's cross the river and speak with the Jizo-sama."

"It's not as simple as it seems," said a voice behind us.

We turned to see the stranger standing behind us, hat in his hands, eyes unblinking behind his glasses.

"Who are you? Are you a hungry ghost? What do you want from us?" My voice came out at a hoarse bark. I was furious that this strange spirit had followed us all the way to the Jizo's temple.

The stranger bowed low.

"I can assure you I am not a hungry ghost," he said, his voice low. "I only wish to help you, Tsuruda-san."

"How can we be sure?" I said. "Your actions have not been those of an honorable man. They are the actions of someone with something to hide, of a thief or one who wishes to do harm." I continued, my voice rising. "Why do you stand outside my family's house? Have you no family of your own?"

"*Gomen nasai.* I am sorry, Tsuruda-san. I have only been following you to learn from you. It is part of the task I was assigned in Yamato, to help you when I was able. And now that time has come."

Benkei crossed his arms. "You haven't even had the courage to offer a simple greeting. How do you intend to help us?"

The stranger bowed again and said, "I can guide you to the Jizo's temple. I know how to avoid the demons and spirits of the river. They do not discriminate, you see—they will pull you under just as surely as they do the newly dead spirits who attempt to ford the *Sanzu no Kawa.* There's very little a spirit can do once he's been pulled into the River of Three Crossings. Your uncle will tell you what I'm saying is true."

I looked at Benkei, who replied with a terse nod. "If he knows a way across the river, we will get our audience with the Jizo-sama without being pulled under," he said.

"What do you want in exchange?" I asked the stranger. I put my fingers around the handle of the dagger Satsuki had placed in coffin before my funeral, wondering how it could possibly protect me. In the sleeve of my kimono, the jingle of something metal.

"My funeral coins?" I asked.

Benkei nodded, and I handed the spirit three of my coins. I now had only one left.

The stranger motioned us to follow him upriver. Around a small bend, a copse of bamboo seemed to grow over the surface of the water.

To the right of the stand of trees was a small trailside shrine to the Jizo-sama set on a boulder, also overgrown with vegetation.

"First, we must request help from the Jizo Bosatsu," said the stranger. He cleared some of the brush away and kneeled in front of the shrine surrounded by statues of red-bibbed Jizo. Before Benkei joined him, he whispered, "You would do well to do the same." I stood behind my uncle and put my palms together, for the first time asking for help from this deity whom I'd viewed as a national curiosity, a quirk of my culture, when I was alive. But now I thought of Haruna, and asked for her protection in the living world, and for Satsuki's, and for my own and my family's, going back to the first Tsuruda. When the stranger had finished praying, he stood and walked to the edge of the river and again motioned for us to follow. Benkei cautioned, "Do not speak, Nephew. We will awaken the demons that live in the river. These waters are under the control of a serpent who is the cousin of *Seiryu*, the same sea dragon you witnessed guarding the *torri* gate in the waters off Yamato."

The stranger began crossing the river at a place where the reeds grew in a dense clump. A rotting bridge stood upriver from us; its blackened pylons decomposing into disrepair.

I peered into the brackish water as we picked our way across. I forgot myself and cried out when I saw the doleful features of Ando-san slide by me just under the surface.

I bent down to see if the face indeed belonged to my former student, but when I looked again, the river only reflected gray sky back at me.

In the middle of the river, small black whirlpools formed around us as we moved. The water was now up to our waists and was climbing toward my chest. We would soon have to start swimming. Dark shapes moved through the water beside us. An unblinking eye the size of an ostrich egg came to the surface near me, then sank out of sight.

The stranger did not look to the left or right but kept moving toward the opposite bank of the river. I followed his lead and, remembering the Jizo sutra my grandmother had taught me, I felt compelled to chant. Benkei and the stranger joined their voices to mine and chanted with me.

So much had changed since the fall from the tree and my birth as a spirit in the afterlife.

The river became shallow again as we neared the far edge of the river. The fog had thickened again, but when it parted we saw the Jizo waiting for us.

We emerged from the water and bowed to the ground on the banks of the River of Three Crossings. The Jizo, whose thin, weathered face—wholly different from the round-faced statues that depicted him—broke into a smile, laughed, and told us to rise.

"Now, tell me what brought you to my temple on the *Sai no Kawara* riverbank," he said. "Not every spirit will risk eternity to ford the River of Three Crossings just to see me."

"O-Jizo-sama, thank you for your protection and help," Benkei said, his voice a hoarse whisper. "We have come to ask if you might know the whereabouts of my nephew's mother and brother. His mother has been here since the end of the last war, and his younger brother for more than a decade."

"*Ararara*," clucked the Jizo, and motioned us to follow him toward the temple. Small spirits swarmed around him like chicks under a mother hen, clinging to his gray robe and rolling by his feet.

"And you," he said to the stranger. "What do you seek?"

Our guide bowed his head. "I have come to rescue my son," he said. "He is here with you. I plan to care for him until his mother joins us in Yamato."

I drew back in surprise. In my arrogance, it had never occurred to me that the stranger had any desire in Yamato other than to cause trouble to my family.

The Jizo nodded, and said, "As I believe you already know, the only way to rescue your child is by receiving the funeral coins from a relative spirit of the child. Since you have succeeded in doing so, *douzo*—your son is free to go with you."

The stranger bowed to the ground again, "O-Jizo-sama, *arigatou gozaimashita*. I will continue to thank you all the days I am in Yamato. And on behalf of our child's mother, I thank you."

I was confused by the Jizo's words. I had given this stranger my funeral coins, yet I was not a relative of his. I'd never met him before he began shadowing me in the afterlife.

"And you, Kenzaburo. As the grandfather of this child, are you willing to help this spirit watch over him in Yamato until your wife and daughter arrive?"

I stared at the Jizo-sama, unable to speak. Benkei remained in bowing position, as did the stranger. Smiling, the deity known at the Jizo Bosatsu reached into the sleeve of his robe and brought a shining ball of light in his palms.

"This is part of your truth," he said, reading my thoughts. "This is the spirit of your unborn grandson, Ken-chan—your daughter's son. Your guide across the River of Three Crossings was known as Akihiro in his mortal life, and he is the child's father. He has been waiting for your arrival in Yamato."

I turned to Akihiro. "That is why you were watching Haruna. You are the one she dreams about . . . "

"*Yurushite kuremasu*," begged Akihiro, bowing to me now. "Forgive me, Tsuruda-san. I loved your daughter, but I was a married man. I did not know Haruna was pregnant with our child when I died. I have been watching you since you arrived, hoping to find a chance to rescue our son, but I was not permitted to tell you who I was until we reached the Jizo-sama's temple."

Light from the spirit in the Jizo's upturned palms illuminated his face: my grandson, my daughter's only child.

I bowed to Akihiro. The anger I felt toward my daughter and her married lover had long since dissipated in Yamato and been replaced with regret. "Please forgive me. I am a stupid old man, a coward who was too stubborn to listen to his daughter when I was still living, too proud to face a difficult truth."

Akihiro shook his head and said, "As living men, we were all afraid of revelations that might have changed our comfortable lives or caused difficulty. I am guilty of the same," he said. "But now I promise you that I will watch over your grandson's spirit until it is time for Haruna to join us here."

I bowed in answer. I could not bring myself to tell Akihiro the truth—that if I was unable to complete my task, my daughter would not be able to join us.

The Jizo passed the glowing ball in his hands to Akihiro, whose cupped palms received his son. I watched the spirit of my unborn grandson roll up Akihiro's arm and sit in the crevice between his ear and shoulder.

The Jizo smiled. "Obon is almost here. You must all make your way back to the Tsuruda home before the holiday begins." He looked at Akihiro. "Your son will want to see his mother, *darou?*"

Akihiro nodded, his face lit from within.

"When you cross the river this time, you will not need coins. The demons will not bother you," the Jizo continued. "You are under my protection. Go back to your own ancestral home and wait for the procession of lights down the mountain in three day's time."

Before leaving, Akihiro bowed to me once more.

"*Ii desuka?*" I asked. "May I?" Akihiro nodded and held out the spirit of my grandson. I cupped my palms and drew the small ball of light toward my chest. My grandson nestled under my chin for a moment, and something that felt like peace filled me.

"He is called 'Akira,'" said the Jizo. "Your daughter gave him this name because she sensed his bright spirit. It's fitting, *darouka?*"

Akihiro, carrying my grandson, made their way downriver on a raft the Jizo indicated. "*Ki wo tsukete*," I called, my hands cupped around my mouth. "Take good care of your spirit, Akihiro-san. And of my grandson. We will look for you when Obon begins." Akihiro waved from the raft, the spirit of my grandson illuminating his face. I watched them both until they floated out of sight.

The river reminded me of Ando-kun again, and I cleared my throat. "Jizo-sama, there is one favor I must ask. I believe I might have seen an acquaintance, an old student of mine, in the *Sanzu no Kawa*. I feel I am responsible for him . . . is there any way I can release him from the river?" I took the last coin out of my kimono pocket and offered it to the Jizo. "Might this help?"

The Jizo smiled. "Even in death, one may learn," he said. "I will see to it that he is released." The Jizo tilted his hairless head. "And now, the real reason why you came here today—you wish to know the whereabouts of your mother and brother," he said.

"*Hai, Onegaishimasu*," I said with a bow, Benkei doing the same at my side.

The Jizo-sama did not speak for a long time. Finally, he let out a long sigh and said, "I am afraid I cannot help you, Tsuruda-san."

"O-Jizo-sama," said Benkei, prostrating himself before the thin monk. "Please take pity upon us, and upon our family line." My uncle paused for a moment, his voice choking. "Each one of our family members who is still in Yamato is destined for an existence as a hungry ghost if we are unable to find my nephew's mother and brother."

The Jizo paused for so long I thought he'd disappeared. When I looked up, his sorrowful eyes were staring back at me. "I cannot help you, Kenzaburo, because they are no longer here," he said, and in his voice, we heard compassion and regret in equal measure. "Obon has begun."

In the distance, we heard the temple bell announcing the start of The Days of the Dead. My third Obon in Yamato, and I had not completed the task Inari had assigned to me. The finality of this realization pulled me down to the ground and held me there.

"Do not give up hope, Tsuruda-san," the Jizo said. "You have until the end of this Obon to finish what you have been unable to complete." I nodded, my shoulders shaking. "Look for your mother and younger brother when you arrive in the living world, Kenzaburo," he said. "But remember, the Buddha said, 'We only lose what we cling to.' Do not cling to what you remember of your *okaasan* and Zaemon, for that memory will bring you pain. Look for them with new eyes and you will find them." The Jizo tapped his staff on the path twice, the signal that our meeting was finished.

"*Arigatou gozaimashita . . . arigatou gozaimashita . . . arigato . . . arigatou . . .* " I heard my voice, dusty and dry as the ground beneath me, thanking him as if I was chanting a sutra, unable to stop even after the Jizo had disappeared inside the temple.

A silent Benkei helped me stand upright. Without a word, he led the way back through the murky water of the River of Three Crossings. The force of guilt bore down on me again, nearly causing me to slip under the water and join the melancholy spirits that slid by. My uncle had waited for me as I came to understand the afterlife, taught me with wisdom and gracious good humor, and still I had lost my way in

Yamato, just as I had in life. The very smallest piece of hope the Jizo of-fered, an ant's meal for a starving man, was all there was to sustain me.

When he reached the far bank, Benkei slumped forward onto a twisted tree, gasping. A subtle change in my uncle's movements as he braced himself against the tree made me pause before I reached him, made me circle to the left when I approached. Benkei's back was to me, but I could see that his limbs appeared to be lengthening. They appeared to grow as disproportionate to his body as the long, spindly arms of a praying mantis.

And then I knew what it was that was giving me pause, caused me to stop in my tracks before reaching out to him, to examine my own hands. I was horrified to see that my fingers had taken on the appearance of gray talons and seemed to curl in on themselves, my fingernails turned obsidian black.

Our transformation into hungry ghosts had already begun.

23
HARUNA
LIGHTING THE WELCOME HOME FIRES

The pounding drums pulled Haruna from her daydream. The young men from the neighborhood were practicing again for the main Obon festival, held on the last day of the holiday. Each strike on the drum skins made the air vibrate around her with anticipation for the pulling of the *Omikoshi*. The portable shrine from their local temple took twenty men and all the neighborhood children to parade through the streets, laughing and calling "Yosho!" as they went. Afterward, the bonfire and dance—her favorite part of the festival—would continue far into the night.

Humming a tune from the Obon dance, Haruna pulled a loose strand of hair behind her right ear, smoothed her shopping list, and reread what she had written.

Eel

Umeboshi

Somen noodles

Hakushika Sake

Flowers for Cemetery and altar

To the list she added one missing item:

Incense

Today, she would light the incense for her father and all the Tsuruda ancestors to welcome them home. Since her mother had fallen ill, Haruna was the one who completed the ritual each year, just as Satsuki had done each Obon since Haruna was a child.

"How will the spirits of our ancestors find their way if we don't light the *mukaebi* for them? They will stumble in the darkness," her mother had always said. "How will they know we are ready for them?"

Haruna hadn't expected Satsuki to realize that Obon was coming, but this morning her mother had surprised her.

"Your father will visit soon," she said when Haruna brought her a cup of green tea. "He is waiting for me, Haru-chan." Satsuki spoke with difficulty, the right half of her mouth nearly immobile now, but her eyes were lit with tiny fires at the mention of Kenzaburo. Haruna nodded, unsure of how to respond, hoping her mother would continue talking. Instead, Satsuki stared at the far corner of the ceiling, seeming intent on listening to a conversation that only she could hear.

It was hard for Haruna to imagine her father visiting them as a spirit, much as she wanted to believe it was so. Her *otohsan* never believed in an afterlife and scoffed at the idea of "*umare-kaware,*" being reincarnated and reborn as another being. She imagined him in the afterlife, arguing with any spirit who dared tell him he was dead, using scientific logic to explain why it was impossible for spirits to exist. Haruna laughed out loud at the image and received a glare from Satsuki in response.

"*Gomen nasai*," she said, and bowed to her mother. "I'm sorry, Mother. Just thinking of something Tae-chan told me the other day," she lied, not wanting to hurt her mother's feelings or dispel her beliefs. If her mother thought Father were coming to visit her, who was she to argue?

Haruna herself was not sure what she believed—like her father, she was a scientist, and yet things had happened since Akihiro's death from cancer and her father's fall from the tree that made her wonder. Recently she'd found a pressed cherry blossom and an old ticket to the planetarium in the brand-new astronomy book she was reading. She was certain she hadn't put it there. One April morning, a huge maroon and gray butterfly alighted on her shoulder, fanning its still-wet wings near her ear, close enough for her to feel the rhythmic push of air on her neck and hear the gentle "whoosh, whoosh" sound its wings made before flying off. And then there were the dreams. Some nights, it seemed as if a revolving door let Akihiro into her thoughts as soon as her father exited, and vice versa. She smiled. The two men whom she'd loved most never appeared together, just as had been true in life.

While she slept, Akihiro would come to her with his gentle smile, whispering her name. "*Shinpai shinai de*," he said each time. "Do not worry. I am here, Haru-chan." She woke feeling rested and at peace. The dreams where she saw her father, who looked troubled, were different. "It is not what I thought, Haru-chan," he lamented. Sometimes he was crying. "Nothing is as I thought," he'd say, head in his hands. There were times she could not bear to see his face.

Satsuki called out from her room and Haruna inhaled and smoothed the front of her cotton blouse. There was no use living in the past, worrying about the ghosts of the men she loved, when her mother was alive and in need of attention.

Later that day, Haruna lit the green *mukaebi* incense sticks and went to clean her father's gravestone. Other families were there, too—some setting up elaborate picnics, or waiting with Buddhist monks—but Haruna had decided to forego the ceremony with the arrogant priest this year, along with his sizable stipend. "*Otohsan*, of all people, would not mind," she told herself, and resolved to recite some sutras for him on her own when she came back to visit his gravesite the next day. Truth be told, the small amount from her father's pension and her tutoring jobs was barely enough to pay the bills. She preferred to make a nice meal and decorate his grave rather than spend all the money on a priest who, it was rumored, enjoyed frequenting the red-light district in Osaka on weekends.

On the first night of Obon, she prepared eel—her mother's favorite—and mashed it up with rice. After she fed her *okaasan*, she put a small cup of her father's favorite chilled sake to Satsuki's lips so her mother could taste it and remember. In this way, they toasted Kenzaburo's memory. *If only,* thought Haruna, Otohsan *could be here with us to enjoy it. If only our rituals could really pull him back home.*

And in the late summer heat, just before twilight fell on the first night of Obon, something inside Haruna shifted. *This year,* she thought, *I will count the stars that fall during the meteor showers of August, just as* Otohsan *and I used to do when I was a girl. But this year, I will also look for the spirits who come to visit. Just as my mother always did, I will open the door and welcome them home.*

Crane

Fox

Boar

Snake

Dragon

二 24 四

KENZABURO
THE FEAST OF THE HUNGRY GHOSTS

The procession of spirits had already begun making its way down to the shores of Yamato. I beckoned to Benkei to follow, but he shook his head.

"I am sorry, Nephew," he said. "This is where you and I must part ways."

"What do you mean?" I asked. "We have until the end of this Obon, Uncle. We will find my mother and Zaemon in the living world. Don't give up now, I beg of you." My voice, high and unnatural, sounded like a child begging a parent to stay with him.

"It cannot be helped," said Benkei. "I have been here for centuries longer than you, Kenzaburo. My transformation is already starting and will soon be complete. You are a younger spirit and will be able to make your way to the living world on the *shoryobuni* boats as usual. I must go with the other hungry ghosts to the underground passage-ways that they use to walk to the living world."

x

247

"Then I will go with you," I said. "It is decided."

Benkei smiled and shook his head again. "You are a good man, Kenzaburo. Akihiro was right. But now you must finish the rest of your task on your own. Just as I cannot take the *shoryobuni* boats to the living world, you are not allowed in the underground passageways. By the time darkness falls, my reversion will be complete, and I will go back to the life of a hungry ghost."

"What do you mean?" I said, sputtering. "You are no more a *gaki* than I am."

"I never told you, Nephew. I could not bring myself to speak the words. I hope you will forgive me, but I will not blame you if you do not. The truth—my truth—is that I had been wandering as a hungry ghost these many years before you arrived in Yamato."

I opened my mouth but had no words. Everything became clear: my uncle's horror and unwillingness to speak of the torture *gaki* endured in the afterlife, his prodding about the scroll, the sad darkness on his face when he didn't know I was watching.

He could not look me in the eyes when he spoke. "Inari chose me to be your guide because, of all the spirits from our family, I showed some awareness, some remorse for my debauched life." His lips twisted into a smile. "She thought I would help you see the mistakes you'd made because I had made so many myself, you see. I was charged with helping you find your mother and brother, Kenzaburo, but I failed you. I always hoped they would be drawn back to our ancestral home." He paused, his familiar voice cracking into pieces like an old ceramic bowl broken into dusty shards. "But for reasons I cannot understand, they did not return. You did not know, nephew, but I began looking for them when you were working on your scroll. I asked every spirit I met for news of them, but to no avail. Their disappearance in Yamato seemed to be complete."

"But the Jizo-sama? He said they would be in the living world this Obon. That we have a chance to find them there."

"Yes, Kenzaburo. I trust that what he says is true, but I'm afraid that is a task you must complete by yourself." His shoulders sagged, and he could not look at me when he said, "*Ki wo tsukete.* Take care of your spirit, Nephew." When Benkei reached out to touch my sleeve, the pearly bone of his right forearm was exposed and glistened in the fading light, as his transformation back to that of a *gaki* began to overtake him.

"Remember, Nephew, I will be in the living world during Obon, for the feast of the hungry ghosts. I will help you as much as the gods allow." When he smiled at me, one of his incisors fell to the ground. He bent to pick it up slowly, polished it on his kimono and placed it in his sleeve. Instead of heading down the road toward the sea, he turned in the dark and moved upward, into the dense underbrush of the mountain, toward the mouth of a small cave that was the entrance to the dank tunnel that the hungry ghosts of Mt. Rokko would follow to the living world.

When I turned and looked back down the mountain toward the procession of spirits, I saw that it was starting to dwindle. I would be last again. With no time to think, I headed in the direction of the bobbing lanterns, following them as best I could. When I arrived on the beach, unlike the mournful departure of souls from the living world, the hubbub of the crowd was like that of a festival—spirits called to each other and laughed, and a lanky man gaily played a traditional tune for the Obon dance on his flute.

I wasted no time in boarding the boat bearing my family name and crest. This time I was joined by my father's youngest sister Tomoe, the one who'd died of the hundred days cough. When the temple bell sounded signaling our departure, Tomoe smiled and nodded. I used the long oar to push off into the dusk. At first, each boat was visible in the fog that surrounded Yamato by the swinging of yellow lanterns tied to their hulls, until all grew silent and I realized we were on our own.

Tomoe looked at me and smiled whenever I glanced at her. "Why aren't you with the Jizo-sama?" I asked, uncertain if she would reply. She had never spoken to me when I'd seen her in Yamato before.

To my surprise, Tomoe giggled and said, "He sent me to take care of you, Nephew." Her small, pale face glowed in the light from the lantern. I turned and bowed to her, grateful that the Jizo-sama had sent someone to help me. She was my aunt, even though she'd only lived to be eight.

We floated on through the night, drifting toward the living world on an advancing tide. The shadow of the ashes from the funeral fire Benkei had lit for me on our last journey were still in the bottom of the boat. My good-hearted uncle, who had been with me since the moment I'd died. The same uncle who was now in a dark tunnel filled with hungry ghosts all heading toward the living world, starving for food that would turn to hot coals as soon as it touched their lips. Some said they were corpse eaters, that they were allowed to feast on human flesh during Obon.

Shivering, I shook my head to banish the thought.

"The Jizo gave these to me after you left," Tomoe said, and I had the feeling she'd been watching me. I looked down and saw that my scroll and fude pen had been placed in the stern of the boat. "He said they were very important to you, so I brought them with me." She handed them to me with a triumphant smile. I bowed to my child aunt, eyes stinging, and silently thanked the Jizo.

As the dark lifted, we saw that we were close to land—the Suma beach of the present rose up before us. Unlike its counterpart in

Yamato, it was modern and covered with high rise apartment buildings. I had never been so glad to see it as I was at that moment. As the temple bell sounded, welcoming us home, a giant hand seemed to pull us to shore. Around us, some spirits yawned and stretched, and others rubbed their eyes. When a gong sounded inside the temple, the spirits of Kobe disembarked. I knew the same thing was happening on each shoreline and each beach around Japan, as the spirits arrived home for the Obon holiday.

"Come on, Kenzaburo, *isoide!*" said my Aunt Tomoe. "Hurry up, the train is leaving."

I followed her as she ran to the Japan Rail station and we waited for the 5:35 a.m. train. Commuters jostled their way onto the platform, some drinking hot coffee they'd bought from nearby vending machines. The smell brought me back to life. Obon, and the journey home. The only time we spirits were allowed to the full range of senses again.

Tomoe sighed. "I wish I could have a *kakigori*," she said and twirled her hair. "I always loved shaved ice in the summer." Without looking up at me she said, "He's waiting for you, you know. On that platform over there. I think you should go talk to him."

I looked across the station to an empty platform, where a businessman in a gray suit was waiting with his back toward me on a bench.

"Well, go on," said Tomoe, impatient.

I took the stairs to the next platform. I wondered who the man was and what he wanted. He didn't turn to me when I reached him but continued to read his newspaper.

He sighed and asked, "You don't recognize me, Kenzaburo?"

"*Eh, Sumimasen.* I'm sorry, but I do not. Who are you?"

When he turned to face me, I saw his amber eyes, so like Satsuki's— but unlike my wife's, the color seemed to shift and change as he talked.

"*Sumimasen*," I said, and bowed low, realizing that I had again failed to see the truth.

"Stand up, Kenzaburo," said Inari, who had taken the form of a portly middle-aged man for our meeting. He looked at his watch. "Your work is not finished, and your time is nearly up. You haven't completed your scroll, and you haven't found your mother and brother," he continued, ticking off my failures. "What excuse do you have for your failure?"

"Inari-sama. I have no excuses to offer you," I said, bowing. "I am a fool and a coward. I have tried, but you are right—I have failed. Please forgive me. I am determined to succeed in the few days I have here in the living world."

Inari nodded curtly. "Let it be so," he said. "If not, I will reserve a special place in Mt. Osore for you, where only the most depraved hungry ghosts are sent." He smoothed his jacket and said, "This is my final offering of help to you. Think, Kenzaburo: What was the first thing your uncle Benkei wrote on your body when you arrived in Yamato. Do you remember?

"*Hai*," I said slowly. "It was 'crane,' 'boar,' 'fox,' and 'snake.' The last character was 'dragon.' And I saw those images again the first night I met you, when you sent me into the passageway back to my home."

"That is correct. Understand that those images hold the answer to all of your questions. They are the key to everything that has transpired in your life." He snapped his newspaper shut and stood. "Because of your dawdling in Yamato, you have only three days to make this right. Now go," he said. "Satsuki is waiting."

I hurried back to the platform just as the train bound for Rokko pulled in. Tomoe was nowhere to be seen. I boarded the train and looked across to the platform where I'd met with Inari, but all that sat on the lone bench was a pale-yellow dog. He swiveled his pointy ears in my direction, panting and grinning at me. I raised my hand toward him and he bowed, ever so slightly, as we left the station.

As I stood by my wife's bedside watching her that first day of Obon, I realized with dismay that Satsuki's condition had deteriorated in the year since my last visit. I talked to her when I thought she might hear me—I sent her visions of her parents in Inari, of our life together, and then the images: crane, fox, boar, snake, and dragon. A frown flitted across her features, a gasp for breath, then her eyes opened wide and she started shouting something unintelligible until Haruna came and put a cold cloth on her forehead.

Startled, I backed into a corner of the bedroom, wondering what it was that bothered my wife so.

Later, I followed Haruna and whispered that I'd met Akihiro and their child, that they were safe and watching over her. I showed her the image of myself, Akihiro, and Akira in her dreams, and watched a warm, slow smile spread across her face.

I did not tell Haruna or Satsuki that I had only three days to secure all of our eternal lives in Yamato. I could not say the words out loud to my wife and daughter—could not let them know that I was failing them, and that our fate rested on my broken shoulders.

It was on my second night home that I heard a strange sound coming from down the hall as I stood vigil by my wife's bedside—a scratching noise, then something small and hard falling to the floor. I ventured to the back of the house, where I heard the sounds coming from—the storeroom on the other side of the kitchen. I slid the door open and felt a flutter where my absent heart once lived.

Kneeling there with her back turned toward me was my mother, unmistakable in her favorite dark purple kimono. On her head perched the wig she wore when she attended society events, bedecked with her family's last heirlooms, two ivory combs carved into the shape of dragons—the only treasure her mother managed to save and bequeath to her when she married my father.

"These combs represent many meals my parents missed. They did this so they could give me something from my family line on my wedding day," my mother told me with pride when she wore them. "It is said they were once owned by a Heian Era empress." I remembered watching her turn this way and that in the mirror to admire the dragons in her hair, each carrying a large pink pearl. "The Kitada's are a noble family, Ken-chan. We are not *common* people," she would sniff, nodding at me before saying, "You must never forget. This is the blood that runs through your veins."

Here she was before me. Hope filled me again—perhaps all was not lost, after all. The last day of Obon had not yet come. There was still time to make right what was wrong.

Not wanting to startle my *okaasan*, I paused and attempted to gather my thoughts. Though we had converted her storeroom into my office after the war, in her presence it had somehow reverted to its former state. The shelves that lined the walls were filled with old records, folded silk kimono in paper, lacquer boxes filled, I knew, with my mother's jewelry and make-up. On the wall hung a large photograph of my mother taken on her wedding day at the age of fourteen. In the picture, she was wearing the traditional white wedding kimono and white hood said to hide the jealous horns of women. Someone had tinted the photo, and her lips appeared crimson red, the hydrangea around her a pale blue. Her face was young and childlike, the pinched, vacant look of the war years nowhere to be found.

Now I realized she was counting something on the floor in front of her. I cleared my throat to get her attention, and whispered, "*Okaasan?* It's Kenzaburo. I have been looking for you and Zaemon for so long now."

My mother's shoulders stiffened, and she sat up straight. "Ken-chan," she whispered, her voice low and hoarse. "Is it really you? I knew you would come." When she turned to me her wig slipped down the right side of her head, revealing a bald scalp sparsely covered with long gray hairs. My mother's face was slack and waxen, and her distended belly and skeletal hands resembled a bloated gray corpse; her mouth was as small as an infant's. When she moved, I could see that she'd been counting her own teeth on the floor in front of her.

"*Gomen nasai*. Forgive me, *Okaasan*. I am too late. I was too late. You are already a hungry ghost, like I soon will be." I shuddered and fell to the floor on my hands and knees. I had failed my uncle, I had failed my wife and child, I had failed the Tsuruda family line. Inari had been wrong to trust me.

"Kenzaburo, you are here," said my mother with difficulty, crawling next to me and lowering her face to the floor. Her eyes glanced toward the door, fearful—of what, I didn't know. "Please, please son, bring me some water. I have had nothing to drink since I arrived in this place."

"It's no use, *Okaasan*. I'm a ghost, just like you. Whatever I give you to drink will only make your pain worse. Don't you see?" I turned my face from hers so she could not see my weakness, my helplessness.

"Why do you punish me," she screamed, her voice shrill. "It has been this way since I arrived in this place. But no one will help me, not Zaemon, not even you. Both of my sons, useless. You sicken me."

I hung my head, realizing how impossible the situation was. My mother was already a hungry ghost, a *gaki*. I was too late, just as the voices had been saying since I arrived in Yamato. It was then that I heard my brother's familiar hacking cough coming from the other side of the wall. My mother sneered in his direction. "Yes, your younger brother is here, too," she said. "No help at all, as usual." Her face tightened, and she turned back to her task, lining up her blackened teeth on the tatami mat. As I was leaving, I saw her attempting to put them back into her mouth.

I knocked at the door that had been our food pantry and said, "Zaemon, is it you?" A weary voice inside said, "*Douzo*. Come in." I slid the door open with a heavy hand, afraid of what I would find.

At first, I could see nothing, the air was so filled with smoke. Ashtrays surrounded my brother, each piled high with fine, gray ash. Zaemon wore a business suit, and the receding smoke revealed sunken cheeks and the stalk-like neck of a hungry ghost. He put a cigarette to a hole in his throat and inhaled. His once handsome face had turned into that of a thin gray spirit, meek and frail. He laughed when he saw the look on my face. "Yes, I am a hungry ghost," he said. "Do you think the way I lived my life would have merited any other ending for it?" His laughter turned into a hacking cough as he went back to his business ledgers, where he was filling in long columns with numbers. In the room around him, which looked like a replica of his office in Hiroshima, were the ventilator machines his company had sold to hospitals in his lifetime, made of discarded weapons from the war and painted an institutional green. He leaned over to strike a new match and his suit jacket swung open to reveal an exposed rib cage. Inside, his remaining lung pulsed like a rotting black mushroom in his chest.

Another bout of coughing overcame him, and I rushed to put a rubber oxygen mask to his face. He pushed me away and held his face in his hands. To my surprise, huge wracking sobs overcame Zaemon, the brother I hadn't seen cry since we were small.

"Look at what I have become, Older Brother," he scoffed. "A soulless ghost counting his money for eternity. I am so sick to death of money, but when I stop counting, my body lights on fire from within. This is the price I pay for the life I led, for my greed," he paused and looked up at me, his eyes gouged and red, "and my jealousy."

"Zaemon, it was not your fault," croaked the voice of my mother. We both turned to her as she shuffled into the room, her form bent and fragile. "The fox vixen seduced you. It was Satsuki's doing," she said, and her voice took on a hypnotic quality. "She bewitched Kenzaburo into marrying her. I knew she was a demon sent to destroy us, but you wouldn't listen to me, either of you. The proof came when she seduced you, as I knew she would."

My brother looked at me, his eyes darting and afraid.

"What do you mean, Mother?" I whispered, looking from one face to the other. "What do you mean to say?"

My brother let his head and arms drop to the desk in front of him, spilling black ink across his ledger. "Didn't you ever wonder?" he said, his voice muffled and choking. "Weren't you surprised that she was able to become pregnant so easily after the doctors told you it was impossible? Your daughter's face, so like mine?"

My mother drew herself up in the doorway, crossing distended arms over her chest, her smile revealing black gums that did not quite cover the bone of her jaw beneath.

With an anguished cry, I lunged across the desk and grabbed Zaemon by the lapels of his dusty suit, but he did not move away. When I touched him, I felt his foul breath inside me. Instead of trying to escape from me, he pulled me toward him in a clutching embrace. At first, I felt dizzy, as if I was falling into a pit, but bit by bit I regained equilibrium and saw images from my brother's life: I watched him being punished for my polio; treated like second best, always; my mother's critical eye and my father's blank one; the closed door of my bedroom. I saw Zaemon as a young boy alone in his dark room, shoulders shaking as tears rolled down his cheeks. Then I saw his marriage to Testuko—his chance to leave Kobe and the disappointment of my parents, and his favored brother, behind.

The next scene was of my Satsuki, beautiful and young, arriving with me in the country house in Hajiyama. The exhilaration he felt, his chest filling with pride that I was now the one on the bottom and he was on top. I was vulnerable, humble—I needed him. Then I was gone, and Satsuki was alone in the house, a scapegoat for the other women, treated like a servant rather than a family member. I saw Zaemon watching her, waiting for his opportunity to catch her alone. I watched him giving her magazines to read, books, seeing his chance when he realized she was unable to read kanji characters, and offering her the false promise of friendship.

What I saw next was almost more than I could bear. Satsuki's face, hopeful, happy to see him, greeting him as a brother. And then Zaemon moving on top of her like an animal. When I heard him say, "A fox is no different from any other woman," and I pushed him away from me with an anguished cry, sickened and shaking with hatred.

"I don't expect you to forgive me," said Zaemon. "I have resigned myself to my fate here. I deserve no better for feeding my jealousy of you for all these years." He shook his head. "Nothing you can do can make it worse."

I remembered the Jizo's words: "You alone have the choice to release your family from their fate, but it will be the hardest choice you will have to make. It cannot be done falsely. All must be laid bare."

"There is another way, son," my mother whispered, her voice pleading behind me. "When Satsuki joins us here in Yamato, she can give her soul to me. That will release me from this hell. You see, it's simple: Her soul for mine." She appraised me. "A fair trade, after all the pain she's brought upon our family, *deshou?*" She nodded and sniffed. "A good daughter-in-law would do this for her husband."

I looked from my mother's cunning, hopeful face to my brother's despairing one. All my life, held prisoner by these two, the one who favored me and the one who hated me. And me, holding fast to my favored status and allowing myself to become the meeting point of all their selfishness and greed. Because I loved Satsuki, they each in their own way had attempted to destroy her. They did not know that my wife was protected in the afterlife just as she was in the living world.

"*Yamete.* That's enough, Mother," I said. And then louder: "You have done enough. You did not deserve my father, and you do not deserve Satsuki. My wife did nothing but show you kindness, in spite of the way you treated her. I see you now, Mother. My only regret is that I did not protect my wife from the venom and lies you spewed."

My *okaasan* shook her head and held her hand to her mouth. "No, no, it's not true," she said, her eyes wild. "She has bewitched you, even in death."

"*Chigaimasu.* You are wrong, Mother. Satsuki was an orphan raised by poor farmers, but she has more nobility than you could ever pretend to have."

My mother screeched and ran back to the store room, banging the door shut behind her.

I slumped and leaned against the wall, my back to my brother. Two broken men, husks of their former selves. Two vain, foolish men who had never understood the importance of light; two men who had died trying to get inside of it.

"It's too difficult. I cannot do it," I whispered. How could I be expected to forgive my brother, my mother? The floor creaked outside the doorway, but I did not move. Whatever my mother wanted, I could not give her. And I had failed again, because my paucity of spirit would not allow me to forgive my mother and brother for what they had done. There was nothing anyone could do now; the Tsuruda line was doomed to an eternity as hungry ghosts, and Satsuki and Haruna would be suffering right along with us.

The floor creaked again, and I looked up.

It was Satsuki, holding her hands out to me. Smiling. She was wearing the nightgown she'd been sleeping in, but her face was young and unlined again, and her feet were bare.

"If I can forgive Zaemon and your mother, you must try to do the same," Satsuki said to me. "And I do forgive them, Kenzaburo." She looked at my brother, her gaze gentle and unwavering. "Zaemon never understood the truth. He was transformed by his own need to cause you pain, to take what was not his and twist it into something unrecognizable. He had a wife who loved him, and that is the saddest part of all." She looked at me, her amber eyes so like Inari's. "But he gave us our daughter, who is your true child just as surely as I am your wife."

Zaemon was hunched against the wall, a sound like wet breathing coming from his chest, his face turned away from us.

"Zaemon," she said in a slow, clear voice, "there is a chance for you to make things right within your own family now. Go to Tetsuko and tell her what happened. It is time for you to help your own children and grandchildren."

I shuddered, weeping, unable to speak the truth to Satsuki.

"It's too late, don't you see?" I said to her. "Even if I can forgive him, Obon is almost over now. It's impossible for me to complete my task and save our family. I've failed."

Satsuki smiled at me sadly and shook her head. "Don't you understand, Kenzaburo? Your inability to see them—to let them go—has kept you living in limbo your whole life, and into your afterlife. It is time for you to see the truth."

I shook my head, still crying, but no tears came. "Satsuki, I want you to promise me that you won't choose to be with me in the afterlife if I am unable to do what is required. You are destined for other things. If you promise me that, I can forgive them."

Satsuki's eyes shone yellow in the low light. Finally, she nodded. I turned toward my brother.

"Zaemon, I forgive you and *Okaasan*. You are released."

Zaemon slid the floor, his forehead pressed to the dusty tatami mat, and whispered, "Thank you, *Oniichan*. Thank you, Satsuki-sama."

We heard a gurgling sound behind us and turned to see my mother pulling at Satsuki's hem. Her wig was sliding from her skull and she spoke through thin lips.

"Satsuki-san, please," she said, her voice wheedling and high. "There is a correct way for you to release me from this state. Give me your soul in exchange for mine; take my place here and free me from this hell. You will finally pay off your debt to our family when you do so. I will consider the ledger clean."

Satsuki looked at her, and on her face instead of hatred and revulsion was compassion. She offered my mother a bowl of rice and a cup of water.

"Today is *segaki*, the feast of the hungry ghosts—the day when *gaki* can be released from their torment," said Satsuki. She spoke to my *okaasan* with the kindness grandparents reserve for their grandchildren. "If you accept my forgiveness, you will be released and free to continue on as a spirit in Yamato." She looked my way, and I swallowed and nodded.

Zaemon bowed low to the floor, his back covered with dust. "I do not deserve your forgiveness. I will do everything in my power to make things right for Tetsuko and my family," he said, his voice shaking. When he sat up, all vestiges of his time as a hungry ghost were gone, save for the same sad darkness I'd seen on my uncle's face.

"I will make sure that Tetsuko knows, Satsuki-san," said Zaemon carefully, humbly, "that what happened was my doing, not yours." He bowed to my wife.

"*Okaasan*, I forgive you," I said. "But you will have to humble yourself and ask Satsuki to forgive you if you wish to be released."

My *okaasan* smiled bitterly. "It is the other way around, my son. It is *she* who must ask forgiveness of me. Your marriage was not arranged properly—you should have married a woman from a respected family in Kansai who would raise our family rank, not an illiterate orphan from Inari. Don't you see, son? We were the laughingstock of Kobe because of her! She did not deserve you, and she was not worthy of our family." She drew herself up and paused, her rotting jaw clenched. "Each piece of bad fortune that befell us was her fault."

"No, Mother," I said, my voice for once not faltering. "You are wrong. No family name can make up for our cowardice, greed, and wrongdoing. The fault was not with Satsuki. It was yours and mine—your hatred and my lack of courage."

My mother tipped her head back and laughed. She tried to cover her mouth but was not fast enough to hide her rotting gums and black teeth. "She still has you under her control, don't you see?" she hissed. "Stay with me here, son—help me. We will remain in the afterlife together."

"I will be with my wife," I said, "who has forgiven you. We hope you will join us when you admit your wrongdoing."

My *okaasan* laughed again, her lips hard and black. "She has given me *her* forgiveness?" She spat the words out as if they were composed of bitter sand. "You are nothing," she said, turning to Satsuki. "You were not fit to marry my son; a demon servant of the fox goddess sent to divide and destroy my family. *You* forgive *me*? You who turned both my sons against me? Because of you, I have been forced to forage for human corpses at night. How dare you presume to forgive me?" As she spoke, she rose to the ceiling, arms outstretched. Swaying back and forth, she fixed Satsuki with a predatory gaze. "Now you will give

me what I demand," she said and moved toward Satsuki with light-
ning speed.

"No, Mother, you will not take one thing more from her," I shouted.
At the same time, Zaemon sprang from his place by the wall with a
roar. His hands reached toward my mother, and when they collided
their forms overlapped. They rolled end over end toward my mother's
store room, and in the places where they intersected, I saw scenes of
our family history—my mother's marriage to my father, the beatings
she gave my brother, Satsuki's arrival in our lives, and my own face,
closed and smug. I followed them, my arms held out—whether to protect Satsuki or shield her from the force of my family's hatred and
jealousies, I was not certain.

When they reached the store room, my mother's form disengaged
from my brother's and they lay on opposite sides of the room. Her wig
had fallen off, revealing sparse strands of long, gray hair.

"I am leaving, Mother," said Zaemon. "You have made your choice
to stay. I warn you, if you try to steal Satsuki's soul again I will trade
mine to have you locked inside Mt. Osore for eternity."

My *okaasan's* eyes darted from Zaemon's face to mine. "You would
have me chained up in a cave in Mt. Osore again," she whispered, "the
last realm of hungry ghosts?"

Zaemon nodded. My mother howled in anger, falling into a purple
and gray heap on the floor. Zaemon turned to me, his face weary and
forlorn. "I will take her away from here now and make sure you are
both safe." He slid the door of the storeroom closed.

"Ken-chan. It is time," said Satsuki. She had seen everything, and
still she chose to be with me. I bowed my head so she could not see
my shame.

"I'm not ready," I said. "I haven't completed the task Inari set for
me. I've failed, Satsuki. Don't you see? I had to write the truth of my

life, and now that I've learned it, I don't have time any longer. I've failed you and Haruna, and I've failed the entire Tsuruda family line." I paused, my voice cracking. "Zaemon's freedom is short-lived. We are all doomed to become hungry ghosts now. Tomorrow we will join my mother and brother in their torment for eternity." A sob escaped my throat. "I am a fool in the afterlife, just as I was when I was alive."

I sank to the floor, and Satsuki sat down next to me. "*Iiwa*," she whispered. "You have not failed, Ken-chan. You have found your mother and brother and forgiven them."

Satsuki stood and moved toward the statue of the Fox Goddess in our living room. She placed the rice and water she'd offered to my mother in front of the picture and kneeled, praying. Satsuki motioned me to come and kneel next to her and pray, and I joined her.

All at once the atmosphere in the room changed, and a voice behind us said, "Like many spirits, your mother is not ready to leave yet."

We turned to see Inari in the corner of the room, a stand of bamboo behind her. She appeared as a young girl on the verge of womanhood. "Some spirits will not leave the Realm of Hungry Ghosts, even when they are given an escape. Your *okaasan* has been here feeding on her hatred for decades, Kenzaburo," she said softly. "She has learned nothing and has only succeeded in creating a hell of her own making."

The next words Inari spoke allowed a tiny seed of hope to grow inside of me. "You have completed your first task, slow though you may have been. As long as you are able to finish your second assignment before midnight and the end of Obon, your family will be safe." She stopped here, and her voice softened. "There is always hope, Kenzaburo. The door will remain open to your mother, when and if she is able to humble herself and admit her wrongdoing."

Satsuki and I thanked Inari, and I found myself believing in the possibility of my mother's redemption.

Now Inari said, "Go inside your house. You will find your scroll and pen on your desk. Finish your story, Kenzaburo. It is time."

"*Hai wakarimashita*," I said, telling the goddess I understood as I bowed. Satsuki bowed next to me, and then reached over and touched her fingertips to my hand.

"You know everything now; you do not need to be afraid," she said. "Write the ending of your story, Kenzaburo. Tell the story of the crane, the fox, the boar, the snake and the dragon. You know who they are now, *deshou?*"

I looked at my wife, startled, realization dawning on me. "You are the fox from Inari, of course . . . I am the careful crane. The boar—you always said Tetsuko resembled one . . . and the snake is—has always been—Zaemon, who was my mother's son more surely than I ever was." I paused and said quietly, "And the dragon is my mother, who is still feeding on her hatred."

I rose and entered the house with Satsuki and lead her back to her bed, tucking her in as she smiled up at me.

"Soon," I said, and she nodded, closing her eyes.

When I reached the desk in my study, I picked up the *fude* pen and began to write. I wrote every detail, I wrote every truth. As the clock edged toward midnight on the last day of Obon, I dipped my pen into the ink stone and wrote the final words of my story:

And at the exact moment of my death, these things I knew:

The wild boar scratched her back with a hairy snout, causing one of her babies to waken and begin nursing.

The ancient snake in our garden slid out of her last skin and slithered off in search of food.

A giant wood spider finished spinning her web over the riverbank.

My wife opened her eyes and felt the futon beside her where my body had lain.

The horned beetles mated.

And at the very instant I died, the cicadas' shrill song began.

I set my pen down and shut my eyes. With a great sighing sound, the wind moved across the garden, flattening the grass and causing the curtains to blow straight into my study. I heard the voices of our family: Benkei, my father, my aunts, uncles, and cousins, calling and whispering around me.

"*Ki wo tsukete,*" I said, running to wave to the departing spirits of my family members. The wind died down just as suddenly as it had blown in.

I looked out over the neighborhoods of the Kobe foothills. At our local shrine, I saw the flames from the Obon bonfire reaching up orange fingers toward the night sky; I heard the young boys pounding on the drums for the final night of the Obon festival, and I danced the dance of an old man who has lived a good life.

When the drums stopped, I stood a moment longer in the garden, looking down the side of Mt. Rokko as it tumbled into the sea. Without thinking, I pressed my filmy palms together and prayed. As always, I would be the last to leave, but this Obon, it did not matter, because Satsuki would be coming with me.

Against a bright full moon
A hilltop pine tree
Is my rebirth
—Oshima Ryota

二25五
SATSUKI

Satsuki lay on her left side, facing the open window. She saw figures slide in and out of the room.

"*Jikan da yo*," they whispered. "It's time."

The nightingale sang "*Hooo-hokekyo*" outside her window. Satsuki heard the maple tree outside her window, swaying in the wind.

Satsuki opened her eyes and saw Kenzaburo standing next to her. Smiling, his hands folded, waiting.

"A horned beetle's wing," she whispered, her eyes never leaving Kenzaburo's face.

"Your hair on our wedding day," he replied.

"This night," she said, and smiled.

"I am finished," said Kenzaburo. "I've done it, Satsuki. We are free to go."

"I am ready," said Satsuki, holding out her hands to Kenzaburo in the dark.

The sound of whispering in her ears was deafening, until she felt buoyed up, her body light and fluid. Satsuki stretched, flexed her arms, and arched her spine. She looked down and saw that she was transparent, bright. Instead of filling her with fear, the sensation pleased her. She was a bubble, dancing on the wind. She was water, light, and sound. She was boundless energy. Released.

Epilogue
HARUNA
OBON
ONE YEAR AFTER SATSUKI'S DEATH

On the first morning of Obon, Haruna walked up the mountain to the gravesite of her parents. She placed memorial flowers there in honor of the one-year anniversary of her mother's death. Two thin granite columns showed their family name, Tsuruda, in letters that still looked freshly cut.

Haruna recited sutras until she was lost in the still humidity of the air, her voice uniting with the sound of thousands of deafening cicadas calling *"min, min, min"* in the heat. When she finished chanting, the insects' voices stopped at the same moment, and Haruna smiled. Her father would have liked that.

Haruna spent the rest of the day making her traditional Obon dinner of chilled somen noodles, eel, salmon, dumplings, seaweed salad, and tofu, which she placed in the refrigerator. All the foods her mother and father liked best, except for the dumplings.

270

Haruna took a bath, letting her weary muscles unspool in the *ofuro*. She exhaled and looked up at the ceiling. She wasn't sure if it was her Aunt Tetsuko's letter or visiting her parents' gravesite, but she felt a kind of peace fill her as she sat in the water.

Haruna heard the Obon festivities beginning as she set her meal on the veranda. The neighborhood temple drums beat loudly, heralding the start of the Days of the Dead. Later, adults and children would dance into the night wearing light cotton kimono and fan themselves when the bonfire became too hot. Young lovers would steal down the lanes two-by-two, counting the stars that fell in the meteor showers of August.

Haruna had come to believe that life was celebrated more fiercely during the Days of the Dead than at any other time of year.

She ate her meal, savoring every bite, drinking the cold sake her father liked best. When she finished, she took out the letter from her Aunt Tetsuko.

Dear Haru-chan,

I hope you are keeping well in the heat of summer.

I would like to invite you to come to my family's country home next month. As you know, your mother spent time here with my family during the war. I would like to show you the house, and a shrine she used to visit. (You will probably not be surprised to hear that it is a shrine to the Fox Goddess.)

Haruna put down the letter and shut her eyes. Her *okaasan* had been gone for one year, and she still missed her every day. When she dreamed of her mother, she was always standing with her father. "We are here, Haru-chan," whispered her *okaasan*. "We are waiting for you."

Each time Haruna dreamed of her father, he opened his hands to reveal a different type of insect. One night, a horned beetle shuffled across his translucent fingers, shutting its black lacquer wings with an indignant click. Another time, a butterfly spread impossible colors across his palm—green, gold, and iridescent blue. Last night, a cicada buzzed before flying off into the heat of her darkened bedroom.

Each time her *otohsan* appeared, he bowed and said, "Forgive me, Haru-chan."

Haruna wiped her eyes and continued reading the letter from her aunt.

> It is strange, Haru-chan. I have been dreaming of your Uncle Zaemon this past year. He talks to me all night sometimes. There are times he is so chatty I cannot sleep! I was never a woman to believe in such things, but I have found that one's mind changes as one grows older. It may sound silly, but your uncle is telling me the story of his life. And I am listening.

Haruna folded the letter along soft linen creases and put it back in the envelope. The next day, she would write to her aunt and accept her invitation to Hajiyama. Haruna had always wanted to see the place where her mother lived during the war. She needed to hear the story from her aunt Tetsuko of what happened when the bomb fell, a time her mother had rarely spoken about to her.

Just before going to bed, Haruna took one last look outside. Fireflies lit up and then disappeared in the dark, reappearing elsewhere. Shapes seemed to shimmer and shift around her in the twilight. At the far end of the garden, where the wall was crumbling, she thought she saw movement in the low light of a neighbor's lantern. The first breeze of the evening ruffled the leaves of the trees. She thought she heard the sound of a familiar voice, and it sounded as if it was comforting a small child.

"Hush, hush," he said. "It's all right. I am here."

"Good night," Haruna whispered softly and smiled. "And welcome home."

ACKNOWLEDGMENTS

Dear reader,

When Beth received that first diagnosis and knew "bad," but not yet "how bad," she shared the news in a note to sixty or so of her closest and most important friends and family. This was a shock because of the cancer and, also, because each of us sincerely believed that we were the one special person in Beth's life.

On some level, it was true. Beth possessed an uncanny and genuine interest in people. An extrovert's extrovert, she listened, she exuded friendliness, and she was kind. Her dry observational humor had all of us laughing, right up until the end. That Beth could make sixty or so people feel important, unique, and like her very best friend is a testament to the impact of her goodness. She saw the best in each of us.

A few days before Beth's death, a visiting hospice nurse explained the process, and, when all the forms were signed and all the questions answered, there was nothing for us to do but hold Beth's hand and make assurances. We would take care of her boys, we said. We would see Alessandro into adulthood. We would support Joe.

Sitting on her bed (blue flowered sheets—funny, what a person re-members) with my arms around her narrow shoulders, we promised to find her novel a home.

Now that promise has been kept.

Beth worked on *The Afterlife of Kenzaburo Tsuruda* for the better part of a decade. Her circle of writer and reader friends saw longer and shorter versions. Her words were spread out in hard copy across a Denny's diner table one night. Her words were sent by email for feed-back. The project evolved tighter and better-shaped, moving from a draft to a manuscript to a graduate thesis to a fully formed novel. It won acclaim with a PEN/New England Discovery Award, as well as the attention of multiple literary agents.

Then Beth got sick. Then she died.

It is a grim sort of humor, as well as a strange comfort, that her book—conceived when her own death was unimaginable—details a rich and vibrant afterlife. When I read Beth's words, I hear her voice, and I remember the vivid dreams she described during the later days of her treatment—the river, the flowers, and the peaceful spirits wait-ing in welcome. It was as if she stepped into her own narrative. Or, as if she somehow saw something we did not.

Neither would surprise me.

There are many people to thank on Beth's behalf, and I request indulgence if any person who played a role in this novel's construction is mistakenly left out. First, her family: her mother Rosemary, Wayne, Barbara, and nieces Lindsay, Kylie, and Haleigh. Rose, Larry, as well as nephews Matteo and little Nico.

Add to this circle Beth's childhood friends and soul sisters: Colleen Hart, Jody Evenson Taylor, Jody Shafran, and Brooke Williams. The circle widens more to include her devoted ex-patriot community: Anders Anderson, Clare Cronin, Kris Repogle, Dearbhla Kelly, Joan

Munson, and Suzanne Julicher. Expanding even more, it includes her writing community—particularly Cathy Kidman, Ann Hood, Suzanne Strempek Shea, Elizabeth Searle, Jaed Coffin, Lisa Takeuchi Cullen, Peggy Moss, Brenda Edmands, Morgan Callan Rogers, Alisia Leavitt, and the entire Stonecoast MFA inaugural graduating class. Her Cape Elizabeth friends, too, who supported Beth in so many tangible and intangible ways: Terri Patterson, Heather Hayes, Sarvi Maisak, Cri Swift, and Lauren Springer.

I must thank the PEN/New England Discovery Award committee for seeing the potential in Beth's words; John Talbot and Karl Krueger for their initial efforts to secure this novel's home; and, ultimately, She Writes Press for becoming that home.

Beth's circle remains big and powerful.

Above and beyond all notion of friends, professional colleagues, awards, and events, Beth loved her boys. Her husband Joe and her son Alessandro were her light and her purpose. It is my hope that when Alessandro reads his mother's words, he will experience her creativity and understand her artistic dedication. His mother had a gift for storytelling. I want him to know how rare this talent is, and I want him to hear her voice in this novel.

Beth's dying brought no pleasure to the world, however, it is my hope that her novel might. It is also my hope that we all remember Beth in her healthiest, most vibrant moments. She lit up rooms and drew people to her. She was hilarious, naughty, witty, and beautiful.

In her novel as well as her life, Beth showed us how to love, how to laugh, and, ultimately, how to gracefully let go.

Sincerely,

Shonna Milliken Humphrey,

one of Beth's many friends

ABOUT THE AUTHOR

Elisabeth Wilkins Lombardo was awarded the 2009 PEN/New England Fiction Discovery Prize for the unpublished manuscript of her novel, *Obon*. She went to Japan as an exchange student in college and stayed for ten more years, traveling extensively throughout Asia from her home in Kobe, Japan, where she worked as a radio and TV personality, teacher, and writer. Her prize-winning essay about the

Great Hanshin Earthquake, "After the Quake," was translated into Japanese and subsequently published in an anthology of the same name. Her stories have been published in *The Japan Times, The Daily Yomiuri, Mothering, Motherhood* (Singapore), and *Kansai Timeout.* Elisabeth received her MFA from the Stonecoast Creative Writing Program in 2005. At the time of her death in 2015, Wilkins Lombardo was the editor of *Empowering Parents,* an award-winning online parenting magazine with a growing international readership of more than 500,000. She lived in Cape Elizabeth, Maine with her husband and son.

SELECTED TITLES FROM SHE WRITES PRESS

She Writes Press is an independent publishing company
founded to serve women writers everywhere.
Visit us at www.shewritespress.com.

The Belief in Angels by J. Dylan Yates. $16.95, 978-1-938314-64-3
From the Majdonek death camp to a volatile hippie household on the East
Coast, this narrative of tragedy, survival, and hope spans more than fifty
years, from the 1920s to the 1970s.

Anchor Out by Barbara Sapienza. $16.95, 978-1631521652
Quirky Frances Pia was a feminist Catholic nun, artist, and beloved sister
and mother until she fell from grace—but now, done nursing her aching
mood swings offshore in a thirty-foot sailboat, she is ready to paint her
way toward forgiveness.

Faint Promise of Rain by Anjali Mitter Duva. $16.95, 978-1-938314-97-1
Adhira, a young girl born to a family of Hindu temple dancers, is raised
to be dutiful—but ultimately, as the world around her changes, it is her
own bold choice that will determine the fate of her family and of their
tradition.

Light Radiance Splendor by Leah Chyten. $16.95, 978-1-63152-178-2
Set in Eastern Europe in the first half of the twentieth century and cul-
minating in contemporary Israel and Palestine, *Light Radiance Splendor*
shows how three generations of the Hebrew Goddess Shekinah's devoted
mission keepers grapple with betrayal, love, and forgiveness.

The Black Velvet Coat by Jill G. Hall. $16.95, 978-1-63152-009-9
When the current owner of a black velvet coat—a San Francisco artist
in search of inspiration—and the original owner, a 1960s heiress who
fled her affluent life fifty years earlier, cross paths, their lives are forever
changed . . . for the better.

Wishful Thinking by Kamy Wicoff. $16.95, 978-1-63152-976-4
A divorced mother of two gets an app on her phone that lets her be in
more than one place at the same time, and quickly goes from zero to hero
in her personal and professional life—but at what cost?